I LOVED A SLAVE

SINMISOLA OGÚNYINKA

I Loved A Slave

by Sinmisola Ogúnyinka

Copyright © 2019

All rights reserved.

Cover Design by Michelle Ganeles Wide Sky Studio © 2019

Author Photo by Babstudio © 2014

Dedicated to Afolarin, my *massa* in love

Slavery didn't start with us, and it definitely didn't end with us - Gilbert Goodling, Confederate veteran.

The way of a man with a maid, I know not – Proverbs 30:18-19 (paraphrased)

Chapter One

Draft article by Gilbert Goodling:

Summer of 1859 brimmed with activity on Holt lands. Edmond Maguerro of Spanish descent was visiting with highfalutin dreams of turning JJ Holt's property into a million-dollar sugarcane plantation. Hundreds of slaves would be purchased to work the lands. Edmond spoke a hundred words in a second and didn't seem to have said enough. Penny Holt, JJ's beautiful wife, entertained all day and night. The two house slaves, Beth and Emily worked till they dropped. JJ had never had slaves work his land and the ones in the house, besides helping with house chores and caring for JJ and Penny's 5-year-old daughter, Katie, were just for status.

Things were about to change forever, and JJ seemed elated.

The first band of slaves arrived in the first week of June. Edmond had purchased two families because according to him, broken-up slave families created more trouble than when they were together. There was the family of Ray and Vivian who had two young adult sons, Dannyboy and Terrance, all tall, and tough-looking; and there were Dee and Anthony, and their teenage daughter, Elisa. Seven new slaves built the slave quarters and did the initial work on the plantation.

With so much work going on, JJ and Edmond at first hired laborers to work with the slaves, but it soon became an unworkable and expensive situation and they purchased more slaves instead.

John Jr was called Johnny, a handsome ruddy young man with cropped black hair and blue eyes and firm, smooth dark skin, he resembled the image of a Greek god. All the girls in the community wanted Johnny, and their mothers fanned their faces when he walked by.

After Johnny was sent to study law at the prestigious King's College in New York, his appeal increased.

JJ Holt, Johnny's father, involved in local politics, often worked with the Mayor Goodling and served on several boards. With the large expanse of land and money in the Holt family, he was important to the Creek View community, a small town north of Louisville. His grand plan though was to have Johnny in Washington, as a Senator or even the president, and Johnny liked the idea as much...

When Johnny walked through the gate of his childhood home, he almost turned back, not sure he was in the right place. The echo of the voices of slaves singing as they worked filled the air, horses galloped to the front of the house constantly and a new frontage had been constructed. Penny hurried to give him a hug and ordered Emily to prepare his bath and food.

"What's going on?" Johnny quizzed. "Am I even in the right house?"

Penny giggled. "I wake up every morning and ask myself the same, but this is what your father always wanted. I have never seen him so happy."

"So, he now owns a plantation? Unbelievable."

Johnny went out to see his childhood friend, Gilbert, the mayor's son, and both talked about the changes in the Holt family.

"Edmond Maguerro comes from a lot of wealth and has a good eye for business," Gilbert said.

"I never heard of him. I've been away for barely two years and it's as though America is colonized again."

Gilbert laughed. "You will get used to it all. Be glad the house is far from the plantation. And you can imagine none of it exists."

"I doubt my father will let me ignore such a massive investment. He probably thinks I should forget about law and join him on this frivolous venture."

Gilbert doubled over, laughing. "Don't sound so forlorn."

Johnny sighed. "I missed home. No one told me all of this was happening. I would have chosen to travel to Italy with friends from King's College."

"I could have told you in one of my letters, but who would have imagined no one informed you?"

"Who indeed?"

"Your father's excitement will soon wane. He will continue to focus on seeing you in Washington, DC."

Johnny sighed. "So I pray."

In the evening, which seemed to wait forever from coming, Johnny walked out in the moonlight and through rows of new plants. He knew the Holt land was massive, but he never imagined this sort of thing, a plantation, could be created. *We have been sitting on gold and had no inkling,* JJ had ranted over dinner. Edmond Maguerro, a 220-pound, 6-footer who ate to feed his bulk, guffawed. Johnny didn't know where to place him yet, but according to his mother, since he left his investments in Georgia and South Carolina, he had lived in their house for over a month.

Johnny walked down the little hill over the creek that formed the name of his town and sat, gazing into space. Soon darkness would envelop him, and he could dream of his future in peace. He closed his eyes and dozed off. Something startled him awake. It wasn't anything in particular, but he found himself conscious.

A sound seemed to come from afar and Johnny had to crane his neck to see the still creek water move, and then a splash, followed by a giggle. The classic Creek View gulf had all the wonders of a large stream and waterfall combined, and many visited as a picnic spot. That a part of it flowed through Holt land had greatly increased its value. He crept through thick brush following the sound of water and human. Someone swimming at this time of the night? There was little light from the moon, and if he hadn't come here so many times himself, he would have missed his step.

He stumbled over a heap of clothing but regained his posture before he landed on the ground, and hurriedly hid behind a tree. In a matter of seconds, the swimmer surfaced, obviously unaware. Johnny could not see well, but by the movement of the waters he deduced this person knew how to swim. He crouched to pick a piece of the clothing. It was a slave dress. A female slave swimming alone at close to midnight! A mean thought crossed his mind - take her clothes and leave, but he wasn't that type of person. Should he reveal himself, and rebuke her? Slaves had no right to the creek unless they were permitted. But who did this one hurt? No one, and maybe this was her way of coping with the hardships of her life.

Johnny squatted behind a tree. There was a splash and for a moment he imagined there were two people. It had been a hot day and warm evening, and he was tempted to hop in as well, but he waited and waited, and after what seemed like forever, with the moon now shining brighter than the sun, a beautiful dark-skinned woman waded out of the water, as naked as the day she was born. Johnny swallowed.

She walked as close as a few feet away from him and picked up her clothing, a relaxed, satisfied look on her face. Johnny's palms sweated, and his heart thudded. She was young, pretty, and had a glorious body, soon disguised by the ugly slave dress. Johnny could not stop staring as he pressed himself harder against the tree. She would see him if she passed by his front, but the slave quarters were the other way, and that was how she proceeded on feet as light as a deer's.

When she was gone, Johnny breathed.

Chapter Two

Elisa sneaked into the wooden shed she shared with her father and mother, dripping wet but happy, shivering from cold and fear. *Would the intruder report her this time?* Dee had warned her to stop going to swim at the creek, but it was the only way she could pass through the day. So, she now waited until they were asleep, which made her trips much later in the night. Her swim was worth the suffering by day at the new plantation. She had never been subjected to so much work in all of her sixteen years on earth. Things had never been easy, born a slave because her mother was, this was the only life she knew, but the previous owners had been established, and they had lived on plantations with many more slaves, tasks had been bearable.

She slid under the single sheet that made up her bedding but could not sleep. He was a white man, and she had noticed him when he stumbled over her pile of dress and improvised padded shoes the slaves wore in winter. He tried to be discreet but being a slave all her life had honed her senses. The question was: Why did he hide? Or was he a slave trying to run away? She thought she saw a flash of white skin, but she could be wrong. Whatever, he didn't want to be discovered, and she neither. Served both their purposes. The next question was: Should she share this experience with anyone? Another lesson about being a slave was learning to be unnoticeable. She had never been whipped but seen many whose inability to shut-up got them into a lot of trouble. Elisa hated pain and trouble and tried to avoid them.

The mysterious man troubled her until she slept and dreamt of ten white men jumping into the creek and flogging her with their horsewhip. She woke up in a pool of sweat.

Johnny quipped over breakfast. "More slaves are being bought today, and I wonder who is paying."

He had refrained talking about the developments on the plantation, because Edmond was always around, and his mother had warned about being rude.

"This man is helping your father live his dream, don't mess with it," she had sternly warned.

But Edmond traveled to Louisville based on some news a slave trader would be holding private auctions and he wanted the best possible.

"I have it on good word strong men will be available, fresh from the south. It's what we need now," JJ said. He had begged to stay back because of hay fever.

"Edmond is paying. We have an agreement on profit-sharing. This land here is worth close to a hundred thousand." JJ coughed. "And I've not even asked for equity."

Johnny smirked. "Is he putting in a hundred thousand?" He didn't think the land was worth half of a hundred, but that didn't matter.

"By the time we start harvesting, yes!"

Penny cleared her throat. "The money he's pumped in has started showing and we are excited."

Johnny faced his bacon and eggs. The slave Beth was a mighty good cook, and she seemed to have improved since the last time he was home. He went in search of Gilbert afterward.

"I need to get away from the house. The Edmond has gone to buy more slaves."

He battled with his secret. Three days in a row, this black beauty came into the creek before midnight and swam for at least thirty minutes. He got away sweating from his hiding behind the tree, but the pain was all worth it. He'd tried to find her in the field, but the slaves worked so hard, and in the sun, they covered their faces from the heat of the day with rags improvised into veils. The only way he could find her would be to ask them all to stand straight for an inspection.

"My dad would let you intern in his law office, if that's what you want," Gilbert said. "Just for the rest of summer."

"I want that more than traveling to Italy, but my father has been grouchy since I voiced my skepticism about this farm thing." Johnny groaned. "How do you wake up one morning and decide to have a plantation. These lands have been in our family for a hundred years and none of our ancestors took farming seriously."

"For you it was sudden, but all of Creek View knew of the impending investment." Gilbert arched an eyebrow. "The richest people in the south own plantations. Your dad may just be tired of aristocracy."

"Give me a break, Gilbert."

"When are the new slaves arriving?"

"Darn if I care. Mom thinks nightfall."

Gilbert chewed on his lower lip. "I have never experienced that before. Would you like to invite me to your house? As a budding renowned historian, it should make for great articles viewing these events." He snickered. "I will write a piece, just for you. What you missed while away!"

"I will read your piece." Johnny rolled his eyes. "You are invited. You may come in for dinner, and afterward I'll take you around the estate. The slaves should arrive by then."

Gilbert chuckled. "Sounds like a great plan, my friend."

They rode on horses after dinner, while the slaves worked.

"I have never done this before," Johnny moaned. "Going through row by row as they work."

"You internalize this. Slavery has been before us and will continue after us." Gilbert smiled at the bent frames of the slaves. "Many of them know no other way of living."

Johnny growled. "That does not make it any more right!"

He was quite close to the edge and a slave leapt at the sound of his voice. Two other female slaves yelped in fear. The foreman, a burly bear of a man called, Doggie, for the way he barked all the time even when he laughed, flung his whip at the hysterical slaves. A cry rent the air, and Johnny turned back.

One other slave on the other side looked up so briefly and locked gazes with Johnny. Within a second, she was bent over the soil with a crude hoe, weeding. Johnny could swear she was the midnight swimmer. Gilbert pulled up beside him as he glared at the bent frame of the slave.

He gazed out over the many heads. "Don't be a coward, Johnny! I will give my soul to have what you got here!"

"What's your name?" Johnny said softly.

He spoke almost under his breath, but she heard the question. As a slave, she had learned never to answer a question not addressed to her. On the other hand, he stood over her, so who else could he be talking to? She hated any day she was posted to the hedge. Whips flew about and caught people close to the end of the row. Though she'd been lucky, but today was particularly close. The new slave who came a week earlier had screeched at every little thing and gotten whipped more for her noise than for her mistakes. Elisa dreaded having to work close to her.

She turned only her head and met with deep blue eyes intent on her. "Elisa, *Massa*."

From the corner of her eye she spied Dee raise her head a little, but anything longer could attract Doggie. There was no way to communicate until nightfall, and everyone was usually too tired to do more than sleep. Sundays were free for all to worship and then they would discuss things, but that was still four days away. She prayed this new master would move on, take attention off her. She lowered her head, the feel of the metal of the hoe in her grip, a reminder of who she was and where.

Thankfully, he continued on his way, the other master on a horse with him. Word had been around among the white foremen and Doggie, he was Master JJ's son and schooled in the big cities. It wasn't likely he would stay and manage the plantation with his father.

"Master JJ wants him to be one of them senators one day," Doggie guffawed. No one understood the joke amongst the other whites, but they laughed because Doggie did.

Elisa bent her head and focused on her work, relieved beyond control.

Later in the night, when she was sure her parents were fast asleep, she stood and wore her padded shoes. Not only did they protect her feet from all the dangerous night crawlers, they helped her make less noise, though they were too warm for the weather. She closed the back door quietly and froze when Dee called her from within. Her mother did sleep-talk and Elisa hoped this was one such incident. She stayed still, waiting for some grunting and incoherent mumblings which would precede Dee's snoring. Instead the door opened.

"Ya still go to swim. After all I warn ya?" Dee whispered harshly.

No use raising a ruckus this late when everywhere was so quiet.

Elisa cried uncaring about how sound carried at night. "I need it to save my soul, Ma!"

"Don't ya see how things are goin' on now? New slaves brought today, this wide-eyed, negro-eaters all o'er the plantation." She heaved. "The new *massa* askin' ya name." Dee grabbed her shoulders. "It is not safe."

Elisa released herself from her mother's grip. "I will be." She stepped back. "What value is this life?" she spat and ran into the night.

Dee was right. In less than a month, a house had become a city. The mammoth work deserved to be done by a hundred, done by not more than twenty. As new slaves arrived, there only seemed to be more to do. The only time she retained her sanity was in the cool water of the creek. Since the night of the intruder, no one else had showed up again. She'd also gone deeper, where the branches were weaker and the rocks slipperier, but she was better hidden, and she made less noise to protect herself. She was safe.

She peeled off her clothes like they hurt her skin and dove into the water with a heavy sigh of relief. Her whole body immersed, she felt like she had died, the soak through her hair presented special relief. Dee's words scared her, and she chose to return earlier than normal. Whatever evil was out there would not catch her.

Elisa swam several laps and reluctantly waded through to where her clothes were. But they were not on the ground where she left them. They were in *his* hands.

"Elisa," he murmured, his voice gruff.

Chapter Three

Elisa shivered from head to toe, from the cold Johnny imagined, and most probably from fear and he realized how insensitive he was to present himself at such a time. In such a way.

"Your dress," he mumbled, the piece of clothing stretched toward her.

She took it without a word and slid it on. He gave her the shoes too, and this time, she collected and ran. Emotions he could not describe whorled through him, weaving a cord of his intestines. Excitement, regret, anger toward himself and the system that treated humans like animals, an untamable desire he enjoyed as much as detested. He only hoped she would be back the following night.

She wasn't. He would not be if he were her.

Elisa noticed the way Dee watched her with keen eyes as she fidgeted and cowered any time any of the overseers came around. The young master had not come again, but his friend visited twice more. Something must have gone wrong but Elisa had no idea how this could affect her family. She feared the worst.   After the negro service on Sunday, the slaves gathered at their quarters for picnics. In the evenings, they would start a bonfire, sing old folk songs and dance around it. This was the best time to huddle, and Dee called Elisa aside.

"What is goin' on with ya, child?"

Dee knew she was strong. Both had seen more pain and suffering than any one person deserved. Elisa's older brother had been hung after he was caught running away with a master's horse, and two other brothers sold to different states. That the family was together now meant so much to each one and not something they wanted to jeopardize. Nonetheless, Elisa burst into tears, and Dee startled.

"The young massa. He know now. He at my swimmin'. He–"

"*Ssh*, child." Dee dragged her aside. "Don't ya let anyone 'ear ya."

"I will ne'er swim 'gain in my life. I sorry. I sorry, Mama."

"Wha'd he say to ya? When was this?"

"Three nights ago. When ya ask me not to go."

Dee gasped. "Wha'd he say to ya?"

"Just call my name. Give me my dress. I run."

"And?"

"Nothin'. I run. Mama, I so afraid. I don't go back. Wha'd he doin' there?"

"Calm down, child. Calm down. We will pretend it did not happen. Ya did not go to the creek. Ya don't know how to swim."

"Yes, Mama." Elisa wiped tears off her face. "Yes."

"Cookies in the big house for everyone!" One of Vivian's boys, Dannyboy, yelled.

The slaves numbering about thirty trooped toward the main house where visitors had been parading in and out all day.

"I ain't goin', Mama. I afraid."

Dee whispered. "Ya have to come. Stay close."

A table was set on the back porch with large plain cookies laid out on simple wooden trays. Penny Holt stood at the end and watched the slaves line up and pick a cookie, thank her, and move on. Besides Beth, no other person from inside the house was present and Elisa heaved a heavy sigh. This was not a trap. Dee, who was in front of her turned to her and smiled knowingly.

The thought had barely left when the young master walked over from the side of the house and whispered into his mother's ear. She nodded and walked away. To make things worse, he walked over to the table and picked up the cookie tray. Three slaves took turns before Dee. She took her cookie, mumbled thanks and lingered. The master looked into her eyes and nodded. Dee stepped away but did not leave as others did.

With her heart in her mouth, Elisa took a cookie. "Thank ya, Massa," she murmured.

"Come tonight."

His voice was so breathy and soft, despite her resolve to keep her face down, it shot up to his, and deep brown eyes clashed with blue ones.

Elisa hurried away, not waiting for Dee. Her mother caught up with her halfway to their cabin.

"What wrong, child? What 'appen?"

Elisa stopped short, tears in her eyes. "He say come tonight. He on to me, Mama. I in trouble now."

Dee looked around. Her husband, Anthony approached with his cookie. "*Ssh*. Ya Pa will 'ear now and there will be trouble."

Anthony got to them and frowned. "Elisa, want more than a cookie? Have mine." He handed it over.

"Thank ya, Papa."

Anthony smiled. "My pleasure. Them cookies too sweet for an old man." He moved on.

Dee sighed. "I think ya should go. Know what this all about."

Johnny stood from the stump he sat on when he saw her arrive. He'd not been sure she would take his request seriously and had been there for almost two hours. He raised the wick in the little lamp he brought and stopped walking.

"Light!" She gasped. "Light!" She turned.

He stepped forward. "Wait. I'll put it out. Please."

She did stop, and he put out the lamp plunging them into complete darkness. There was no moon tonight, and Johnny would have to depend on his words to calm her.

"Do you want to swim?"

"No, Massa."

"My name is Johnny. Please call me Johnny."

"Yes, Massa Johnny."

He moaned softly. This wasn't going to be easy and though he had revised a million times, being here with her was just as tough as he had imagined it would be.

"*Huh*, I brought a piece of Beth's lemon pound cake for you." He cleared his throat. "She makes the best pound cake in the world, believe me."

Her silence rankled. Did she leave? From prior times, he knew she could be exceptionally quiet when moving.

"Elisa?"

"Yes, Massa Johnny."

"I said I brought some–"

"I hear ya, Massa Johnny. I just don't know why?"

He chuckled. "Why? I... the pound cake is really good. I thought you may want some."

"No, thank ya, Massa Johnny."

She said something else under her breath. He didn't quite hear her, and he took a step forward.

"Sorry, I didn't hear that."

"I say, no thanks, Massa Johnny."

"Yes, I heard that. What you said, afterward?

"Nothin', Massa Johnny."

He chuckled. "Are you lying now, Elisa?"

"No, Massa Johnny. I say nothin' more."

"You said you don't want to take poison." He laughed. "Isn't that what you said, Elisa?"

"I don't wanna, Massa Johnny."

There was a little laughter in her voice, and it made his insides bubble. "Good, I don't want you to take poison either. So, to prove to you there's none, I'm going to take a bite."

His eyes now accustomed to the darkness; he could see her frame. She stood several feet away, a sure sign she didn't trust him. He stepped toward her and took a bite of the cake.

"*Hmm*, so good. We had it for dinner." He reached out. "Here, taste."

Never had Elisa tasted anything so creamy, and soft and moist. It melted in her mouth and she moaned.

Johnny laughed. "I told you so."

Her heart pounded harder. She would never understand what was going on, and she feared this meeting was the beginning of a lot of trouble. She hated trouble. It never amounted to anything. They had heard of uprisings by slaves, it usually ended in unwarranted casualties. Her parents never got involved in any discussions about leaving slavery. They heard about the news and the executions, and Dee and Anthony had vowed never to be a part of it.

"If the slave owners don't want slaves no more, they won't 'ave slaves no more," Anthony always chanted. "Nothin' a slave goin' a do to change anythin'."

Whatever the case, Elisa loved the pound cake and ate more. And more. When the cake was finished, Johnny produced a bottle of fresh-squeezed oranges and they drank together.

"Do you want to sit down?" he asked.

"Yes, Massa Johnny. Thank ya."

"Over here. There is a stump." He pointed toward where he had been.

She avoided him and sat on the stump. She hadn't noticed this before, but then she'd never had to sit under any tree here. He remained on his feet and all she could think of was getting away. His tone and manner reminded her of Dannyboy. Dee told her the boy was interested in her, but she had vowed never to fall in love, not even with a free man. Her children would be slaves by virtue of her status as one, and that was something she couldn't bear to see.

"The other woman, today. The one who got the cookie before you. Is she your mother?" Johnny said.

"Yes, Massa Johnny."

"I thought so too. She's like a mother hen." He chuckled. "I got the eye from her." He changed his voice. "Like if you go near my baby!"

His efforts to amuse her didn't work. She could not be entertained out of her nerves. What was this about? Dee had stood by the door and watched her leave. She knew her mother would not sleep until she returned. If she returned. Her final words rankled, *"If ya go, trouble: if ya don't go trouble. Go so we get this trouble o'er with."*

Johnny crouched. "When I was a child, I would sneak here and jump in the creek. It scared my mother to death when she discovered. She did think I would drown one day."

Elisa said nothing because it was not her place to make conversations with him.

He stood suddenly. "I think you should start to go back so you can have some time to sleep. I promised myself not to keep you."

She stood, curbing a heavy sigh. "Yes, Massa Johnny. Thank ya."

He escorted her to the edge of the woods. "Please, come tomorrow."

The following night he brought Beth's apple pie and Elisa had never tasted anything so good. He brought the pound cake again. And a pumpkin pie. And truffle. And sugar. Every day for the next week, he brought sweet things she enjoyed. Dee warned her she would get into trouble and had to stop and she told Johnny.

"My Mama think comin' 'ere should stop, Massa Johnny."

Johnny sighed. "I know. We can't be caught. But it doesn't have to stop. We just need to be careful."

For another week, they continued to meet. When Dee threatened to tell Anthony, Elisa stopped going for a few days, with consent from Johnny, and then they resumed at midnight when everyone would be asleep.

On one night, Johnny brought with him milk chocolates and red wine. And a small dress. He prodded Elisa to change into it and swim with him. He gave her the chocolates and they drank the sweet red wine. High and excited, clad in the small dress, Elisa jumped into the creek. Johnny took his clothes off, and wearing loose pants jumped in too.

Chapter Four

Nothing made Johnny happier than the evening time when he would go to the creek to be with Elisa. He started working at the mayor's law office, but as soon as dinner was over, he would go for a long walk. Sometimes he would return early to talk about the plantation with his father. Most of the time, he would wait until the house was asleep, then he'd go into the pantry and take something sweet for Elisa. Her sweet tooth amused and pleased him too. They would swim, play in the water like children and talk until it was necessary to go back.

"I want to find a way for you to work in the house," Johnny told her one night.

"No, my mama will not be happy."

"I want to see more of you, Elisa."

She shook her head. "No, Massa Johnny. 'Tis too dangerous."

On one other occasion, he brought her a bracelet.

"No, Massa Johnny. My mama won't lemme 'ave it."

The more they met, the more they wanted to meet. After the first planting period, some of the slaves were sent to the stables, and Elisa was one of them. This gave Johnny the opportunity to see her during the day.

Throwing caution to the wind late one afternoon, Johnny came back from work and went into the stables. The slaves were preparing to take a break for dinner. He cornered Elisa and they escaped into a stall deeper inside, stifling laughter like teenagers. Johnny had honey-coated almonds from his lunchtime at work, and Elisa ate almost all.

"I will get more for you, tonight. I will go back to town and buy them."

She giggled. "Tis so sweet all of 'em."

Johnny nodded. "I'm going to teach you how to read and write too."

"No, Massa Johnny. Slaves ain't s'posed to read and write."

"How are you a slave if you're here eating my almonds and giggling?"

Elisa jumped; her face filled with horror.

Johnny turned and saw Dee standing at the entrance. He fully faced her and bowed. "Miz Dee."

Dee growled. "Massa Johnny, are ya tryin' a get my daughter *killtt*?"

"If you'll excuse me," Johnny sidestepped her and walked away.

Dee stepped up to Elisa and slapped her hard. "Ya fool child. 'ave ya been lettin' him touch ya everywhere?"

Elisa screamed. "No, Mama. He not touchin' me."

Dee dragged her by her ear and pushed her out. "I am goin' a tell ya Papa. He goin' a whip foolishness out of ya head before ya get yaself killt!" She pushed her forward. "I'm goin' a tell ya Papa what ya been up to, foolish child," Dee cursed. "That whippin ya been lookin' for, ya a goin' a get from ya Papa." She pulled Elisa along.

"Please, Mama. Don't tell Papa."

But Dee was beyond approach. The slaves were winding down and clearing up dinner when Dee and Elisa got to their cabin.

Anthony growled. "And where did ya all go?"

Dee whispered harshly. "Ya child been lettin' the young Massa touch her."

"No, Papa. No massa touchin'–"

Anthony's slap cut her off and she fell on her knees.

Dee moaned. "She been hidin' around playin' with a white man. She goin' a get all of us killt or worse sold off like chickens."

Anthony pulled out his rubber belt. "Lie on ya face, child."

Elisa sobbed but obeyed. "Papa, please."

"This 'ere is no punishmen', Elisa." He flung the belt and it hit Elisa across her butt. "This is correction."

Elisa screamed through six lashes. When her father was done with her, she scuttled to the corner and wept.

"Ya get up from there and come 'ave dinner." Dee shouted at her. "We run late and ya get the real whippin'."

She had dinner and returned to the stables with the others. JJ had a new herd of horses arriving and there was a lot of work going on in preparation. Shortly before they were done, Johnny showed up again, and this time walked over to Doggie and asked permission to take Elisa off the work.

Dee glared as the two walked out of the stables.

Alone at the back of the huge shed and out of view of anyone, Johnny brought out a bag of honey almonds.

"I just got back. Here."

Elisa swallowed. "No, Massa Johnny. I can't take it."

Johnny searched her face. "Why? Your Mama?"

"And Papa."

Johnny arched his eyebrows. "She told him?"

"And I got whipped."

"*Oh* darling, I'm sorry. Will you come tonight?"

She shook her head. "I can't play with ya no more. Ya a white man, I a black slave."

Their gazes locked and Elisa had never felt such a twisting in her belly before.

Especially after Johnny whispered, "Please."

Elisa dragged her gaze away. "My Papa will kill me."

"Come to the house, then."

"The house! Massa Johnny!"

He scratched his scalp. "You're right. That makes no sense."

He started to pace, which made Elisa really nervous. What was on his mind? Dee had told her the massa wanted to have sex with her, but they had been "friends" for more than a month now. If he wanted such a thing, he could have had it without her consent. His father always went to Vivian and she had nothing to say about that. Her husband and her two boys had nothing to say to it either.

She felt she needed to know what Johnny was after. She really liked him now and didn't want anything to spoil their relationship, but Dee was right. Such a relationship would lead to no good.

"We will find something for you to do at the back of the house." He stopped suddenly. "My sister just got two pet dogs. What kind of pet do you like?"

Elisa shrugged. "It make no difference. Chicken, maybe."

Johnny laughed. "Chickens are for food, not petting. I can get a kitten to add to Katie's two dogs, and you must come and care for them in the evenings."

Elisa shook her head. "Massa Johnny–?"

"Yes. That's it." He threw a punch in the air. "That will work. And I will just happen by to take a walk in the yard while you care for the dogs and cat."

"Mama will know." Elisa shuddered. "And Papa too. And Missiz Penny will never agree."

"Leave her to me. She takes a nap after dinner. I will tell Doggie you are reassigned after dinner."

"Massa Johnny, I don't want trouble."

He came close and cupped her cheeks. "You will have no trouble. And now run along. I'll see you tomorrow at the dog pen."

She heaved a sigh, unable to catch on to his enthusiasm. "Yes, Massa Johnny."

He beamed. "Good girl."

Johnny watched her go, his heart swelling with more affection than he had ever felt for any other human being. She was beautiful, and this drew him to her, but even more she was fun to be with. His gifts excited her, and she was so grateful for the littlest things. He enjoyed his conversations with her as well. Despite all the differences between them, they were alike in many ways. He didn't see color or status when he was with her, he only saw a soulmate. Someone he could relax around and be himself with.

Thoughts of the future crossed his mind, and he pushed them aside.

Chapter Five

The first three days went as planned. Elisa came to the back of the house and cleaned out the dog pen. There was no kitten as expected, but Johnny came smoking a pipe, and lazily walking around and talked to her. Anyone seeing them would think he was either taking a leisurely walk or supervising her. He talked about teaching her to read, and even called letters to her, asking her to repeat them after him.

Cleaning the doghouse wasn't a lot of work, and after an hour of loitering over it, he asked her to go back to the stable to avoid suspicion.

On the fourth day, Johnny brought a cute brown and white kitten. Elisa fell in love with it so much. But it was supposed to be Katie's, so while Elisa took care of the dogs, Katie played with her kitten and the two could not have any conversation.

When this happened the next day, Johnny ordered Katie to go inside, making the girl cry as she ran inside.

Elisa giggled. "She be mad at ya, Massa Johnny."

"She's had enough of time with her pet," Johnny said. "I want some time with mine."

Elisa giggled. Johnny paced. "Now, do you remember the song we sang with the letters?"

"*A,B,C,D,E,F,Geee,H,I,J,K,L,L,M,O,Peee.*"

Johnny laughed. "Goodness, Elisa. You tease. I have a book for you."

"With the song? Massa Johnny, ya know I can't be with a book."

Johnny looked around. "Come with me. Quick." He waved at her and she looked around and left the doghouse to follow him.

Elisa entered the big house for the first time and gasped. The smell of lavender and roses accosted her, and she took a deep breath. Added to the beautiful fresh air was the smell of freshly baked cookies. Johnny led her to a large room, with a big bed made with fancy and silk fabrics. A large polished wooden table was at one end with many books on it and tucked into the table was a matching chair.

"This is so beautiful, Massa Johnny. I 'ave never seen a room so glorious."

Johnny chuckled. "You now have many colorful words, Elisa. I should bring you here every day." He walked over to the table and pulled out two books from the shelf. "Here. I bought them from town. For you."

She shook her head. "I can't 'ave books. My Papa will whip me to death before them massas get me."

Johnny sat on the bed. "Then you can sit here and read. When it is dark, I'll lead you out and you can go back."

"Massa Johnny, I scared."

"No one can harm you here with me, Elisa darling." He stretched out his hand to her.She reluctantly took it. He pulled her to him and made her sit on the bed beside him. "You'll be alright, Elisa. I promise."

"Bed so soft." She giggled and threw herself back, lying flat on the bed. "So smooth."

Johnny laughed and smoothed her cheek. "Come on up. Let's do some reading."

The door to the room pushed open slowly and they both stood, their laughter cut off. Katie stood in the doorway, tear streaks on her cheeks.

Johnny snapped. "Go on, Katie. It's past your bedtime."

The small girl turned and ran off.

Elisa shuddered. "I gatto leave, Massa Johnny. No body must see me 'ere."

"I'll lead you out," Johnny said, and took the books back to his shelf.

But Elisa did not wait for him. She took to the door and ran out. The corridor led two ways and she took the turn she thought was right. It led her into a large kitchen. She remembered she didn't pass through the kitchen and turned around. She bumped into the mistress of the house, and Penny screeched.

"What are you doing in my kitchen?"

Johnny came up behind her. "I asked her to come and help with–"

Penny was hysterical. "A field slave in my kitchen." She turned and hurried away.

Johnny followed her. "Mother, calm down."

Elisa shivered to her toes. She knew there would be trouble. She ran out of the kitchen but had no idea where to go. The house was big, and no one was in sight. Unsure, she ran back inside the kitchen and cried. No one came. She wished Johnny would just come back and take her out, but he didn't. Dee's angry and frustrated voice of caution rang in her brain. She heard the big bell ring and knew Penny had gotten Doggie. The bell informed everyone there would be a whipping, and they had to come out to watch.

Her wait was cut short when Beth entered the kitchen, but before she could ask for help, Doggie and JJ Holt walked in. Elisa would have fainted if she knew how to. Penny followed with Katie, and then Johnny.

"Please, Massa Doggie–"

Doggie grabbed her by the arm and led her out into the yard. Everyone followed. Johnny made a single protest word and said nothing more.

Tears streamed from Elisa's eyes as Doggie took her to the backyard where they had been served cookies several times. There also was the stakes Massa Edmond had had them erect. Several slaves had been tied to it and whipped until they dropped.

Elisa wailed. "No, Massa Doggie, please." Fear of the pain terrified her more than the pain she anticipated.

Other slaves stood around to watch, which was mandatory. From the corner of her eye, Elisa saw Dee run up to join the others, and her insides turned. Before the first lash touched her bare back, she screamed.

On the third lash, a loud crack got everyone turn toward the house. Johnny had a baseball bat with him and was smashing all the windows in wild rage. Beclouded by pain and tears as thick as blood, Elisa understood what he was doing. Another lash hit her across the back, and she screamed more.

Penny yelled. "Johnny, stop it! Somebody stop him, please. He's going to burn the house down."

JJ ran over and pulled Johnny by the shirt, tumbled him down the steps toward the stakes. He growled. "Somebody give me a whip!"

No one did. Elisa turned her face and saw Johnny tied to the stake beside her, a big smile on his face.

She didn't know what to say. A lash hit her and another hit him.

Penny screamed. "This is madness. Somebody stop this."

There were loud tears everywhere. Elisa knew hers was one and Dee's would be too. Johnny's face scrunched, but not a sound came from him. Elisa didn't know how many lashes he took, but finally, the lunacy stopped due to Penny's hysterical pleading. Penny ran over and loosened him from the stake. He could hardly stand, and she let him lean on her shoulder and led him away. His blood-stained shirt turned to shreds at the back.

Anthony came over and carried her into their cabin.

Chapter Six

"I 'ave ne'er seen a white man take a wippin' for a slave in my fity years of slavery. Ne'er," Anthony moaned. "Not even for his Mama."

Dee dipped a blood-stained rag into the bowl of hot water, squeezed and pressed on Elisa's back. Elisa yelped.

"That why I know this goin' a lead to no good," Dee moaned. "*Ssh*, child. Do ya still 'ave some of that honey of yas, Anthony?"

"Yes." Anthony leaped toward the small cupboard with their crockery. "Here."

Elisa groaned. "Mama, no. Please."

"The honey work fassa, Elisa and not hurt like salt or the white man's gin." She took the bowl from Anthony. "Ya goin' a be on ya belly for seven days the way I see this 'ere." Then out of character, Dee giggled. "I bet no meetin' with lover white boy for seven days." She gently spread the honey over Elisa's back. Elisa moaned at the soothing feeling of the honey with a little prickly ticklish feeling.

Anthony shook his head. "I ne'er seen, Dee Anthony Holt. Ne'er seen."

Johnny lay on his belly while the family doctor examined the pelts on his back.

"Not too bad, Mrs. Holt," Dr. Al Gadson said. "With the iodine soaked in, he should be up and about in a few days."

"Thank you very much, Dr. Al." Penny walked him to the door. "I'll see you soon."

"You're welcome, Miz Penny. Please make sure he eats well."

"I will." Penny closed the door after the doctor and returned to sit beside Johnny. "What was all that about, Johnny boy? Why did you do that?"

Johnny turned his head to face Penny. "I told you to let her go. You disrespected me, Mother. You disrespected me in front of a slave."

Penny gasped. "She was punished–"

Johnny lifted himself up sharply and groaned from the pain. "Dang." He growled. "I told you she was innocent. To let her go."

"She was in my kitchen looking for something to steal."

"She was in your kitchen because she missed her way!"

Penny cried. "She is a field slave with no place inside the house."

Johnny waved. "Please leave, Mother. I need to think."

"She drove JJ Holt to raise a whip to his own son!" Penny drew in a shuddering breath. "Your father forbids you to see her again. You have a million and one beautiful ladies in Creek View, and Louisville, and a million liberal minds in New York. What does this girl do to you?"

"Please go."

"You cannot see her again, Johnny Holt Junior," she said. "Unless just for physical escapades, which I have come to realize with men mean nothing."

Johnny did not reply. When he heard the door close behind her, he dragged himself off the bed, wincing as he pulled on a robe. He wanted to know if Elisa was okay. She must have taken double his whipping, and for him to feel so sick, he wondered if she had not been killed.

The house was pitch black, and he didn't take a lamp to avoid detection. Edmond had talked of getting the vigilante to parade the Holt plantation, but no concrete arrangements had been made. No slave had yet tried to escape, but with this, he could only imagine how paranoid they would get.

He found his way to the slave cabins and realized he didn't know which belonged to Elisa's family. Frustrated, he took the long painful walk back. He needed to find a courier. Soon too.

Chapter Seven

Honey worked magic on Elisa's back and on the seventh day as her mother had predicted, she could sit and was able to wear her dress. Doggie insisted she returned to work in the stables and revoked the permission to work at the doghouse.

Just before dinner, Beth came inside the stable and spoke with Doggie. Shortly afterward, Elisa was called upon and asked to follow the short, skinny house slave. Dee and Anthony were back in the field and she hoped they would not get the shock of their lives again. She had promised her parents not to see Johnny again. Beth was among the party that led her to be whipped a week earlier, and she hated the way the much older woman carried her thin shoulders high and nose in the air like she wasn't a slave as well. Pride stopped her from asking Beth why she was being led to wherever she was being taken to. She also didn't have the courage.

They got to the front of the house and Beth told her to wait. She stood listlessly, half-hoping Johnny would walk out. She had kept her feelings to herself since the events of the previous week, though her father came back every day talking about how much respect he had for Johnny, and if she was sure he had not seen her "undergarments" as he chose to put it. She didn't know what it was to fall in love with anyone, but she knew Johnny was so special to her. His skin color made no difference, but Dee kept on saying, *"No good goin' a come off this."*

Massa Edmond and Massa JJ walked through the front of the house, and Elisa's heart sank to the pit of her belly. They were going to whip her again. Edmond was so mean-spirited and there had been rumors amongst the new slaves he was wanted in Georgia for killing two slaves in cold blood. JJ would be mad at her for having to whip his son for her.

Her hands and lips trembled. These two men knew Johnny was probably still too sick to move around. A third white man with a heavy beard walked out of the house behind the two masters, and Elisa's eyes darted from one to the other, her heart thudding hard and fast.

"She looks strong." the third man came down the few steps to her. He circled her, and then pulled her dress down, tearing it at the shoulder. "*Whoa*, welts!"

"She took a whipping last week for being stubborn, but you see how strong she is. To be back to work. It's not quite five days." Edmond turned to JJ. "Five days, *yeah*?"

"Four," JJ lied. "Thirty strokes."

The inspector touched her back gingerly. "Healed well if you say four days. I have fool slaves take twenty and they lay for a month." He looked at her over. "Skin is good." He traced a finger over her arm and breasts. Tweaked her nipple. "Hmm."

"She works very hard. A whip here and there keeps her sane most times," Edmond said.

"I really would have wanted a man. I told you this, Edmond." The buyer sighed. "This looks good, but I want a man. And your asking price is too much, with all those welts." He headed back into the house.

JJ followed him. "I'll give you a twenty percent discount."

"Go back to work," Edmond barked.

Elisa turned and walked back on shaky legs. She couldn't believe what just happened. They were going to sell her and there was nothing she could do. If Edmond and JJ convinced the buyer, she could be gone from the plantation in a day. She couldn't bear the thought of not seeing her parents again. And Johnny. What would he do? He'd be so heartbroken. Elisa couldn't hold her tears and couldn't wait until she fell into her mother's arms and they could weep over this together.

The end was near.

A soft knock came through and Johnny looked away from his desk. It had to be his dinner. Though he had been up and about for two days now, he continued to refuse to have dinner with the family. His father owed him an apology and he had told his mother so. He was as much master in the plantation as Edmond or JJ, and he had a right to bring in the house whomsoever he wished, whensoever. This was his argument with his mother on a daily basis.

For days all he did was write poems to Elisa. He didn't know when he would see her again, because he still didn't know who to trust with information. Beth could have been a good ally, but she had led Elisa out with Doggie, and much as he loved the woman's cooking, he could not trust her. She was too loyal to Penny. And he wondered why. Back when he was younger, Penny had had her three children sold off one by one, insisting they didn't need to keep many slaves as there was nothing for them to do. The last sold, a six-year-old boy had broken the woman and Johnny suspected that single event had turned Beth into a cold-hearted, unfeeling woman.

He closed his journal. "Come in."

Beth walked in with a tray of hot potato and mushroom soup and freshly baked rolls.

"Missiz Penny say ya want a light tonight." She placed the tray on his desk. "I sneak in a lil blueberry muffin for that lil girl ya take a whippin' to. She may be gone in the mornin'." She headed out.

Johnny leaped off his seat and blocked her exit, breathing hard. "What do you mean, Miz Beth?"

"Ya the only massa that call me Miz Beth. Not e'en ya lil sis call me. I feel I owe ya."

Johnny grabbed her shoulders. "What do you mean gone in the morning?"

"*Ssh*, ya loud as a bell," Beth whispered. "Massa Edmond and Massa JJ, they ask me to bring her. They goin' a sell 'er either way tomorrow. A buyer wanna take 'er for $30 and they goin' a sell 'er." She opened the door.

Johnny shut it.

"I'll be right with ya, Missiz Penny." Beth raised her voice. "Massa Johnny ask me to put out the soup."

Johnny lowered his voice to a bare whisper. "Take me to her. Tonight. Midnight. Meet me at the stakes." Johnny cleared his throat. "Thanks for dishing, Miz Beth."

Chapter Eight

Elisa said nothing to her parents until everyone was ready to sleep. She had been sad since she returned to the stable and had no idea what to do. She didn't want to be sold to go to live on another plantation. Her father always said it was better to die than to be sold, and since it was against the faith to commit suicide, all they could do was to live one day at a time. She didn't want to leave her parents or Johnny. Did he know about this? Had he given up on their friendship? Or maybe his parents had convinced him she was better left alone.

He was a fine young man, and anything with her would lead to nowhere. The society would never accept their relationship, even if he bought her. Moreso, she had never heard of a white man marrying a black slave. He would marry a white woman who could keep his home and have children for him. The best she would ever be to them would be a slave. She could have his children, but they would all be slaves too. That she prayed never to happen to her.

Dee gripped Anthony's hand when Elisa finished talking about what happened to her. "Don't let 'em take 'er away, please, Anthony."

Anthony groaned. "Wha'd I do? What can a slave do?" He stood. "Run. We need to run."

Elisa wept. "Run to where?"

Dee screeched. "We don't know where we at, Anthony!"

"I can speak with some men on the field in the mornin'. Start a plan."

Dee covered her face and wept. "The end is 'ere." She sobbed. "I goin' a lose my last child. I goin' a killt myself."

Elisa had never felt so helpless. Slavery was such a hopeless situation. She blamed herself for putting the family though this misery. If only she had listened to her mother's advice and not gone to the creek. If only…

One loud knock rang through and the two women huddled. Anthony stood like a man, but Elisa knew he felt none of the bravery he mustered.

Dee sobbed. "They come for her to killt her. Just like they killt my Noah in the middle o' night."

Anthony stood before the door but didn't open it. "Who knock? Tis late."

"It Miz Beth. Massa Johnny 'ere with me."

Anthony jerked the door open. Johnny entered the room not paying attention to him and rushed to Elisa. The two hugged tightly, both weeping.

Dee rushed to Beth. "Thank ya."

"I need a 'urry back." Beth disappeared into the night.

Johnny cupped Elisa's face. "I'm sorry, darling. For all the sorrow I brought to you."

Dee came to stand beside him. "Ya know they sell 'er off? She be gone tomorro'."

"I just got to know this evening, but I have a plan. I'm taking Elisa now with me. We will go into Louisville and I will find a place for her. Tomorrow, I will contact friends in New York–"

Anthony whispered harshly. "Ya do not think I will let ya take my daughter like that!" He snapped his fingers.

Johnny's tone matched Anthony's. "What do you propose? Tomorrow my father plans to sell her for as little as $30 if he can't get a better deal."

Dee sobbed. "Take 'er with ya, Massa Johnny. We will meet one day in 'eaven."

Elisa stepped back. "I'm not leavin' without my mama and papa. I will die."

Johnny looked at her as though she had grown wings. "Did you hear what I said my father plans to do with you?"

"Yes. And I saw the man. He look mean, and ol'. But I'm not leavin'." Elisa left his embrace and stood between Dee and Anthony.

"Get sense, child!" Anthony paced. "If Massa Johnny take ya now, we can meet in future. We will find ya!"

"No," Elisa cried. "The massa will think ya hep me run. He will sell ya or whip ya, or killt ya."

"No, when he no see Massa Johnny, he will know he run with ya," Anthony argued. "Is easy to run with one slave, not three."

Elisa folded her arms across her chest. "I'm not goin'."

Johnny stepped closer to her. "Listen to your father. He is right. I don't have a plan yet; I have to think as we move. And the bundle I packed can be enough for just two of us. I'm heading to New York and I don't know how many friends will have board for three extra people."

Elisa turned her back. "Go, Massa Johnny. I a slave. I will live and die a slave."

There was silence for several beats.

Johnny walked to the door and turned. "Well, what are y'all waiting for. We don't have all night!"

They snuck through the back of the cabins, with Johnny in the lead. He grew up on this land and had many options for escape. He could take them to the stable, but he wasn't sure Anthony could ride a horse, and this would make some noise. He could go around to the back of the house and take Edmond's carriage, but that would be easily noticed missing and draw unnecessary attention. Besides, a carriage would be slower. They could pass through the creek, but that would leave them all wet. He had packed a small bag for himself and Elisa, which contained some dry foods and clothing, now he had two more and he just needed to think on his feet.

A figure appeared in their path, and Johnny stopped.

"Lemme go with ya. I'av no life 'ere," Beth whispered harshly. She held a small bundle.

Johnny shook his head. "Where are we going? This is the fastest way to get caught." He turned to Elisa and her parents. "I'm not doing it. I'm not on a suicide mission."

Johnny was not going to be roped into what he could not handle. Beth stepped up to him, her voice trembling.

"When I was bought by Missiz Penny and Massa JJ, I was married to a slave in the other plantation. They let me visit and he visit too. We got us three chilren, and they massas start to fight over 'em. They settle the fight by sellin' off our chilren and sharin' the money. We try a run away. They found us and Matthew took a bullet." She gripped Johnny's hand. "I'av nothin'. Hep me."

Dee stepped forward. "We know the prolem this can cause. I and my Anthony will stay back." Elisa started to protest but she stopped her. "Go with Massa Johnny. When ya all safe, we will find ya."

"I will come back for you. It's just that this is all so sudden." Johnny nodded. "Thank you for your understanding."

Anthony's voice was laden with emotion. "We know ya mean well, Massa Johnny. Please take care of my baby."

Elisa shuddered with tears. Johnny held out his hand and took hers. "She'll be safe with me. I will defend her with my life."

His words evoked emotions and Elisa parted with her parents tearfully. He still could not take a horse, which was his initial plan, so he took the carriage. The women hid on the floor with Johnny's bag tossed carelessly over them. It wasn't much of a camouflage and when they reached Louisville, Johnny buckled.

He parked the carriage under a deserted commercial stable and spoke as though someone sat beside him.

"We can't continue like this. I am not confident of any plan. And if we are stopped before we cross into Ohio, we all will be in trouble." When none of his passengers replied, he continued. "I have Gilbert here, and the kind Dr. Al but how much can they do?"

"I know a famly who hep escape slaves on the other side of town," Beth murmured.

"Do you know the name of the street?"

"If I see where we at, I can take ya to 'im.'"

Johnny thought of the options and drove to a deserted highway not far from town. Louisville was such a large city; Beth could be taking them to any part. They could be minutes or hours away. He jumped down from the carriage and helped the women out. Beth walked a few feet away and then turned toward the south.

Johnny frowned. "Do you know where we are?"

"I do now, Massa Johnny." She nodded. "I follow Missiz Penny 'ere all the time."

Johnny held Elisa's hand and they followed Beth off the road, their load flung on their backs.

Elisa couldn't stop crying despite Johnny's reassuring murmurs and gentle squeeze of her hand. She knew she had no reason to be afraid with him. He had given more than anyone ever could, proven he loved her and wanted her safe, but she had only been separated from her mother once, for a few months, and those had been the worst days of her life. It would not have been better if she was sold, but what if JJ never got a buyer for her? What if it was just a way to intimidate her and not a real threat? What if they had panicked for nothing?

"I want my Mama," she mumbled.

Beth led them through the woods, and they continued for what seemed forever. The sun started to come up and Johnny stopped them.

"We can't be seen once it's light. Where are we going, Miz Beth?"

Beth sighed. "Acroz the road, Massa Johnny. Over the'e." She pointed.

Johnny frowned. "The church?"

"Behind the church. The good doctor will help."

"Let's hurry, Massa Johnny," Elisa whispered. "The sun gets up real fast when it does." She remembered Dee's words.

They dashed across the road, Johnny first, and went by the side of the church to a small farmhouse. Beth walked to a back window and knocked three distinct times, while Johnny and Elisa remained pressed against the wall. A window opened, and Beth climbed in like she had done this all her life. She leaned over and waved the two over, and they climbed in as well. The room was dark at first, then a white man walked in with a lamp.

Johnny gasped. "Dr. Al?"

Chapter Nine

Johnny had never felt more relief in his life. He stepped forward and gripped the shoulders of the heavily bearded, middle-aged medicine man.

"Thank you, sir."

Dr. Al didn't seem as enthusiastic. He shifted from Johnny. "Why, Johnny. What are you doing here?"

Beth moved closer and spoke softly. "Massa Johnny hep us to get 'ere."

"Us, Beth." The doctor took a deep breath. "Well, come with me, Beth, I'm glad you got here safely. The others are ready."

Johnny frowned. "Wait, not only Miz Beth. We…Elisa and I–"

"Beth?" Dr. Al turned to the slave woman and she looked down at her hands.

Johnny could not believe what this seemed like now. "This was a plan already?"

Beth stared at her feet. "Am sorry, Massa Johnny. But I 'ave wanted this from the day my first babe was taken from me. They tell me I goin' a see my babe again. I–"

Dr. Al straightened. "There's no time to waste, Beth. Come with me."

Johnny blocked his retreat. "What about us?"

"I'm sorry, Johnny. There is room for only one." Dr. Al bypassed him and left, Beth hurried after him.

With the doctor gone, the room was thrown in pitch blackness.

Johnny swore. "I can't believe this. She made us leave two people, brought us here knowing there was no plan for us!"

Elisa's voice came from a distance; he'd almost forgotten she was there. "A slave life tough, Massa Johnny," Elisa sighed. "I dunno what I'd do if me was Miz Beth."

He scratched his beard. "I don't know what to do now."

"We just 'ave to wait till they come back."

They had long to wait. But finally, a young black woman came in with two rolls of bread and hot soup on a tray, with drinking water in a clear jar. She placed it on a small table Johnny hadn't noticed earlier in the empty room and set the small lamp in her other hand on the floor. She would have left, but Johnny cleared his throat.

"Excuse me. Please wait. My name is Johnny. I came with Beth. Miz Beth." He could not articulate his thoughts or words.

"Yes, Master Johnny," the young woman said in a clear and strong voice, her diction perfect. "My name is Savanna, and I work as Dr. Al's maid."

"You are educated?" Johnny paused. "Are you free?"

"Yes, Master Johnny. Dr. Al has no slaves. My family has worked for his family for years. Since my mother was free, I was born free."

"Glad to meet you, Savanna." Johnny held out his hand to her. She shook it hesitantly. "I need to know what is going on."

Savanna smiled. "Ms. Beth has been taken with the others. They will go through the Underground Railroad to freedom."

"Do you know what plans are made for us?"

Savanna's gaze darted from him to Elisa. There was a story behind that exchange and Johnny stepped closer to her.

"Please, we need help too."

"I'm sorry, Master Johnny. I do not know." She stepped back. "Please excuse me."

Johnny turned away, more frustrated than ever. "This is ridiculous."

"Am 'ungry. Ya should eat too, Massa Johnny." For a minute, Johnny's stomach twisted, and a slow growl followed. "Ya see?" Both chuckled.

"Yes, we should eat."

They sat together and dipped the rolls in the soup. Johnny's stomach growled more.

"Did you hear how the young lady speaks?" Johnny smiled at her. "You will speak like that too. And our children will be free, because you will be."

Elisa mumbled. "She a mulatto."

"That is not a good word to use for how our children will be."

Elisa shrugged and continued eating.

Johnny stopped. "You know I want to marry you, Elisa, don't you?"

"Ya talk of a futcha we cannot see, Massa Johnny."

"I see a future with you. It's the only future I see." Johnny went on one knee. "Will you marry me, Elisa Anthony?"

"Massa Johnny, no!" Elisa exclaimed. "Eat and think o' today."

Johnny swallowed and sat. The food was tasty, but he'd lost appetite. This was not the time to propose and he had no ring, but what better time to let her know how committed he was. He didn't come here to save his own neck.

The door opened and Dr. Al walked in. "It's time to leave. Are you done eating?"

They jumped to their feet.

"Yes, sir. Where are we going?"

"Slave catchers set out. They saw Edmond's coach, which you stole, and I have the information they are searching for you." Dr. Al's gaze was fixed on Johnny. "Your mother has been very worried for you and I can only do what is right."

Johnny's mouth dropped open. "What are you saying? What time is it?"

"It's time to go home, Johnny, I'm sorry."

Instinctively, Johnny moved to stand in front of Elisa. "You sold us out?"

"We protect justice and the law. You cannot steal a slave and a carriage and imagine I will support you, Johnny."

"But you will help Beth to escape. You work both sides!" Johnny trembled. "Dr. Al, please don't do this to us. I plead with my life. Elisa will be sold or killed if taken back."

The doctor looked at her as though she sprouted out of nowhere. "Why would that be a bother, Johnny?" He frowned. "Why would you want to risk everything? A beautiful education and a life at the Senate?"

"She is the love of my life, Dr. Al. I risk everything if I lose her."

The doctor laughed, a low sound synonymous to that of mice having babies. "You cannot be married to her, even in Europe such a relationship will ostracize you from society."

Johnny swallowed. "I don't care about society. My happiness and hers is most important."

His words seemed to bounce off the wall. Dr. Al took a deep breath. "We waste time, Johnny. The men are willing to let you go if you both come out of your own volition."

"The men." Johnny gasped. "They are here? You let them into...here? How do you help people like Beth to escape and refuse to help us?"

"Beth needed help. I knew her from when she had her children with her. She has suffered–"

Johnny exclaimed. "And we don't need help?"

"We have limited resources and contacts. We help people who really need help."

Johnny closed his eyes briefly. "Please, Dr. Al–"

"Will you follow me, or I should ask them to come and get you?"

Johnny exhaled. "When I took Elisa and left my father's plantation, I didn't plan to walk out and return today–"

Elisa stepped in front of him. "Is me they want, Massa Johnny. Lemme go." She smiled and touched his face.

It was the first time she would ever touch him. Her palm felt rough against his cheek and a sob escaped his lips. He pulled her into his embrace, and whispered harshly, "Never!"

They did not see Dr. Al leave but heard a soft click of the door.

It jolted Johnny. "Come!"

The door opened the same time Johnny slid open the window they had come through. He pushed Elisa out and jumped after her. She landed on a black man on guard and Johnny fell on her. In the confusion, they ran toward the church building, shouts of demands to surrender preceding them. Men scuttled heavy footsteps. Johnny dragged her, holding her firmly by the hand. The back door of the church did not open, and he threw himself against it twice as three armed men closed in.

One of the men shouted. "Holt!"

Elisa whispered. "Massa Doggie!'

Johnny knew Doggie could kill Elisa and get away with it, any of the men could. He screamed and threw himself against the wooden door with all his might. It splintered in the middle, but it was enough. With strength from nowhere but from the place of fear, he shoved Elisa through the broken door and blocked it with his body.

The men stopped their advance.

Doggie snarled. "Get out of the way, Holt! If you don't want to get hurt."

Johnny breathed hard, calculating his next move. He pressed his back into the broken door and lost balance falling inside. A hand, Elisa's, dragged him out of the way just before the men burst through, shouting orders on how to proceed.

Inside, Elisa had discovered a wooden staircase by the door and stood ready to run or aid Johnny. They stumbled down, making so much noise the three men followed them. The staircase led to a maze of a basement. Obviously, this was used by abolitionists to help slaves escape, Johnny thought. He realized too late coming here could burst the bubble for many, and unlike Dr. Al, was not going to risk such a decision just to save his neck.

He yelled. "Run! Meet me at the creek."

Elisa disappeared down the corridor just as the three men appeared. On the way down the stairs, a plank had loosened, and Johnny had taken it. Did Elisa know which creek, he didn't, but all of that didn't matter in this moment.

Doggie stopped with his men and laughed. "Your father thought you were smart enough to go to college. He should see you now!" Doggie guffawed his bark of a laugh. "See you now! Fighting on your life for a slave we all had!" He *brouhahaed*. "How many times you had her, Scotty?"

The stout redneck, Pat, with his face covered in shaggy hair, grunted. "Take him, Doggie, we don't have all day. The little *nigger* will get away."

"They are cornered." Doggie laughed. "This place leads to the dead house where she'd soon end up."

"When we are done passing her around," the third guy, called Scott, said.

Pat stammered. "Take him, Doggie, you make a fool a yaself at the wrong time."

Doggie swung his hand to the left and caught Pat's jaw with a punch that sent the latter staggering backward. Johnny flung the wood plank at Doggie in that moment of distraction and ran in the direction Elisa had gone.

Doggie was right. The dead house was at the end of a long narrow corridor, and it was cold and quiet. And stinky.

"Elisa!" Johnny whispered as loud as he could.

"Massa Johnny?"

She crawled out from behind a slab and ran into his arms. Johnny couldn't care now. He took her lips in a desperate kiss.

Chapter Ten

Doggie was no fool and made no mean jokes. They were stuck in the dead house and if he didn't get to them first, the stench and cold would. Johnny hugged Elisa on the bare wooden floor, unable to think of the next steps. No one had thought of proper clothing when he left in a hurry. Elisa was even barefooted! They were caged in and whatever luck he might think they had earlier, run out. For several minutes after his kiss, he just held her not knowing what to do or think. The energy he had from fear and desperation was now depleted. He was cold and wished he'd eaten more of the rolls and hot soup.

"That first night," Elisa whispered. "When you fall o'er my shoe?"

"You knew?"

She nodded, the motion tickling his chest. "Yes." She giggled. "I thought I'd die in that wa'er."

He pressed a kiss to her forehead. "You're cold."

"I was cold more in this in that wa'er." She shuddered with suppressed laughter. "Who'd a think a be 'ere now, dyin' with ya."

"Does that mean you will marry me?"

She turned her head up and he caught her lips again. "If am dyin' with ya, Massa Johnny, I better die a Missiz Elisa Johnny."

He remembered part of the wedding vows and told her to repeat them after him.

"You may now kiss the bride," he said, and they kissed again, then chuckled together.

They squeezed closer to share body heat, but it was futile.

"'Ave ya near died before, my hasband?" She moaned. "That sound good. Hasband."

"I've never near-died before, my wife. But it's good to have a first experience with you."

"That only experien'. Cos ya be ded by the time ya're done."

Johnny smiled. "We'll meet on the other side, my love. Missis Elisa Johnny Holt."

"Why do ya wanna die with me?"

"*Ssh*, someone is coming."

They froze like they had another choice. The voices grew louder but hushed.

"Dump him under a dead body, you fool."

"He's not dead, Doggie. Why are you doing this?"

"You want to join him in hell?" Doggie spat. "Drop him here! Now let's find those idiots."

"They'd be freezing dead by now. And how do you take 'em out. The church is starting!"

Doggie sniveled. "The cold here ain't killing nobody. Let's get back, then! After the church service we come for 'em."

Johnny was quiet, cold and stiff, his cold hand stuck to her neck. Elisa feared he was dead, but she could hear the two men talking. They continued to argue about the person they brought. She deduced the church service would be on. She'd thought she could hear singing but wasn't sure. Was today Sunday then? It wasn't. Last she remembered, they left Holt Lands on Friday night and they couldn't have been here for more than an hour. She couldn't think. She couldn't cry too. Never in her life had she been this cold.

A voice too close for comfort whispered. "You'll join him, Scott. If you don't shut that dirty trap o' yours."

Footsteps retreated and all was quiet again. Elisa tried several times before her mouth opened.

"Hasband Johnny? Are ya alive, 'oney?"

He did not respond. She pressed her face to his chest and heard a slight breathing.

She cried. "Don't ya die on me, darlin'."

Summoning all willpower, she slowly stood and found his hand. It was cold and dark, and she had no idea what she was doing, but she was ready to die too. Johnny was only about a half of a foot taller than her and she didn't think he weighed much more but pulling him took every ounce of her freezing bones. This was not by strength, but sheer determination.

Elisa dragged and with the exertion of energy, she felt herself begin to sweat. She still didn't know where to go or what to do if she made it, but then those questions would have to be answered when the time came. She hoped Johnny was not dead, then she'd be accused of killing a master, and that would be hanging. She could not even bear to have such a thought. She had come to care for Johnny and would rather die with him...especially now she was somewhat married to him.

She stumbled and fell over a body and screamed involuntarily. For a moment, she imagined the dead house would fill up with people who heard her, but besides an echo all went still. Then a deep groan.

She wished her tired eyes would at least pick out a form in the darkness. "Massa Johnny?"

She seemed to be on top of a body and it near-drove her hysterical. She let go of Johnny's hands hoping to find her bearing first, but he gripped it.

"Ya alive," she sobbed. "Thank ya."

"What happened?"

"We freeze. Thot we'd die."

Johnny moaned. "I can't see a thing, but there is someone here."

"I 'ere."

Johnny made a ghost-chuckle sound. "He's warmer than you and I." He let go of one of her hands.

She cried. "Don't lea'e me."

"I 'ere." He mimicked her voice. "He's really warm. I think he's still alive, just knocked out."

"Yea. I 'ear a man talk, sound like Massa Doggie."

Johnny gasped. "Doggie is still here?"

"I 'ere him talkin' to Scotty. They argue and leave us 'ere. Say we are goin' a die anyway."

Johnny stumbled into her and pulled her. "Let's get out of here, honey,"

Elisa resisted. "What 'bout him?"

"Who?"

"The one. Man. Ya say he alive."

"We can't take him. We don't know where we are going!"

"We can't leave him too. He wounded."

She freed her hands from his and traced the wounded man in the darkness. When she pulled on his shirt, the man grunted. She continued to drag, and soon the weight became lighter when Johnny joined her. They got to an unexpected entrance to a corridor. A small lamp burned at the far end of a narrow passage.

Johnny stopped. "Wait here, let me check it out."

"Don't lea'e me!"

He cooed. "*Ssh*. We'll be fine, darling."

But she was having none of it. They let go of the unconscious man and he crept down the corridor, with Elisa right behind him. They could not stand because the path looked more like it had been carved to take the full height of a child, and medium-sized adult. About twenty yards on they came to the lamp. It was placed on a small bench. Another bench was turned over on the side of the wall and Elisa exclaimed.

"Door, Hasband! Ya see the door!"

The door was hidden and only a good eye would have spotted it. Johnny pushed and it gave way to another short passage. Johnny gripped Elisa's hand.

"The man."

Johnny rolled his eyes and returned to get him.

The passage led to a train track, and Johnny concluded this must be a route the abolitionists used to get slaves out. A dead house could just be a cover. If Beth had been rescued earlier in the day, then no train may be passing by any time soon. He didn't know anything about such.

They hid in the bush for a while and Pat, the unconscious man, regained consciousness. When he saw them, he startled and cursing out loud, crawled to his feet and staggered away. Johnny and Elisa watched him go. They followed the opposite direction, not sure of their location, and heard the sound of water.

"Has to be the creek or a stream linked to it." Johnny groaned. "A curse and a blessing."

Elisa remained mute, her lips pressed together. Johnny could smell the fear she must feel, but he said nothing about it. Right now, the only reassurance he could give her was to know what he was doing.

He squeezed her hand. "We will wash and see where this road leads. I don't even know if we are headed north or south yet."

The sun rose and Johnny used this to determine their direction.

"We're going south," he moaned. "Heading back home." He drew in a ragged breath.

"I see bush closin'," Elisa said. "Maybe we shoulda... We'd just die 'ere of 'unger."

"The stream continues. So we have water." He patted her cheeks to lighten the mood, though he didn't feel any better. "The path is not closed. Once we get to a settlement, I will go and find help."

"If they white. They black and I be the one to get hep."

She'd barely stopped speaking when they saw smoke from a distance. Johnny ducked. "We go slow and careful. Don't panic."

His toes went cold in his shoes and his heart thudded. Smoke from a chimney could be anything. Whatever it was, they were fugitives, and his father had sent slave catchers after him, whether they were real or just Doggie. If he could cross to Ohio State, he'd feel better. One thing was sure though, he needed to find food, either by stealing or otherwise. More than once it had occurred to him taking her was a mistake, but he'd rather die here than have her sold off.

"I smell food. Because I 'ungry?"

"Yes, my love. Because you're hungry." His stomach rumbled. "I smell food too."

The bush thinned and they crawled toward the smoke and smell. A small fire burned and there seemed to be a small animal on a spit. Johnny felt movement before he saw it. Six men surrounded them and he covered Elisa with his body.

The men all dressed like bounty hunters held their rifles pointed at the couple. Johnny could not recognize any of them, and remained on the ground, making no attempt to do anything else.

"You're coming with us," the one who seemed like the leader said.

Johnny growled, "Tell me when to stand."

"Stand." The man bit off the top of a cigar and chewed it. "Holt."

He helped Elisa stand and they were led to the small clearing where the meat was on the roast. Elisa was yanked away from him and tied, hand and feet. Johnny reached out to take her, but two men held him.

He snickered. "You'd have to hold me all day because I won't stand and let you keep her tied," he yelled.

"Shut up, Holt. How about I blow her brains out."

Johnny struggled hard and one of the other men walked over and punched him in the stomach. He slumped.

Elisa knew better than to get involved when masters tackled one another. She wanted to scream for them to leave Johnny alone, but even her tears she hid. The smell of the meat roasting turned her wild with hunger, and her stomach twisted with pain. That she knew how to control as well, so she closed her eyes and pretended she was in another world in another time. She imagined wearing the beautiful, flowing dresses the white women wore with their fancy hats and umbrellas, and she didn't come out of her dream world until one of the men nudged her with his boot and commanded her to open her eyes.

She did, and first saw Johnny seated on the ground, holding a piece of meat, and glaring at her. She shrank from his gaze. Did he despise her already? She always knew it would come to this but didn't know how soon.

"Johnny here say he married you," the bully leader said. "Take, Miz Johnny." He shoved a chunk of meat in her face and laughed.

She grabbed it with her mouth and tore a piece off. "Thank ya, Massa." She chewed noisily, unable to curb the low groan that emanated from her belly, joy at tasting food. It must have been two days now since she ate.

The captor continued to stand in front of her and fed her the meat twice more, then walked off. It wasn't until then she looked at her husband again and smiled. His eyes twinkled and though he wasn't bound like her, she felt a reassurance which was soon deflated when the man said,

"We'll rest a little and return to Louisville."

They came from Louisville?

The city elicited fear in Elisa. She had only heard about how busy it was and how slaves hardly ever got away with the sins they committed. Well, that was true of everywhere. Why had she agreed to this foolish plot? The mere fact that her parents couldn't come along should have been the sign not to follow Johnny. What had she gotten herself into?

The group gathered after what seemed like only an hour. Elisa's feet hurt, and the hunters kept her bound hand and foot despite Johnny's, who they allowed to walk freely, plea.

Thankfully, the hunters didn't know the track that led them here, and soon they could see houses. Without provocation, Johnny pushed the man closest to him and fled. One of the men wanted to go after him, but the leader stopped him.

"He's a farm owner. He'll find his way home."

They made her walk while they rode horses and entered Holt Lands close to midnight. It seemed everyone already knew what had happened. She was tied to the whip-stake facing forward, faint and thirsty, and she feared they would whip her on the face. What other form of cruelty would that be? At least it would mean no one would sell her easily. She wanted to die. Maybe they'd just hang her as they did some runaway slaves.

Where was Johnny? Since he ran off, the hunters decided to return her instead of taking her to Louisville, where she knew for sure she would be lynched at night. They had joked it would be better to return her to her owner and get the ransom. JJ Holt placed a ransom on her? That still surprised her. She closed her eyes, resigned.

Slaves gathered for some time, but she was so tired and weak, she couldn't make out faces. Not a single sound came from the onlookers, but she knew her parents would hold to themselves and weep silently. Doggie walked to her and spat on her face. He said several things, but she couldn't make out a single word, then he started to pour a liquid on her. It smelt like dung. She threw up on herself.

"Elisa? Wife? Let's go. I have the cart."

She startled awake. What a dream? Still tied to the stake, she thought she had died.

"Come on, baby." Johnny heaved her up. "Here."

Her throat was so dry, she couldn't speak. At this point, nothing mattered. She let him carry her. He laid her on the floor of the wooden cart, under what seemed like a blanket. A hand put a cup to her mouth, and she drank cool water.

"My babe," a familiar voice said.

Elisa knew then she had died and was in heaven.

Chapter Eleven

Johnny abandoned the cart with its two horses close to the church building, and when he was sure the coast was clear, led his regrouped escapees, Dee, Anthony, and Elisa, through the broken door of the previous day, the narrow corridor, and dead house, out onto the rail trail. At this time of the day, he suspected escaped slaves would be in the doctor's house, preparing to leave by whatever means. They would not have anyone watching, and he was probably right.

Probably, because he chose the opposite direction from their journey the day before because of the direction of the sun. The trail continued for a long while and then tapered. The rail continued but the path didn't.

"We have to decide how to proceed." Johnny stopped to survey the area. "If we get on the rail, we will be easy to spot."

Anthony breathed. "Ya done well, Massa Johnny. Ne'er knew we could come this far."

"We still have two days to cross the border into Ohio." He looked at a still-weak Elisa. "How are you?" She nodded. "Hold up. We'll soon get rest," he said softly.

He pulled out the map he got from Gilbert and memorized the path he had spent all of the day before studying after he ran from the captors. Gilbert had not heard about his escapades as he had been busy helping with his father's political aspiration, and they had not spoken since before the whipping. He'd sent a message to take time off work at the mayor's office due to ill-health and no one had bothered to check on him. His friend had given him the map and answered simple questions he thought were out of curiosity.

They continued for less than an hour before they heard dogs barking. Johnny panicked. "We need to find a place to hide."

They scrambled until they located a hole, but it wasn't big enough for four.

Anthony offered himself. "Lemme go."

"No!" Dee stood behind him. "Ya know they kill ya. Ya go, I go."

"They go, I go. I ain't lettin' ya run off on me 'gain," Elisa mumbled.

"If I didn't run, you'd be burning on a whip-stake," Johnny snapped. "Now, be reasonable. This space can take two. Miz Dee stays with her husband. You stay with yours."

Elisa snickered. "That ain't no kind o' marriage. In a dead house."

"I kissed your cold lips, didn't I?"

Dee stepped forward. "Ya two are goin' a let them catch us." She whispered harshly, "Go and hide or we ded."

Johnny gripped Elisa's hand and dragged her further away. They found another hole and lay flat in it. Within minutes they heard the dogs bark louder. Elisa started crying when she could see one of the dogs.

Johnny closed his eyes. "Not again, Lord. We had this."

A pair of feet appeared beside the dog, and without consulting or thinking, Johnny crawled forward.

"Stay here," he whispered.

Elisa whispered harshly. "Johnny!"

He stood as soon as he could and crept away from the hole. The dog barked louder and followed him. It didn't take a minute and he stopped moving, his hands up in the air, his back to the dog.

"Turn around." The man with the dog shouted. "Slowly."

Johnny gasped. "Gilbert?" And swung around.

"Johnny?" Gilbert's eyes widened. "What are you...you are the white accomplice? You're helping a slave to escape?" He lowered the gun he had aimed at Johnny's chest.

"Gilbert, let me go, please. They are my...she is my slave."

"There's more than one?" Gilbert smirked. "You will never cease to amaze me, Johnny. Why?"

"It doesn't matter. Are you a slave catcher now?"

"The money is good, and your father offered a lot." Gilbert paused. "Does he know it's you?" His eyes widened. "Is this why you took the map and asked all those questions about routes?"

Johnny heaved. "I don't have the time for small talk. Let me go, please."

Gilbert raised his handgun. "Go? You are aiding slaves to run. Trying to ruin your father and his business–"

"Don't you think that is a family affair." Johnny turned as though he would walk away. He knew he couldn't, but it was just to call Gilbert's bluff.

"I'll shoot you in the head, Holt, and no one will do anything about it. As for the slaves you stole, they will be tied to the stakes and skinned alive."

Johnny flung around. "You wouldn't dare."

"Look at you, Johnny Holt, golden boy, a student of the prestigious King's College with a full scholarship," Gilbert snarled. "What more do you want?"

"Nothing you can ever understand." Johnny walked to his friend. "I won't give you the pleasure of shooting me in the back like the jealous coward you are."

"You fool. Even if I let you go, these grounds swarm of hungry men ready to turn you and your stolen slaves in for a thousand easy bucks."

Johnny stopped short. "My father put a thousand on my head?" *Where did JJ get that kind of money from?*

"On each of your heads, dummy. Now raise your hands."

Johnny did, but his eyes were fixed on the gun. He only needed one quick movement, get the gun and kill the dog. He knew Gilbert was no good with a gun.

Elisa watched Johnny risk his life for her again. If she had not loved him before, she did now. She had crept out of the hole, hoping the dog did not sniff her, but she suspected this particular dog only followed Johnny's scent. It also accounted for the reason why the dog did nothing, though she was close behind, hidden from view.

She shut her eyes in fright when Johnny jumped the talkative man. A shot went off and Elisa burst into tears, but then heard grunts. The shot missed, and the two men were engaged in combat. She thought of what to do to help Johnny, but had no weapon, and feared she'd hurt him instead, so she rolled up on the ground and wept.

Johnny tapped her shoulder moments later, breathing hard. She knew it was him because it was such a gentle touch.

"We need to leave. There are more people according to him."

"Are ya 'urt?" She clung to his neck. "I'm sorry. Are ya okay?"

"Yes. And I'm wearing Gilbert's clothes. We..." He breathed hard. "We need to go."

"My parents–"

"Let's get them now. The dog is dead. We will rub its blood on all of our clothes."

Dee and Anthony were not in the hole Johnny left them in, and Elisa burst in another bout of tears. They searched around, but when they heard shouts from the catchers, decided to leave.

"They will be fine," Johnny told her, but she could not be comforted.

"They be ded. They goin 'o tie 'em to stakes n skin 'em alive."

Johnny cut a branch off a tree by the way and dipped it in the dog's blood. He let it soak in her dress.

"I'm safe. No one is looking for Gilbert yet."

Elisa hiccupped. "He ded?"

"No. But he won't talk for–"

Elisa yelped when Anthony came up behind Johnny.

"Dee a little 'urt, but we escape. They everywhere," Anthony said. "Dee 'urt 'er ankle."

"Come here." Johnny let their clothes soak the dog's blood.

Elisa murmured, "What good that do?"

"I don't know, but a dog won't try to catch the blood of a dog. I think." Johnny looked at Gilbert's gun in his hand. "And we have this now to aid us."

Chapter Twelve

The escape was not easy. The dog blood stank after a day, but the group trudged into Ohio. Elisa hid in the bushes with Dee, and Johnny entered the towns with Anthony posed as his slave. They got food, and clothes, even stole two horses at a time and rode them hard until they couldn't move that way anymore and continued to hide and run.

Thirteen days after their narrow escape, they got to Pennsylvania, and then had to find their way to Philadelphia. But new laws encouraged ordinary people to report runaway slaves. Johnny continued to pose as a slave trader on a journey. He continued to be seen in public with Anthony, his slave. They all agreed it would be unusual for a young slave trader to move with three slaves, so the women remained in hiding at every point. At night, they hid in shacks and abandoned building, and on one of those days, a runaway slave ran into the shed they were in.

The boy couldn't be more than fifteen years old and had pelt marks all over his face and body, exposed by the torn rags he wore. He would have run because he stumbled into Johnny first, but Johnny grabbed him, and as he begged and whimpered, Elisa came out in the open, followed by Dee.

Dee grunted. "He a spy?"

The boy's eyes widened. The shed was so well-hidden, only someone looking for it would find it.

"We're yet to find out." Johnny held the only part of his rags not torn. A piece about his neck. "What's your name?"

"Nat, Massa."

Johnny let go of him, and he fell to his face. "I'm not your *massa*!"

"Remind me o' my Lucas. Healthy-looking, handsome. Scared ta hell." Dee moved closer to Nat. "What ya story, boy?"

Nat trembled, but said nothing.

Elisa sighed. "He look like he goin' a need some food."

She went back deeper into the holes they kept food and supplies and removed a roll of dry bread and jerky. She beckoned on Nat to come forward and the boy did. After he had eaten, she gave him a bowl of water to wash in and he slept off.

"Only 'eaven knows how long he goin' a be out for," she murmured.

Johnny stared at the boy. "We have to leave here. If another person discovers this place, we're done." He summoned Anthony. "It gets dark in a bit, then we can go searching."

He moved away to prepare.

"I don't think he mean any 'arm, but where we comin' from, anyone is the devil," Anthony said.

The two men left shortly afterward.

"I'm goin' a wake 'im, Mama. Afore the men return."

Dee nodded. "We woman know better than those men."

Nat grunted several times when Elisa nudged him, but he finally came awake and sat with his knees drawn up to his chin.

"Tell us ya story. Our men are gone," Dee said.

Nat spoke in a low, muffled tone. "I run from Maryland. Was s'pposed to join a group but couldn't," he sighed. "Been on my own for a month, finding my way 'ere."

Elisa exclaimed. "From Maryland!"

Dee snorted. "So, where ya goin'? What group?"

Nat shot his gaze in between the two, his dark eyes widened with fear, but he spoke all the same. "They say they goin' ta the old city. 'Ere. I want ta find it...them. They'll go ta Canada where there ain't no slavery." His tone thickened with excitement. "We goin' a get jobs in factories."

Dee beamed. "Canada."

When the men returned, Dee was all giddy and ready to move with Nat to Canada. Johnny listened to the story again.

He nodded. "I know where they call the old city. We can leave immediately."

They packed the little food and clothing they had close to midnight, and Johnny led them to the old part of town. The doors were all closed, and the street deserted.

Elisa hugged Dee's side. "This don't look good. Where e'er'body?"

Johnny turned to the group. "We'll find some hiding place and I'll move with Nat."

Elisa moaned. "Please, Johnny hasband. Don't leave."

Johnny pulled her into his arms and kissed her forehead. "I'll be back as soon as we find the group."

He and Nat walked off briskly, while the rest pressed themselves against the wall in a dark alley. It was as close to a dangerous risk as they had taken throughout their trip. It took what seemed like hours and Elisa sobbed quietly. No one came by the alley, but they all feared morning would come, and daylight would expose them. Anthony tried to reassure the women he knew enough of the town to get them out if it came to that, but it was futile. Fear made his voice wobble.

"Maybe we should return to the shed," Elisa fretted. "At least we safe there."

Anthony shrugged. "Till a lad come by. No longer safe if someone couln' find it."

Dee covered her mouth. "Ssh, I 'ear voices."

Johnny showed up, but he was alone.

Elisa jumped on his neck and wept. "I thot ya'd ne'er return."

He hugged her back. "Even if it will cost my life, Wife, I'll come back for you." He looked at the others. "We found the place. Let's go."

"And Nat?" Dee asked.

Johnny nodded. "Is safe. We'll be with him. Soon."

"Ya talkin' to yaself when ya comin'?" Elisa whispered.

"Yes, darling. To alert you I was coming." He pulled her closer. "Come on, let's go."

They wove a track in between several houses and dark streets, walking fast and close to the buildings. It was a long walk and by the time Johnny gave three distinct knocks on a wooden door, the first signs of daylight were upon them.

Someone opened the door and they rushed inside. Elisa did not see anyone inside the well-lit and simply furnished parlor they entered. Johnny walked straight across the room to another door and opened it. This room was dark except for a single lamp by the window. It looked like a bedroom with a large bed laid with silk. Johnny walked briskly to the small woven carpet at the head of the bed and pushed it aside. A small knob surfaced, which he turned, and then asked them to get in through a small square hole with a winding wooden staircase in what was just a tunnel. Then he followed and closed the hole.

Someone would have to put the woven thing back in place, Elisa thought.

They descended as quietly as they could, and Johnny opened a door at the foot of the stairs. They entered a room that looked like a church with wooden pews.

"We'll sit here and wait for someone," Johnny said.

Chapter Thirteen

Elisa looked tired, and soon slumped on Johnny. He let her sleep. That way, she could have some peace. The journey had taken such a toll on her and he suspected there was more. She could be sick, and he hoped to heaven they'd reach New York before she broke out with anything. He'd succeeded in sending a telegram to his roommate and the young man awaited his return. That he would return with a woman was in the message. Omitted was a black woman. As a man, he fought the urges for his wife daily, but he couldn't consummate his marriage yet. Not until they could be alone at least.

A door behind what could easily be converted to an altar opened and a white woman hurried over to where they sat. Johnny was the only one awake, but everyone came to at the sound of the opening door.

"Mr. Holt. We are ready for you. You will go through the water. Final destination is Canada, but they will drop you off in New York as you requested." Her gaze dashed toward the others. "Your companions will not have a fantastic accommodation," she heaved. "But I believe that should not be a problem."

Her words rolled over fast and rehearsed, like something she said every day. Johnny clasped her gloved hands.

"Thank you, Miss."

She nodded and waved them toward the door she entered from but did not follow them. "God go with you."

"Thank ya, Miz." Dee curtseyed. "Thank ya."

To everyone's surprise, the woman hugged them each. "God go with you. God bless you."

Johnny led the way again, as though he'd been here before. The door opened surprisingly to a deck, and right at the end of a wooden dock, a small boat waited with two oars. They hurried to the boat, and the men helped the women to get in.

"Where we goin'?" Elisa whispered.

"We're going to row out. They will meet us," Johnny said.

Dee gasped. "Meet us? Were?"

"Trust me, please," Johnny snapped. "This is all hard enough!"

He closed his eyes for a second and swallowed to put his temper in place. So many things could go wrong. It was broad daylight, and the sun was high up in the sky. The river was a small one and they could see the other side.

"You ladies lay flat. Me and Massa Johnny goin' a row," Anthony said softly.

The rowing seemed forever, but they got to the other side. In his mind, Johnny thought, now what? But he didn't have long to wait. As soon as the small boat hit the bank, Nat showed up from behind a tree.

Nat waved. "This way, Massa."

As they hurried out of the boat, a young white man dressed like a businessman got into it with a black man about his age and rowed the boat back the way they came. Nat led through the brush, running wildly until they got to the bank of another river, much bigger, and one that seemed endless. The group of five were allowed to enter a steam boat without any scrutiny.

"This way," Nat said. "Not you, Massa Johnny."

Johnny stopped him from moving. "What do you mean, not me?"

"We slaves have our place." He looked to the rest. "The cap'ain will take care of you, Massa."

He began to walk down the narrow passage off the deck of the boat. Johnny gripped Elisa.

"I'll find you, darling." He kissed her on the mouth. "I love you."

The place for slaves was no place. Elisa had never had to sleep on the floor next to a steam engine. It was hot, stifling and not enough space for a bunch of men and women of all ages. Yet, they all were grateful to have it. Elisa curled up in a corner and listened to slave stories too unimaginable to comprehend. For the first time, she appreciated Johnny's father for not being as crude and mean as some of these other masters.

Once before everyone fell asleep anywhere they could, an elderly black man Elisa had not seen earlier came in with a large bowl of broth and fresh rolls in a big sack. The women shared it and all had a healthy helping. It only made the gathering more like a party. Then afterward, Dee and Anthony found space beside Elisa.

"Elisa dear," Anthony said. "Ya ma and me been talkin' 'bout movin' on to Canada."

Elisa could imagine where the conversation would lead. Moving to Canada would probably be the best thing to do, but what about Johnny. He would not want to leave New York, his school, give up his scholarship…he had given up too much already. Johnny Holt would never be able to go back home, and the rest of his life would be spent looking over his shoulder. He would ever be wary of slave-runners, angry at him. Someone like his friend, Gilbert, would never forgive him for the way he was beat up and left naked with Johnny's dirty clothes tossed over him.

"We know ya and ya Massa Johnny got that marriage thin' goin'." Dee's voice faded. "No 'ope for us 'ere, child."

Chapter Fourteen

A hand tugged at her and she moaned.

"Elisa, darling wife, it's me."

She roused and hugged his neck before she could make out his face. "Where are we?"

There was laughter in his voice. "Home. New York, darling."

She leaped. "New York."

Someone groaned beside her and she realized she was in the steam engine room sandwiched between a wall and her mother. Two big lamps placed at each end provided some illumination. She pushed him off.

Elisa snapped. "Don't ya come playin' nassy jokes at me, Massa Johnny."

He lifted her easily. "Come, wife. I have a surprise."

She rolled her eyes and wished she could wipe away the smirk on his face. "I done with ya surprises, sir."

He kissed her forehead. "*Ssh.* You'll wake up the whole steam engine crew."

Elisa grunted. Did he think this was all funny? She felt light in his arms, and much as her heart thudded, she wanted to ask so many questions. He took a winding metal staircase up one flight and continued to walk through a narrow passage. She lifted her head and saw the dark water beneath, the moon shining on it. The steam boat seemed to be floating or maybe her head was floating. She just wanted to disappear. She remembered the tales some of the old people told of the trip from homeland, and how many died and were thrown in the water. Everywhere there were small lamps to light the boat. She had been happy the steam engine room was lit too, but she soon hated it because it took all privacy away. She'd wanted to weep, but then her giddy mother would have wondered why she wasn't happy.

"What are you thinking, sweetheart?" Johnny mumbled.

"Nothin'."

"I don't believe you. Your sweet little head always has something going."

Despite herself, she giggled. "Thinkin' of 'em old people who come by the big rivers from the homeland."

"Bad thoughts. I would be thinking of living in New York as Missis Elisa Johnny Holt."

"Bad dream if I gerrout of 'ere." Then she giggled into his chest. "I must smell like a pig now. Them horses done–"

"*Ssh.*"

He stopped walking and let her down. She saw where he'd brought her before she could ask, a small empty room by a corner. A big basin filled with water lay in the middle of the floor. A half of the room had a wall, but the other opened to the river with only the railings.

"I have soap for you too," he said.

Elisa leaped on him and kissed his face. "How did ya do it?"

"Well, shall I say, the good captain does not know I have a beautiful wife down in the steam engine room." He chuckled. "I told him my beautiful wife needed a good bath."

Elisa rushed to it and took her clothes off as though no one was there with her and got into the cool water. A gasp of pleasure escaped her lips.

Johnny gave her a bar of scented soap and she rubbed it all over herself.

"How lon' we got 'ere?"

Johnny shrugged. "As long as my beautiful wife wants to stay. The captain said I should let him know when we're done."

She shrieked. "O! I could be 'ere fore'er."

Johnny squatted beside her and twirled her long strands of hair through his fingers. "You are so beautiful, Miz Holt."

He kissed her neck and she stopped soaping herself. "Ya wanna come in? The basin big 'nof."

His voice thickened now. "Okay."

He stood and took all of his clothes off too. Elisa had never seen him naked and stared shamelessly. She had never seen a naked white man, but most of the men hung that she'd seen were black and nude. Her mind reeled. This was it. Johnny was going to do what her mother warned her about men.

He stepped into the basin, and a small sigh escaped from his mouth a second before he clamped it over hers.

Chapter Fifteen

The trip took two weeks and finally one evening, the elderly black slave who always brought food, twice daily, rushed down the winding iron stairs and shouted,

"New York!"

The slaves broke into dancing. Of almost thirty men, women and children cramped together, none had died. The children took ill, but they had all arrived. Some ran to the old man and asked about plans to move to Canada.

"We all get off 'ere," he replied, and turned to answer other questions.

In two weeks, Johnny had managed to get Elisa four baths, and four love-making sessions in a basin. She liked it and looked forward to them, though it couldn't be planned.

After the first night and Dee smelt her hair, she winked and told her, *"Ya a Miz now, babe."*

Elisa smiled and no one made a mention of any of it anymore.

The steam boat docked on a bright and cool morning. People ran helter-skelter in the steam engine room. Elisa, Dee, and Anthony stood by one side at the foot of the iron stairway unsure of what to do. Johnny had not come around for several days, and though Elisa was sure he would not leave her, she only wished she knew the plan. Nat hurried by and Dee grabbed his arm.

"We goin' a Canada too." She held his gaze. "We tol' ya."

"Then come." His voice high-pitched and excited, he didn't wait to hear what they had to say. "Come." He shouted, not even looking back.

Elisa hugged herself. "Go."

Dee shuddered. "We ain't goin' a leave ya 'ere all by yaself."

"I'm a Miz now, Ma."

"No way are we leavin' ya alone to yaself." Anthony growled. "That boy Johnny may be ya–"

"Johnny!" Elisa screamed and ran to him. Too late she stopped herself and bowed. "Massa."

Johnny drew her aside and laughed. "No one heard you. It's time to go."

Elisa heaved. "Ma, and my Pa. They wanna go to Canada. I tol' ya."

She had never been so confused in her life. She so badly wanted to go with Johnny. He had done too much for her and she loved him even more now. But would she never see her parents again? Would even the New York society ever accept a black woman married to a white man? Their children would never live a normal life. It made no sense. Canada would give her the opportunity for a new beginning. And Nat had made more than one inference to settling down with her. He was perfect at just two years older and already trained as a carpenter.

"The steam boat goes on to Canada. We have to get off here." Johnny took her hand. "Let's say our goodbyes."

She tugged her hand. "My goodbye is to ya, Johnny."

He froze as though he'd been hit by a bullet. "To me? You're my wife."

"Only in the dead house." She stepped back. "I sorry, Massa Johnny. Slave life 'ard and no one will e'er see me better."

Johnny breathed hard and his face turned red. "Elisa!"

She couldn't stay and look at him. The tremor in his voice tore her heart. She was only doing what was best for both of them. One day he would appreciate her decision. She ran to her mother's arms, just a couple yards away and burst into tears.

"I told 'im, Mama!" She wailed. "I told 'im I can't!"

Anthony stepped forward. "Massa Johnny, I cannot thank ya 'nof of all ya done for my famly."

Johnny cried. "Tell her to stay with me. She's my wife!"

Dee shrieked. "We gotta leave now!"

Most of the slaves had left the steam engine room. Dee wrapped her arm around Elisa, and they climbed the iron stairs, with Anthony close behind. Elisa raised her head to steal a glance at Johnny, who remained at the same spot, an abundance of emotions flashing across his face, his body rigid, with only his hands clenching and unclenching. She tucked her face back on her mother's shoulder.

One day he would appreciate her decision.

Johnny watched Elisa leave him. More than anger, fear engulfed him. He wanted her. He loved her. More importantly he feared she would not be safe. Something terrible would go wrong in Canada and he would never be able to forgive himself. He had brought her this far, who would imagine she would walk away from all they had? Fear.

He understood her plight. In fairness, Canada was a better option for her. New York may be a free state, but he'd never seen a bi-racial marriage. The racial divide was as strong here as back home, and though people were far more tolerant, everyone still stayed in their cultural paths. Blacks married blacks and whites married whites. And attended their churches separately. How would they live? She could be a housewife, and take care of home and children, but how would they ever socialize? She would never be accepted in white circles, and the blacks would always suspect him.

Johnny watched as the absconding slaves scampered all over the place until the steam engine room was empty. He sank to his knees and covered his head. Deep sobs wracked his body. What did he have left? A doomed future. News from home would reach his school, especially if his father had the mind to send a message to find out if he returned when the fall session resumed in a couple weeks. If what he did reached the college, he would be expelled. He'd seen students with less "mischief" as his president called it, suspended, and disgraced out of a successful future.

Most importantly, he wanted Elisa. The desire for her went beyond physical, it was a spiritual connection he had never felt with anyone. His days were filled with thoughts of her and he only slept well when he was sure she was alright. He climbed up the iron stairs with only one thought in mind. He started living when he met her and had no desire to continue if she was gone.

Dusk had descended while he wept down in the steam engine room. The deck was busy with people still getting off or coming in, he wasn't sure. The captain had told him the steam boat would move on to Canada, so why did Elisa and her parents need to leave it? He regretted letting her go so abruptly. Maybe if he'd had time to think it through, talk her out of it...maybe if they'd discussed this when she first mentioned it...? Johnny found a spot at the end of the deck and stared longingly into the water. No one noticed him, and who cared. He was an outcast if he chose to live. In a little while, darkness would envelope the world, and he Johnny Holt would jump into the water. Anyone who cared would think he was going for a swim on this late summer night. He would swim until death took him.

"Mister Holt!"

He turned and came face to face with the captain, a middle-aged wiry man who had allowed him to set up the baths with Elisa on four occasions and pretended he didn't notice Johnny's beautiful wife was a runaway slave. These people knew and saw everything, he never took chances with them. It had amazed him when the man muttered under his breath about the color of her skin. *"She must get tanned often," he'd said.*

"Captain Ingrid." Johnny arched an eyebrow. "I believe all is well?"

"I searched for you everywhere. I got you the carriage you requested." He smiled. "Your good woman awaits."

Chapter Sixteen

Johnny's mouth dropped open. "Well, thank you, Captain."

Ingrid stood with a grin on his face, and Johnny felt compelled to leave. He had mentioned in passing a few days earlier he would need a carriage to take him and "his beautiful wife" to the campus of the prestigious King's College. He didn't think the older man took him seriously. He walked a few steps and then turned. It was only appropriate to show appreciation to the captain.

"And Captain, thank you. For everything."

He pushed a few cents into the man's hands. Surely Ingrid would know he didn't have a lot and should not expect anything. He'd taken out all his savings from his job when he escaped his first capture and pilfered some money from Penny's room but most of it was gone in the weeks of their journeys.

Ingrid beamed. "Why, thank you, Mister Holt! And say me well to your missis."

One of the sailor boys walked on to the deck and began to light the lamps. Johnny hurried away. Maybe he would be better off jumping in the Harlem River. Even with the newly built bridge, and many plying it just to brag they were on the bridge, no one would care if they saw him. It was a better plan than the one he had previously. He would see the beautiful city one last time. Remind himself of why he gave up his dream for a woman not his color.

Excitement filled the dock as men and women, white and black hurried into the berthing steam boat. Eager passengers chattered about the trip, and several references to Canada filled the air. Johnny pushed past, surprised he might as well be the last to disembark. Everyone else moved into the boat. Off the dock and out in the street, he took several deep breaths. Maybe, just maybe, he could get what he lost back, go to his father and beg for forgiveness, like the prodigal son, continue with the remaining year of his study and work into getting admission into law school, write his bar exams and become a city lawyer. He would not pursue litigation as his father had wanted but go for human rights, become an abolitionist, for Elisa. Probably marry a Southern woman, but one who was educated in the North and shared his views.

A carriage stood in-waiting just outside, and a woman wearing a simple green dress with laced short sleeves over a cotton chemise, stood by it. She carried an elaborate fan, which she used to swipe her face several times in an attempt to stir the air around her.

"Mr. Holt. I've waited hours for you. The good Captain Ingrid thought I was your missis, and why not?" She giggled. "I would take a ride to the city with a handsome young man any day!"

Johnny gagged. He couldn't even remember her name. She was one of those high-class ladies of questionable means he met at dinner several times. They'd chit-chatted, but nothing more. How could Ingrid imagine this old hag was his–wife! Especially after a hint about Elisa's dark color.

"You can have the carriage, Madam." Johnny heaved. "I will rather take a walk. Feel the city again."

"Why, Mr. Holt–?

He hurried off before he heard any more.

If he craved any company tonight, it wasn't hers. The streets were just as he remembered and though he had only been to the harbor a couple times with college friends, he knew his way around. A figure hovered at the corner of the street just a few yards away from the carriage, and he turned in its direction. He suspected harbor urchins willing to steal anything even if they didn't need it and clutched his worn coat closer until he could feel a breath of air right at his shoulder. He spun around, wishing he had a knife or something to defend himself. It was dark now, and many of the lamps lighting the streets were either broken or stolen.

"Johnny."

Elisa wept all the way out to the dock where the old black man put everyone to work preparing the steam boat for the trip to Canada. They stocked crates of dry foods, warm clothing and cleaning supplies. It was like being on the plantation again, but this was the only way they could pay their way to freedom. The men helped with some repairs on the boat while women beat out fabrics too heavy to wash. Evening approached fast and Elisa could not make herself stop crying. When they stopped work to have supper, Dee had some tough words for her.

"Ya been cryin' o'er a man that don't care none. He coulda come with us to Canada, couldn' he?"

Elisa had no appetite for food and pushed thick chicken broth about with her spoon. She didn't have the mental or physical capacity to argue with her mother either. Dee continued her rebuke.

"When a man love a woman, he'd do anythin' for her. He'd die for her." She took several spoons of her broth and bit into her roll. "Ya Johnny not man 'nof. No man goin' a let the woman he love go. No man." She finished her food. "Now ya clean up ya plate and smile. Canada callin'!" She stood and left.

Nat walked over as soon as Dee left. "Hey, I hear Johnny ain't goin' a Canada with you."

Elisa glanced at him and took a spoon of her broth, just to do something other than speak.

Nat took the seat Dee just vacated. "I'll take care 'o you." He touched her hand and she flinched. "I know he done a lot more than any white man I'd seen do for a woman. But I'll beat him to it, Elisa."

Big Old Man shouted. "Last run, ya'll!"

"We'll soon get back on the boat, ready to leave." Nat stood; his joy unhidden. "Com'on Elisa, finish your food and let's join the others."

He sprinted off without waiting for her reply. His delight was contagious, and a small smile split Elisa's gloomy face. A tear slid down her cheeks and she wondered if she could ever be happy with him or in Canada. He'd gotten some education while being apprenticed as a carpenter. He definitely had better prospects than most of them escaping, even her father. She could hang on to him and make a family, but could he ever make her laugh like Johnny. Could he give up his life for her? After all, he was born a slave. It was no secret they were wired to fight for their own survival before that of any other.

A first whistle blew, and everyone hurried toward the steam boat. Elisa stood, and her bowl of broth, which had been on her lap fell. She bent to pick it, not sure of what to do with the mess on the ground.

"Com'on, girl. Time to go!" Dee's voice breezed over her.

Anthony's followed. "Canada, my *nu* 'ome!"

Elisa straightened and watched them move. At the entrance of the boat, Dee turned and waved her on. She confessed in her heart she had never seen her mother so relaxed, so happy. Dee's default face all her life had been glum. But all through the trip from Philadelphia, she had loosened up more and more. Elisa even caught her having intimate moments with her father. Something she had never seen. She was sure Dee and Anthony would do well in Canada. It was only proper for her to follow them. It made no sense not to leave. Johnny didn't run after and beg her or offer to follow her. He would be long gone to his old life. She would never forget him or all he did for her and her family.

She would never forget their intimate loving too. But it was time to move on.

Elisa stirred toward the trail of people she believed were passengers. Some were white families, and every single person seemed excited about the journey. She swallowed and would have gotten into the flow to enter the boat if she hadn't seen Johnny Holt make his way out. She waited and watched him walk to the waiting carriage. Hot tears slid down her cheeks and she fought the urge to wail. Johnny did not get into the carriage, but spoke to a woman, and then walked away. Elisa could see him right across the road, his shoulders slightly slouching.

She did not make any decision, her feet did.

Chapter Seventeen

She stepped back into the shadows and Johnny followed her with such a force he thought he'd choked her by the time his mouth found hers.

"Elisa," he breathed. "My love."

"I couln' leave ya, Johnny. I just couln'." She kissed his face as he did hers. "Ma and Pa goin' a loose their minds but I wanna be with ya."

"I wanna be with ya too, Elisa my wife. My sweet love." Uncontrollable tears streamed from his eyes. "I thought I'd just kill myself. I don't want to live without you."

"I don't wanna live without ya, too." She cried. Then laughed. "Ya couln' sound like a slave Massa Johnny. No matter how 'ard ya try."

He clasped her hand and pulled her forward. "Come with me to my room at the college." He laughed. "Come Elisa. Our future will be very bright."

The walk to Johnny's college was long, but Elisa didn't feel any stress at all. She had never felt so happy and knowing she did the right thing before. Dee would fret, curse, and then resign herself. Anthony would call her a fool, nothing more. Her parents would conclude she'd die and mourn her, but as soon forget about her. It was the way of slavery. To keep sanity, they got over tragedies as fast as possible. But she promised herself one day she would go to Canada to find them. Maybe with their grandchildren. That would make them happy.

"We're here!" Johnny announced.

Elisa stared at the huge building; her mouth wide open. It had so many stories, she bent her head all the way to the back to see all of it.

"Woah!"

Johnny laughed. "Come."

He ran with her through the manicured hedges of the walkways and through the back of his hall. It was close to midnight and the college was all quiet. Johnny opened his wallet, which he'd carried all along and removed his key. Together, with Elisa gasping intermittently, they climbed three flights of stairs, and knocked on one of many doors on both sides of a long corridor.

"Cole Truse, who requests entry?"

Johnny whispered at Elisa. "He says that all the time." He raised his voice. "John James Holt Junior, friend. And his beautiful wi–"

The door jerked open and Cole, a tall, thin man with red hair and a long thin beard, about Johnny's age, pulled him into a hug. "I indeed got your telegram. You got married." He pushed a laughing Johnny aside and stepped into the corridor only to stop short at the sight of Elisa. "You married a–slave?" Cole frowned, and took short deep breaths. "You didn't say that."

Johnny, holding her hand firmly, stepped into the room. "Of course, I would not say that in the telegram. What does it matter? Elisa, meet here Mr. Cole–"

"It does matter." Cole stood in the hallway. "This is–we are–does your–"

Johnny moved a chair out from where it was neatly tucked into a desk, and motioned Elisa to sit. She did, but on the edge.

"Come in and close the door, Cole, and stop been so uptight. This is New York. A free state." Johnny leaned on the edge of the table. "*Oh*, well. You need to excuse us tonight. You did make plans for where to stay, didn't you?"

Cole straightened. "I'm not sure it will be appropriate to leave the room for you. Don't you think? Without at least informing the hall president or someone."

Johnny frowned. "You've brought lady friends to stay over the night many times, Cole, and I excused you."

Cole gesticulated. "But not–this."

"I thought you were free-spirited and liberal. I was more conservative than you, Cole. What's wrong?" Johnny stole a glance at Elisa and she quickly dropped her gaze to her fingers.

"*Oh-oh*, this has nothing to do with free-spirit. She is a–slave." Cole walked in and closed the door. "I hate to be a jerk, but how do you imagine she will stay here, John Holt Jr?"

The two men stared hard at each other and it was Cole who budged. "I'll leave for a couple nights." He opened a closet and stuffed a leather bag with some things. At the door he turned. "I'm glad you're back, Mr. Holt." With that he opened the door and closed it behind him.

"Him's goin' a rat ya in, hasband." Elisa stared at the door. "Where do we go?"

"We stay here." Johnny turned to her and squatted before her. "He won't say a word to anyone. Unless they ask him. But he'll want us to go somewhere else by tomorrow or the day after it."

She inhaled. "Is this a big problem?" And let it out in a soft release.

"No. Cole is from New York. He'll help us find a place." He cupped her face and kissed her mouth. "You must be very tired. My bed is soft."

"A'right. Thank ya." She stood and took her shoes off. "Please lock the door."

"I will." He smiled wryly. "There's a small basin in the corner. It normally has clean water. Freshen up."

She complied. He walked to a small cupboard pushed against the wall. He brought out a tin of assorted biscuits and some fresh milk. He poured some into a cup and placed it with the biscuits on the desk, then he locked the door.

"I don't blame Massa Cole, Hasband." She chuckled in between squishing her mouth. "I'd be scarred too if ya were some black man and I be white."

Johnny laughed. "Maybe in Canada and Europe a black man will marry a white woman, but that will never happen in this great country of ours. Cole must be thinking along those lines. I feel like a pioneer."

She returned to her seat. "I left some of 'em water for ya."

"Thanks, love." He walked to the basin. "I'll go out tomorrow and find Cole. He can help us get a small room until we know our next move."

"Next move?" Elisa stopped chewing a cracker. "We movin'?"

"Not moving out of America. Just what we need to do with our lives."

"*Ow.*"

But she didn't understand. He had spoken so well of his roommate, the reaction she got didn't only not add up, it scared hell out of her. She imagined Cole Truse would return in a few hours with a battalion of slave catchers, and they would take her back to Holt Land, this time to be hanged on a tree and left for food to the birds of the air.

"I'd like to settle down, have kids." Johnny drew a chair from the other reading desk to his and sat with her. "And you need to get an education. I want you to get a job."

A giggle escaped from her. "Job. How?"

He caressed her cheek. "I think you will make a great schoolhouse teacher."

She turned her face away. "Now we should be thinkin' of a angry Massa Cole who can be tellin' 'unters ya bring a black slave 'ere."

"Cole is from New York. But let me tell you his story, darling, and you will understand why he won't bring any slave catchers here." He took a healthy gulp of milk from the cup. "His father met his mother on a visit to Georgia. She was the daughter of a wealthy plantation owner. They had a short, wild love affair, and he married her, brought her to New York. But she missed home and would fall sick and return to the plantation.

"After Cole was born, she took him south and refused to return so his father joined her." Johnny arched an eyebrow. "Things went well for a while. Cole's father even started to enjoy living on the plantation. Then there was a slave-rising."

Elisa waved her hands. "No. Don't te-ell me."

"The slaves burst into the main house and set fire to it." Johnny paused and studied her. "Cole's mother was so badly burnt, one day her father walked into her room and put an end to her misery."

Elisa clasped her hand over her mouth. "*Oh*, my Lord!"

"Cole was six. He never talks about it, though." Johnny took a biscuit and bit into it. "His grandfather shot himself afterward. Cole's father took him and left Georgia. They've never been back."

"I'd 'ate ever' black I see too."

"Cole doesn't hate blacks. He hates slavery. His father is a leading abolitionist here." Johnny finished his biscuit. "Come to bed, my love. You look so beautiful. I want you."

Elisa let him take her to bed, but could not forget the tragedy Cole's life was wrapped in.

Chapter Eighteen

The following morning, Johnny woke a little late, and stared at Elisa. She was so beautiful with her long, curly hair framing her face, and her mouth set in a soft pout like a baby. He kissed it a couple times and she roused. He was so grateful to God to have her here.

"I'll be going to find Cole and ask him about accommodation for us." He smoothed back her hair. "I didn't want to disturb you. But you'd be worried when you wake up alone."

"Thank ya," she mumbled. "What time is it?"

"It's almost noon. We slept a lot." He chuckled. "Well, when we decided to." He kissed her forehead.

"Will ya be safe?"

"Yes, darling. And you too." He stood. He'd been awake a lot longer and was dressed in one of the few clothes he left behind. "There's more biscuits in the cupboard. I'll bring some soup back."

"Ya say I shouldn' worry? 'Bout ya, us?" She sat up fully. "What'd I be doin' when ya is gone?"

"Sleep some more, eat. Then sleep. Pray." He grinned. "Be ready for me tonight."

"Pray. That one I'd do."

"Be ready too." Johnny chuckled. "I have to run now. I love you."

He hurried out of the room, not willing to have to answer questions he could see in her eyes. They would be fine, he was sure. If they could cross the forest through three states to get to Pennsylvania, and then survive the steam boat and a brief separation, he knew they would be fine. When he woke up on his bed, with her all curled up in his arms, a new resolve to get her a life she deserved enveloped him. Maybe he was doing something no one had ever done, or succeeded in, but he had no intention of backing out now. He left everything for her, and she just did the same for him. They were even now. No going back. They would escape and get a decent life together or die trying.

Johnny went in search of Cole at his father's arms store in downtown Harlem. The store looked deserted at first and though the welcome bell rang, no one came, then Trevor Truse did, a mid-forties, gray-haired man who looked more in his sixties than forties.

Johnny straightened. He didn't expect to meet the older man who was always busy and hardly in his storefront.

"Good afternoon, sir."

"Good afternoon, Johnny." Trevor took his hand in a firm handshake. "Cole said you'd come. And I wanted to see you."

"*Huh*, thanks sir. Is Cole here?"

"Yes. And we are in a meeting. Please come with me."

Trevor did not wait for a response. He returned the way he came, and apprehensively, Johnny followed him. The older Truse had been quite radical in his views since tragedy struck his family and, on many issues, differed from even the most committed activists. Johnny had hoped to not get him involved.

Johnny followed Trevor into a small conference room with just about ten chairs. The two chairs at either end of the table were empty. Trevor took one and motioned Johnny to the other.

"I will save us all time and not introduce each person," Trevor said. "But you know my son, Cole." He pointed at Cole who sat to his left side. "And Quaker Peter the Great." On his right.

Everyone knew Peter the Great, as he had come to be addressed, a wanted, yet free man whose radical views and actions had gotten a long list of slaves, not as long as his waist-length beard though, killed instead of freed.

"*What do we be doin 'ere, hasband?*" Elisa's voice rang in Johnny's mind.

"We've been here all morning, discussing about you, Johnny Holt. Cole wasn't sure what time you would seek him out, but he knew you would."

Johnny cleared his throat. "Sir, what am I doing in your meeting?"

"Edmond Maguerro, your father's partner, is wanted in Georgia for the murder of two black men, who were freed and working for him. He shot them both in the head when they asked for their wages," Peter the Great answered. "Your wife must have some stories to help us catch him."

"My wife?" Johnny struggled to his feet and shot Cole an accusatory glance. "I do not want to be a part of this."

"Sit." Trevor snapped. "Your father knows about Maguerro's crimes and still continues to do business with him."

Johnny sat, despite himself. "I do not wish to be a part of this, sir."

Peter snickered. "Because you do not know that your father has written to the President of your college, asking that they expel you? That in Kentucky you are wanted for crimes against one Gilbert Goodling?"

Johnny gasped. "Gilbert?"

"And a bunch of other slave catchers you assaulted. Besides stealing and aiding plus inciting slaves to escape." Trevor leaned back in his seat. "Your father is not as keen on protecting your crimes as he is his business partner's."

Johnny swallowed. "I was wrong to do the things I am accused of."

He couldn't be a part of this movement, and it would be too dangerous to involve Elisa. He tried to remind himself why he hadn't followed her family to Canada and found no reason.

Trevor passed a piece of paper until it got to Johnny. It was a notice with his likeness and a five-hundred-dollar ransom posted for anyone who found him. Johnny blanched.

"When the school session re-opens late next week, that will be posted all over campus. Your dean will call you to his office and expel you, if you are stupid enough to stick around until then. And a couple students will be happy to make a few hundred dollars to rat you out." The Quaker clasped his hands together. "But we have an offer."

Chapter Nineteen

Elisa balled up, her hands shaking so badly she doubted they would ever be normal again. "So, they wanna put me in fron' o' a judge?"

Johnny leaned against the wall. "It will be a closed meeting. An artist will paint you, and you will give a testimony of what goes on…on Holt Land, Creek View, Kentucky."

She gasped. "But that be like reportin'! Massa JJ and Massa Edmond goin' a be in trouble."

He pushed back his hair. "What should we do then? Move out of here and find accommodation?"

"Like ya say before!"

Johnny closed his eyes. He had never felt so betrayed in his life. By Cole, by his father, and now he was the betrayer.

"Ya agreed for me to do this?" Elisa wailed. "I can't!"

Johnny opened his eyes and rubbed them. "They will give us a house outside of town. We will be safe. Cole's father will give me a job, writing out invoices for him from the safety of our home, and you can learn to sew." Johnny threw his hands in the air. "A lot of what we hoped to have."

She didn't mind sewing. She had always been intrigued by the frills and laces that made up beautiful dresses.

"Who'd I be sewin' for?"

Johnny pushed his hands into his pockets. Her eyes followed him as he began to pace.

"There's been a lot of talk about a war between the North and South." He stopped in front of her. "They promise you can sew military uniforms."

Elisa covered her ears. "Wha'd ya think ya sayin', Johnny? Wha'd we get ourselve in?"

Johnny sat beside her on the bed. "I'm scared out of my mind, Elisa. I never imagined my father would have sent a message to the college. What do you want me to do?"

She'd never been asked for her opinion about anything. All her life, someone took the decision for her. Until when she followed Johnny off the dock instead of getting into a steamboat to Canada. That was when she got herself into a big mess she feared she'd regret for the rest of her life.

"How'd I sew uniform? Who'd teach me?" She shuddered and Johnny drew her into his arms. "Wha'd we do if n we refuse?"

Johnny massaged her scalp the way she loved, and she relaxed in his arms. "We have to leave here if we refuse their offer. I can go down to the pub I visited as a student and speak to a friend who can find us a place temporarily." He pressed a kiss on her head. "I'm sorry for putting you through this." He sighed. "Angel looks white, but her mother is mixed, and her father is white. She ran away from home after she saw her father kill her mother by mistake, she says. She runs the pub and is very influential and will be sympathetic."

Elisa raised her head. "A white-lookin' black woman? No. She goin' a take ya from me." She pressed her lips to his.

Johnny laughed. "You just reminded me of why I fell in love with you."

"I ain't goin' a watch some woman hep my man." She hugged his neck. "I'd sew for *soljas* if tha'd what ya want, my hasband."

"You want us to take Mr. Truse and Quaker Peter's offer?"

Elisa nodded. "Yes. Or leave America to Canada."

Johnny kissed her deeper than she could remember he ever did.

A carriage waited just outside the west side of the college premises. Johnny had been told to come with his wife at the set time if they agreed to take up the offer, and they would be taken to their new home thirty minutes outside New York City. No questions asked, they got into the carriage, and rode out. He trusted the movement Trevor Truse supported, but he feared many things and could feel no relief. To think he was now probably a national fugitive terrified him, but the offer from Trevor was too good to refuse.

After he told the group he had to get Elisa's consent, they delved into the trending news of the day. The war was on the top of the list and the elections coming up the following year. Everyone agreed whoever won the race would determine if slavery would end in America or not. Much as Johnny had found himself excited about being in the Senate previously, the whole discussion left a bad taste in his mouth. An hour later, the meeting dismissed, and Cole walked up to him.

"I'm sorry for the way I spoke to your wife yesterday. I just never imagined...you only said you got married and would be arriving with your...her."

Johnny wanted to tell him it didn't matter but realized it did. "How can you fight a cause and hate the people it affected the most?" He bit out.

"I do not hate them!"

"You can never convince me otherwise, Mr. Cole Truse." He brushed past ignoring the curious gazes he got by the tone of his voice and hurried off. He needed to get back to Elisa with the news.

The carriage rode up a drive and stopped in front of a townhouse in a residential neighborhood. The lamps were lit and bright enough for Johnny to notice the resemblance with other houses they had passed by. There was nothing special about it and could be occupied by anyone in the neighborhood. The carriage driver said nothing, and after a few minutes of confusion on his and Elisa's part, he helped her to get down. The carriage left.

"Tha' strange," Elisa murmured.

Johnny held her hand and walked to the wooden front door. He knocked twice and turned the handle when they got no response. It opened. He stepped into a small furnished living room with a brightly lit lamp hung on a wall and closed the door. The smell of pot-pie filled his nostrils and he looked around. Two wooden seats were tucked into a table and pushed against a whitewashed wall. An open door led into a passage and at the end, a narrow stairway. Just before the foot of the stairs was a kitchen, with the door open as well. Johnny peeped briefly and holding Elisa's hand tighter, walked through. They climbed the stairs and found a small washroom facing the staircase with a room on either side.

The first room opened to a bedroom with a double bed, a table and chair. Johnny walked to the table and found a bottle of ink, a pen and several pieces of loose sheets. The lamp was lit. The second room had a sewing machine set up and ready to use. Elisa yelped.

"Well." Johnny sighed. "This is our new reality." He pulled her into his arms. "Why don't we go find the source of that pot pie smell."

There indeed was freshly baked chicken pot pie in the kitchen and a pantry full of supplies. They carried the food and a jug of water back into the living room and ate.

Elisa giggled. "*Hmm*, if e'er! This is the best food I eaten in my whole life."

"It tastes really good." Johnny ate thoughtfully. "Wonder if they will keep bringing food.

"Not with that there pantry full like that." She smiled. "I cook so worry not, hasband."

It was late already, and it had been a long day. Johnny found the key to the front door and locked it, then they went up into their bedroom. There were some clothes for both of them in a closet and they changed into nightwear. Johnny pulled her into his arms, feeling romantic and needy, but Elisa stopped his advance with a whispered request.

"Can we pray, hasband?"

Johnny moaned. "Of course."

Elisa repeated the prayers her mother prayed every night on Holt Land for protection against the evils of the night and that in the minds of humans.

"Amen."

Johnny answered. "Amen."

"Johnny?"

His hands moved over her body. "Yes, my love."

"Massa Cole's Mammy. Did anyone die in the fires?"

Johnny stopped caressing her. "In the initial fire, no. But then, she died, shot by her father, who then took his own life."

"The slave who done it, run?"

"Yes. But they were caught."

She gasped. "*Oh*, my Lord. All o' them?"

"All of them." Johnny sighed. "Four slaves planned it. Eleven were hanged and six whipped to near-death."

Elisa burst into tears.

Chapter Twenty

Early the following morning, Peter the Great came with a colored woman only known as Nan, and told them she would teach Elisa to sew, and in essence, read and write. He also had a parcel for Johnny.

"Your work for the next week," he said, and left without waiting for Johnny to open the bundle or ask questions.

Johnny tore the package open and found stationery and a note from Trevor. It also contained a folder with the account details Johnny had to work on; several numbered loose sheets.

"Well, I'll have to excuse you ladies. I have my work cut out." He gave Elisa a peck. "I'll be in the bedroom if you need me."

Elisa stole a glance at Nan. "What of breakfast?"

"We can have a late one. Let me see what this job is about." He bowed to Nan. "Excuse me, Miz Nan."

"Show me the room where you'll take lessons in," Nan said in a crisp foreign accent.

Johnny arched an eyebrow. "You sound foreign, Miz. Are you from Europe?"

Nan clenched her hands at her sides. "No."

"This way then, Miz."

Johnny led the ladies up the stairs. At the entrance of the "sewing" room, he bowed again, and proceeded to the bedroom. He closed the door behind him.

The three went into the kitchen before noon for brunch and later for an early dinner. All remained in their rooms until dark, and Nan left on her own.

Johnny couldn't wait to get an update from Elisa after Nan left.

"She left on a horse. She rode." Johnny laughed. "I will have to get a horse too. Teach you how to ride."

"That there will make me faint," Elisa laughed. "She a stron' woman."

They stood in the kitchen and snacked on dried dates and almonds Elisa found in the pantry.

"Did she say much about herself?"

Elisa shrugged. "She not talk 'bout 'ersef. She talk 'bout sewin'." She smiled. "She good. Really good."

Johnny tucked a curl behind her ear. "Do you like it?"

"Do I like it?" Her eyes widened. "I love it!"

He picked a date and put it on his lips. Then he motioned to her to get it. She shook her head, but he pulled her in and kissed her all the same.

"Are you happy?"

Elisa nodded.

"I'm very happy, too." Johnny kissed her again. "We're safe here. I noticed from the invoices I got, though, Trevor seems to be doing a lot of transactions. They are getting a lot of guns into New York City."

"Why?"

Johnny shrugged. "The war? I do hope not, though."

"Miz Nan," Elisa sighed. "I don't kno'."

He cupped her cheeks. "Tell me. What happened?"

"I don't think she like me. She ask how I let a white man kiss me." She looked at him. "But she almost white 'ersef."

Johnny arched an eyebrow. "That's quite surprising. I expected her to be...more civil?"

"I just be careful."

"Well, she's not here now, and I cannot be bothered if she doesn't like us." He picked her up in his arms and took her upstairs.

The following week, Elisa broke out in a sickness neither she nor Johnny could understand. It started in the evening shortly after Nan left and almost all through the night. She could not keep her food down, and had a strange craving for Beth's pound cake.

Johnny was confused as to what to do. "I have no idea where Beth is. Can I go into town and find pound cake for you, darling?"

Elisa nodded. "I'm sorry, Massa Johnny," she whispered.

Autumn had set in early and it was getting cold, but she had him wrap her up in a thick blanket they found in their closet as though it was freezing.

"Don't apologize, my love. You're not to blame." He lay beside her and cuddled. "As soon as Nan comes in, I'll ask her for her horse and go in search of the pound cake."

In one week, they hadn't gone anywhere, but Trevor had visited to give him an advance on his salary. They didn't need to restock the pantry or kitchen and didn't feel it was safe to be seen walking on the street in daylight. During the previous days, they'd both stare out of their kitchen or living room and bedroom to see what the street was like where they lived. It was mainly deserted, but there were signs of people living all around, and they'd even spotted children running in a yard a couple houses away.

"Ya be safe and come back to me."

He pressed a kiss on her forehead. "Ya know I come back."

"It don't fit ya." They laughed.

Nan was not too keen on lending Johnny her horse, but she agreed after he begged Elisa was ill and there was no medication in the house. He returned shortly after with some potion and a pound cake to find Elisa seated in bed sipping hot tea.

She smiled when he walked in. "Ya back."

"Of course." He pecked her forehead. "How are you?"

"Miz Nan find some tea for me. I feel good now."

"I brought you a pound cake. I also now know where to get our supplies." He sat beside her. "Where's Miz Nan?" He placed a slice of pound cake on the bed with her.

"She be in sewin' room." She squeezed her nose. "Tha' there pound cake smell bad. I hate pound cake."

Johnny frowned. "It's freshly baked."

"No, no. I hate the smell." She turned from him.

He took the cake and strolled out of the room, unsure of what to do. How would she make him go out to find something and then on his return, "hated" it? He dropped the cake on the kitchen table, fighting the urge to throw it in the trash. He'd have some later, maybe when she was asleep.

"She's with child."

Nan's voice startled him, and he turned. She leaned against the wall and folded her arms across her chest.

"She is?" He gasped. "Does she know?"

She walked fully into the kitchen, and the small space seemed to shrink betwixt her hard gaze. Johnny stepped aside because he felt a need to.

"Why are you surprised?" She snickered. "All that kissing you'd been doing everyday does have consequences."

Johnny snapped. "She's my wife."

A full laughter wracked Nan's body. "Where'd you marry her from. England? France? Not even Canada has a single priest who will join you to a black runaway slave."

"We got married before God."

Nan glared. "You evil white man." She swallowed hard and straightened in a concerted effort to compose herself. "I wanted you to know I'm leaving. When she gets better, I will return."

Johnny blanched. "Is she too sick, like that? She seemed better with the tea you gave her."

"Yes, she's too sick, thanks to you." She turned. "Tell Trevor when she gets better."

"Please." He followed her to the door. "Did she say she was too sick to learn. If it's just her condition–"

"Burn in hell, Johnny Holt," she growled. She opened the door and slammed it after her.

Chapter Twenty-One

Elisa had finished her tea and was fast asleep when Johnny returned upstairs. He stared at her curled-up posture and a new love swelled for her. She was going to have his child and a deep urge to fight for her rose in him. Whatever had Nan riled wasn't a good thing. He didn't want such a negative person around Elisa. Her skin was white, and her hair long and dark. If she wasn't called colored, she could fit into any white society. To cap it up, she worked with a group of extremists. Some of their members had been tried and executed for defending the cause of eradicating slavery. Why would she be so much against him?

It wasn't noon yet, and Johnny fought the urge to go in search of Trevor Truse or Cole. Why would they send such a woman to teach Elisa? Though she was good, and Elisa had picked up a lot on reading and taking measurements. She was eager to start cutting and sewing. But he had to wait. She would be terrified if she woke up and found no one in the house. Since he didn't have Nan's horse, it would be a long walk and that was time he couldn't predict. So he sat and admired Elisa in her sleep. She was the most beautiful creature he had ever seen, and now she was going to have his baby. Nan's hatred couldn't demean or tarnish what they had.

He traced his finger over her lips and she stirred. Maybe he wanted to wake her, tell her the news. Did Nan even know for sure? Would Elisa know? She was just sixteen. Innocent beauty he'd found to be a virgin.

She moaned. "*Hmm*, ya 'ere?"

"Yes, darling. I'm right here. How do you feel?"

There was a thin film of sweat on her forehead and he mopped it with his bare hand.

"Good. The tea hep mighty." She sat up. "Miz Nan? She mad with my sleep?"

"I don't know. She was mad, though. She left."

She clasped her hand over her mouth. "*Oh*, I'm sorry."

"Not your fault you don't feel well."

She started to raise herself and he helped her sit up. "I feel good now. I can sew some."

"She said you're too sick to sew."

"I ain't too sick to sew. Just the food. Now I'm fine!"

Johnny smiled and gathered her into his arms, then he cupped her face and looked into her eyes. "Yes, darling." He swallowed. "But, Miz Nan. She thinks you're with child."

She jerked. "With child? Me havin' a babe o' my own?"

Johnny laughed. "Yes, my love." He pressed a kiss on her lips. "Yes."

She screamed. "*Oh*, my Lord! Me havin' my own babe?" Then she stared at him. "She goin' a be colored. Is why Miz Nan mad at me?"

"I think she was mad at me. Maybe...well, she doesn't believe we're married."

Elisa nodded. "She said that too when I tol' 'er we married." She mimicked Nan. "No priest on earth goin' a join a *whaaht* man to a *nigger*!"

Johnny jumped to his feet. "What? She used that word at you?"

"I don't care. I goin' a have me a babe, and I goin' a love 'im weather he black, *whaaht* or colored." She threw her chin up.

Johnny laughed. "I'm going to love you and our baby with all of my life too." He resumed his seat. "I'm going into town to find Trevor. Miz Nan has to come back to finish teaching you."

"Ain't nothin' she goin' a teach me I don't kno'."

"*Hmm*, that sounds like the strong black woman I fell for."

Despite her pleas, Johnny left as soon as it was dark. Elisa cried a little, but he promised her he'd be back or die trying, which made her laugh with the tears in her eyes.

"Ya'd be dead and leavin' me anyway," she said.

He knew his way to Trevor Truse's house because he'd been there with Cole a few times, but never at night. Still, he found the house quite easily. It was buried in the heart of uptown Harlem, where many of the rich people of New York had private homes and townhouses. Though the single-family house was expensive, Mr. Truse had bought it. Besides the wealth he made selling guns in small and large quantities, Cole's maternal grandfather had left a large estate for his grandson, which Trevor sold off. The capital had been invested into Trevor's business and what an irony, money from a slave-owner would be invested in a venture that sponsored radical anti-slavery movements. Half of the profits went into a trust fund for Cole.

Johnny didn't know what to expect, but what he found surprised him. Trevor was home and in his library with a young man with light green eyes that reminded him of a pet kitten.

"John Holt! Well, I am not surprised you're here." Trevor waved him in. "Come right in, and meet Henri Pierre Jean, the next big name in art!"

Johnny and this man could not be more than in the same age bracket. A year or two older, maybe. Henri stood and shook hands with him.

"I just got a hold of Henri to get Elisa's painting done. He has some grand ideas about how he wants to go about it." Trevor pulled a chair closer, so the three men sat in a circle. "A half-nude showing the welts on Elisa's back."

Johnny blanched. "Welts? How would you know–?"

"I am not a child, Johnny. And I do not fight this cause from a blind spot." Trevor clapped. "We start tomorrow?"

"Of course, Trevor. I will be in New York for only three days," Henri said in a soft, heavily-accented voice.

"Henri travels through Europe and the Americas. He's the best."

"I believe I have seen a painting by him before and we are privileged to have him." Johnny knew he had never seen any painting by the artist before. He frowned. "However, Elisa is sick."

"Better," Henri said. "She will not look good, which is what we want to portray."

"No, not sick in that way. She...*huh*."

Trevor arched an eyebrow. "With child. Nan told me."

Henri pursed his lips. "Well, that is good too. Her breasts would be full."

Johnny gasped. "You will not paint the naked body of my wife!"

Trevor smirked. "Anyway, we will be in your house, say noon? Henri may choose to spend the night and finish the sketches before he leaves."

Johnny wanted to tell him Henri was not welcome, but he remembered the deal with the movement. Would he have declined if he knew Elisa would be painted without clothes? Probably not. He was a wanted man, and Elisa, an escaped slave. Their options were limited.

Henri stood. "Will your servant show me to my rooms?"

"Yes, Henri. And enjoy the luxuries of my home." Trevor pulled a bell beside his desk and a young uniformed black man walked in. "Take Henri with you, Ola."

Ola nodded. "Yes, Trevor. Henri?" The men left.

Johnny arched an eyebrow, surprised the "slave" called Trevor by name. But what else would he expect of Trevor Truse?

"Ola was a little boy when I took him from Cole's grandfather's farm. His parents were both hung for the fires." Trevor pushed his chair back into place and leaned against it. "Is there something you wanted to tell me?"

"Nan," Johnny heaved. "I–"

"You want to see her?"

"No, she...well, I thought you could speak with her. Elisa is fine now." He blinked rapidly. "She was very sick in the morning but she's fine now."

"You can tell her that yourself." Trevor pulled the bell twice.

Nan walked in a moment later casually dressed and in a housecoat. "The boy-lover shows up." She snickered. "How's the baby-mammy?"

Johnny clenched his fists at his side. "She's fine now. Would you come tomorrow?"

Nan looked at Trevor. "Thought the painting starts tomorrow."

"It does," Trevor said. "You can resume after two days?"

Nan returned her gaze to Johnny. "What time'd you say she got better?"

"About noon. Shortly after you left."

Nan shrugged. "I'll just be there at noon then. She's going to be sick until noon every day for another three months, believe me."

Johnny gasped. "Three months? Why?"

Trevor laughed. "The way of womanhood."

Nan moved closer to Trevor and gave him a peck on his lips. "I'm turning in. No more calls."

Johnny's eyes widened and he blurted. "You're married?"

Nan pressed her lips together. "Kept."

Trevor chorused. "Lovers."

CHAPTER TWENTY-TWO

His jaw hanging down, Johnny watched Nan leave.

"She hates the fact that I married Elisa. Is that not hypocrisy?" He turned to Trevor. "Who is she?"

Trevor took a seat behind his large cedar desk. "She hates the fact that I didn't marry her." He smirked. "And won't. Marriage is over-rated."

Johnny's eyes widened. "Why?"

"You think what you do matters? She's my lover and has been from before Lily died."

Johnny slumped back in his seat. "You cheated on Cole's mother?"

Trevor smiled. "What did it matter? She died anyway."

Johnny stood and paced. "How can you fight for a noble cause and in your personal life you do something so...so dishonorable."

Trevor leaned back and studied Johnny. "What is so honorable about what you do? Marrying a young slave girl in your mind alone? Or do you have a document to prove your marriage?"

His words hurt Johnny more than he wanted to admit and he swallowed the urge to defend his actions. He had acted nobly under the circumstances he found himself.

"Tonight, as we speak, the posters for your ransom are being pasted on every surface on the college premises." Trevor narrowed his eyes. "If you have nothing more to discuss, you may leave."

Johnny breathed hard. "Who is Miz Nan?"

Elisa watched for any movement at the front of the house and saw none. Tears slid down her eyes. Johnny had been gone so long. She even slept off and woke with a start to feel for him. He wasn't back yet. She slid her hand over her flat stomach. After the cup of tea, and sleeping, she had been fine up until now. Was she really pregnant? Dee had never told her anything about these things until after her bleeding started. And all she'd said was that if any of Vivian's boys "touched" her she was going to be carrying a babe. And her life would be finished. What was she to do if she was pregnant and Johnny was gone? Johnny had done much more than just touching her since they got on the steamboat. Sometimes she wondered if some of the things he did to her body were even normal. Did her father do all these things to her mama? No one to ask. She liked most of it though, and that made it more difficult to talk about.

She hadn't seen the bleeding for some weeks now, but could that be the reason she was sick? They'd never been regular since she started barely a year ago, anyway, though her mother told her they should happen every month. She peeped out the window from their bedroom again and saw a horse race through to the front of the house. Fear gripped her heart and she ran to the foot of their wooden bed. Johnny couldn't have known riders would come for her, or did he? Was this why he ran off without her? Or was he afraid of being the father of a colored child.

The front door burst open with a loud bang and Elisa covered her ears, her lips trembling so badly.

"Elisa! Wife!"

Johnny's heavy footsteps rang all the way up the stairs. He was back. Elisa stood with such speed, she almost lost balance in her haste to go to him.

"Johnny!"

She ran into his arms and wailed. "I thot ya'd ne'er return."

He caught her lips with his and kissed her hungrily. "Don't you ever, ever think that. I will never leave you." He kissed her longer.

She giggled and sniffed when he released her. "Thank ya."

He wiped her tears. "There's so much to talk about." He led her into their room. "How are you? Do you still feel sick?"

"No! I'm 'ail as a log."

He laughed. "Never heard of that." He sat on their bed and pulled her into him. "Trevor gave me a horse to return with."

"*Oh*, tha' so kind of 'im."

"I don't think he's a kind man but listen to this. He's in love with Nan. They live together, like us."

Elisa exclaimed. "Ya don't say? Why she hate at us?"

"It's a long story and I milked it out of him." He paused. "She was his wife Lily's little sister. Her mother was a colored slave the master was sleeping with."

"The way o' slaves."

"There was a lot of emotions, hatred. Lily hated her sister, Nan, and when Nan was ten, Cole was born, and Nan was asked to come and babysit in the main house." Johnny breathed in. "At the time of the slave-rising, Trevor was having intimacy with the now-sixteen-year-old Nan and Lily knew of it. More hatred everywhere."

"Why'd he do tha' to his wife?"

Johnny rolled his eyes. "I asked and he said he was in love with Nan."

Elisa gasped suddenly. "Nan and–they start the fire?"

"It was a suspicion, but four slaves had entered the house. Two of them were Nan's brothers. Her mother was accused of being an accessory and was hanged along with her boys." Johnny shook his head. "Trevor took his son and Nan and returned to New York after Lily was shot by her father."

"Lily's mammy?"

Johnny frowned. "Trevor never mentioned her. Must have died before all of this happened."

"I think Trevor knew!" Elisa shuddered. "Like, he was touchin' with the lil sister. And her brothers come in and burn the wife room." She shrugged. "I don't know."

"It's a good theory. But he's the master's son-in-law and the master is intimate with his mistress's mother!"

Elisa wiped imaginary sweat from her forehead. "Tha'z stron'!"

"Well, Lily there is burnt all over and dying from pain. The slaves are tried and executed. Lily's father changes his will and leaves everything to Cole. Enters Lily's room one evening gives her a bullet in the head, and then swallows one." Johnny tightens his hold on Elisa. "Trevor takes his son and his mistress, sells off the estate, slaves and all, returned North."

"He not kind as ya say," Elisa sighed. "So why Miz Nan hate at me? She been kissin' a *whaaht* man longer than me!"

Johnny laughed long and hard, and Elisa joined in.

"They get chil'ren?" she asked.

Johnny coughed. "A teenage son. Schools in Europe."

"*Oh*, they good. Wha'd her problem with me?"

"She jealous, Miz Elisa. *Jes* jealous."

Chapter Twenty-Three

Elisa was sick until noon the following day. Nothing stayed down, then she was as strong as a horse. Much as Johnny hated it, he let Henri paint a naked Elisa draped in a loose rag. He couldn't stay in the room to watch after five minutes and Henri was still gawking at the flawless figure of *Madame* Holt and making comments about it. Even the supposed welts were fading already.

He slid his hand down Elisa's back. "I'll have to create ugly images of beating here," he murmured.

Johnny stomped off.

Though the main sketching for the painting seemed done, Henri wanted to spend the night. He was a talkative and asked a lot of questions from Elisa, but Johnny answered them all. When it became unbearable, Johnny took Elisa's hand and retired to their bedroom without showing Henri where to sleep. In the morning, he found the French man seated at the canvas working on Elisa's sketch. Elisa was throwing up again and complaining he had an odor about him she hated. It gave him a reason to leave her for a time.

Johnny cleared his throat. "I'm sorry about last night. The way we retired. She was tired."

"Don't apologize, Monsieur Holt. If my wife was half as beautiful as yours, I'd be twice as, *huh*, possessive?" His gaze remained on his work. "She's the most beautiful thing I've ever seen."

Johnny swallowed. "You leave today?"

"Right now." Henri spared him a glance. "I will finish this in the privacy of my studio."

"Thank you."

"Nan did say she gets ill in the morning. So, I don't expect her to sit for me?" When Johnny didn't respond, Henri arched his eyebrow. "Can she sit for me?"

"No." Johnny clenched his teeth. "What else did Nan tell you about my wife?"

"That she's learning to sew for soldiers in preparation for the war." Henri busied himself with packing up his wares. "The war, *hmm*. If I had a beautiful woman like yours, I'd take her out of here before it starts." He rolled his eyes. "*Huh*, that skin!"

Johnny ignored the inference. "Even if there is a war, and I very much doubt there will be, it will not come to New York."

Henri stopped short and glared at Johnny. "You don't get it do you? You Americans want to kill yourselves over a bunch of burnt-by-the-sun people? You should send them all back to where you got them from."

Johnny flared. "Don't be rude!"

"You have a beautiful wife, so I guess she's worth the fight." Henri straightened. "I want to invite her to the new art center down at Manhattan. I will love to have her model for me."

Johnny could punch his nose and break some teeth. Instead, he held his breath. "You said you'd be in New York for three days."

"Trevor's New York, that is. I have a private studio in the attic at the center. Too expensive if you ask me." Henri held his bag, ready to leave. "Will she be available in another three days?"

"Well, Nan says she can be sick for another three months, but I don't believe her."

"Believe Nan. She talks too much, but never says what she doesn't know." He walked to the door. "Three months? I will take it over nothing."

Johnny arched an eyebrow. "You'll still be here in three months?"

Henri snickered. "I live here. Do we have a deal?"

"What deal?"

"Bring Elisa to my studio to model for me, Johnny?"

"No."

"I'll pay her a thousand American dollars."

Johnny gasped. "What will she be doing for you?"

"She'll sit or stand or lie down, depending on how I want it, in her naked glory," he moaned. "And I will paint her."

"Get out of my house!"

Henri scoffed. "Your house." He opened the door. "The new art center down at Manhattan is where to find me when you get sense." He left without waiting for a response.

Elisa was sick every morning for three months as Nan had predicted. She had lessons from noon and slept strong, but in the morning, nothing helped her sickness. One morning she woke up and rushed down to the pantry for some almonds, and then had a hot chocolate drink. Johnny watched her from where he stoked the wood in the fireplace. Winter seemed to set in faster than they envisaged, and Elisa constantly complained of cold in the mornings. Upstairs would be a little more of a challenge, though he got fire going in the passage as well, and this seemed to keep the rooms there warm.

"Watch how you take all that food, dear." He smirked. "Or we'll be mopping the stairway of your vomit as well."

"I don't feel bad. My body stron'." Elisa sipped her drink. "The drink good today."

Johnny straightened. "Is it three months yet?" Then he laughed. "Should be. I'll ask Nan for her next prediction when she arrives."

"She ain't comin' no more. Said I good now with my sewin'. She left a bundle a cloth."

Johnny frowned. "She's done with you? How come no one told me?"

"I thot she'd tell ya."

"Well, you're my wife!" Johnny snapped. "I don't need to beg for information from you."

"I sorry."

Johnny turned away from her and finished setting the fire, then he brushed past and left the house to get more firewood. Her sickness had brought a lot of strain in their relationship. Most nights, she pushed him away when he touched her, complained her body felt sour. He didn't know what to believe, whether she was lying or not. If this was just an excuse to not get intimate. His desire for her drove him into her arms every day since they got off the steamboat. Could he continue to do without her? Most nights he would ride out on the horse Trevor loaned to him, for as long as he could to burn off his anger and frustration. Elisa made no fuss and would avoid him by escaping into her sewing room. He'd caught her feigning sleep several times as well, and this drove him mad.

He knew Nan had been teaching her a lot about being with child and motherhood, and though Henri made it look like Nan had the truth, Johnny didn't believe someone with so much jealousy could be able to tell it. Nan must have poisoned Elisa's mind some, and he was helpless to do anything about it. They had a safe comfortable accommodation and what more could he ask for?

The horse wasn't one of the best he'd had, but it served its purpose and Trevor had not asked him to pay for it. With Elisa able to sew now, he was happy she'd be gainfully employed. They may not need whatever income she made, because though Trevor could be a man of double standards, he paid wages on a timely basis. Their lives were simple as it was and he had no ambitions besides to be married to Elisa and live quietly with her and have many children. The baby on the way made him so excited too, though it didn't show on Elisa yet. But her body had changed. Her hair was longer, and her skin silkier, and her breasts were so much bigger in just these few months, it hurt to look at them and not be able to touch.

Johnny drove the horse hard and when he got into the woods, gathered some extra logs and returned. With a day after three months, he may not need to wait any longer to love his wife again. Maybe the sour feeling she complained about would be gone too. The mere thought excited him, and he rode home with anticipation.

For some disgusting reason, there was no back door to the house. It was a security risk and Johnny wished he could enter and exit his house without being in full view of the street. Not that it had been a bother before. Until today. When he approached the house, a carriage was parked in front of it, with two men on guard. Johnny panicked. Elisa was home alone.

Elisa watched him leave, her lips trembled with fear. Johnny had never raised a hand to her, but his angry tones had replaced his probing hand in the past three months, until there was none of the loving longings and only sarcasm and wrath. She had to find a way to get back the man she had fallen so much in love with, though she had never had the confidence to tell him. After all, she was a wanted slave and any pressure on him may make him give her away. She wasn't sure how a woman should treat a man. She could reference her mother, but Dee and Anthony were slaves, bound by conditions beyond their control. When Johnny came home, she had to let him have her. But what if he wasn't interested anymore? She didn't know what to do. Was it proper for her to reach over at night and kiss him?

A loud banging on the door startled her and she turned toward it. They rarely had visitors, and not so early. The sun just rose, and Johnny should not be gone too long. Whoever was at the door banged on it again, and a voice called, "Open up!"

She walked to the door, but the person behind kicked it down before she could reach it. Elisa screamed.

Chapter Twenty-Four

The two men guarding the carriage ignored Johnny as he pulled the horse to a stop and leapt off it, and he decided not to ask any questions. His door had been broken into which scared him even more. Elisa had no means of protecting herself and he cursed the stupid anger that drove him away when it was unnecessary. He stumbled over the door into his living room and stopped short.

His mother sat at the table, while Elisa cowered at the side against the wall, still clad in her nightdress, shivering.

Johnny gasped. "Mother! What are you doing here? How did you find us?"

He wasn't sure what the men outside were doing and if there were other people. Penny Holt had always been a very temperamental woman. If he went to Elisa's side, which was what he really wanted to do, would it not aggravate Penny?

Penny stood. "*Oh*, Johnny!"

An emotion he didn't believe existed within him rose and he fell into his mother's arms, sobbing.

Johnny heaved. "You found us."

"A woman called Nan sent a telegram to your father," she said with a trembling voice. "I intercepted it because I wanted to see you again."

Johnny stepped back. "Nan!" He fought the urge to look at Elisa. "I know her."

"She also believes there is an influence in your life, Johnny!" Penny cried. "I've watched you grow to become such a handsome young man, full of life. What happened to you? How did you become this hopelessness personified?"

"I don't believe there's anything I can say that would convince you." He pushed his hair back. It had grown to shoulder length and made him feel more mature. He liked it.

"Nothing, Johnny! Look what you threw away. A future in Washington. Or a life on Holt Land controlling hundreds of thousands of invested wealth in cash and property!"

Shame overwhelmed Johnny. When last did he get a scolding? Three months ago, by Trevor Truse?

Penny Holt clasped her hands together. "I am here, and it only means in a matter of time, your father will be too. Nan, and I must thank her, will not stop until she gets you delivered."

She drew in a long deep breath. "When you took that whipping, I thought you were just being juvenile. But this has gone beyond anything anyone imagined or comprehended."

"I am not a child anymore." Johnny raised his head and glared at Penny. "What do you want, Mother? Why are you here?"

Penny blinked rapidly. "To deliver you. Save you from yourself. Take you back home!"

"I am wanted in the State of Kentucky. If I get lucky, I will live the rest of my life in jail." He steeled his voice. "Is that what you want me to return to?"

"If you let me take her, you will be free. She will be the negotiation for all of the loss and misery and shame you have put your father and me to," Penny sighed. "And I can have my son back. You can have your soul back."

"Give me tonight, Mother. When do you return?"

"I don't have tonight. I should have taken her when you were not here. I should have known you will be unreasonable, that the potions you are being fed will not make you think properly!" Penny stomped to the door. "I leave you to your fate. You are dead to me." She wept. "I am a childless woman."

"Mother, please." Her words suddenly hit. "What happened to Katie?"

"Nothing! She is alive and well and obedient, not at all like you!" Penny yelled. "I hate you."

She stepped over the broken door. For a moment, Johnny panicked the men with her would come in. He could not fight two men at the same time. He put himself between the door and Elisa. If it meant he had to fight though, he would. But the men followed Penny and helped her into the carriage. Several minutes after they were gone, Johnny continued to stand and stare. He knew that would not be the end of his mother. Penny was not a forgiving woman. She would never understand why he did not choose to follow her, so he could stay with Elisa. Nan's telegram got to JJ and probably Edmond. And Penny couldn't be right about taking Elisa to negotiate. They may not kill him, but he would never be a free man.

Cold wind blew into the room and he came to himself. He lifted the door and pushed it into place. The damage was only at the hinges. Whoever kicked it down knew how to handle a door. It also reminded him this door was the only thing that protected him and his wife from the wicked world outside. A kick alone would be all it took. He was just one man, with one gun he had bought weeks earlier, against a world of mean people.

Nan. How could she?

He strode by a still-cowering Elisa to get his toolbox. In his heart, he really loved her and wanted her, but how long and what more would he risk and give up for her? If his mother believed he had been given potions or was under a spell, it would be ridiculous. There were many tales on plantations and farms about the slaves casting spells, but Johnny never believed any of it. If a slave had the power, then they would have cast a spell on their owner and be returned home free. He didn't think Elisa, or her parents had any super powers over him. She was just a beautiful girl who had no iota of bitterness in her, and who made him laugh. She was pure inside out, not a grain of darkness resided in her. She found light even in the darkest night and she made his body burn.

Johnny managed to put some nails in the door and got it to close again, though it wasn't strong. He then went to tend to his horse and keep it warm in his makeshift stable. He brought in the extra log he had gotten and locked the door behind him. He needed time to think and plan. They may return, and they may not. He had never been able to predict other people's actions.

"I'll be in the room working," he mumbled, as he walked by Elisa and went up the stairs.

Elisa stayed in the sewing room, first to have her privacy and nurse the wounds inflicted on her by the man who broke down the door. The first thing he did when he saw her was give her a punch on the head. She fainted. When she realized herself, she had a small cut on her temple and Penny was seated at the table. If they wanted to kill her, or take her away, it would have been the simplest thing. No, they wanted to punish her and Johnny before they did whatever they planned. *The way of massas*, she thought bitterly.

Johnny stayed away for a long time. Maybe he never took note of time, but for those several hours she had to stand and wait, she had several thoughts about giving up. She could offer to go with Penny and be hanged, rather than let Johnny find them. But she had learned that silent slaves fared better than talkative ones and she didn't want to be murdered with her innocent, unborn baby. What was Johnny's mother's plan? She had no idea. The fire in the fireplace went out and with the door open, the room got chilly, but Penny never said a word. She wore her heavy coat and was probably warm, and Elisa had no problem with that. She was warm too. The only chill she had was from fear.

Elisa touched pieces of the cloth she had worked on with Nan, the evil one. Thoughts of this betrayal tore at her heart. At some point she had taken the older woman as her mother and shared her deepest desires for her baby. Why would a woman be so conceited? And was it a coincidence Penny showed up the day Nan told her she would not return? Perhaps the other woman knew Penny Holt was already in town. And all the talk about a telegram seemed wrong to her. She didn't know much about these things, but after more than three months learning from Nan, she was no longer an illiterate.

It suddenly dawned on her. She had spoken too much. Maybe Penny was right. She'd told Nan a lot about her life and Holt Lands. She knew she mentioned JJ, Edmond, and Penny, and Nat, Vivian and her boys and of course, her parents, Beth and Dr. Al. She had told Nan everything about her life as the older woman warmed up to her. What a traitor! Shame overwhelmed her and she wept into her hands. She had sentenced herself and her unborn child to death while learning to sew. Only one option remained. She could no longer be the reason for Johnny's failure. She carried a baby, but what future could such a child have?

There were several ways, but she would choose the easiest. Johnny always kept his gun under the bed where she could see it. He'd taught her how to use it too, so she could feel safer when he was away. Funny how every thought of the gun had disappeared from her mind when she heard the knocking earlier in the day. She would use this gun once, on her stomach and her unborn child. But first, she owed her husband an appreciation.

Johnny was fast asleep when she walked in. He liked to undress her, so she kept her long nightdress on. Her hands were sweaty, and her heart thudded in her chest. She took a minute to check the gun. It was right there under the bed where he kept it, easy to reach. She would use it after he left to gather wood in the morning. But for now, she slid into the sheets beside him, and did what she thought was right.

Her cold hands cupped his face and he started awake. He reached under the bed, but Elisa kissed him on the mouth.

He opened his eyes and touched her. "Wife?"

"It's me, hasband," she whispered. "Don't talk."

She'd been practicing her speech, trying to speak more like Nan and Johnny, though she slipped in unguarded moments. But now was not the time for a conversation, learned or not. She hoped she didn't annoy him more afterward. This would be a farewell gift, as well as her way to thank him for all he had done for her. She needed to be dead for Johnny Holt to change the direction of his life, but he didn't know any of this, and would never know. He would leave her in the morning to gather wood, happy, fulfilled, ready to continue to live a normal life, but would return to find her remains. And she'd have a note ready to let him know why. It would be the ultimate sacrifice, but one she gladly gave.

Johnny grunted, and Elisa took it as a good sign. She found an opening in his nightwear and slid her hands inside. He moaned again and sought for the edge of her long dress. That was it. She felt she had done the right thing when he lifted himself and positioned her underneath him.

Chapter Twenty-Five

They were a tangled wreck and it took Johnny the most-needed minute to unlock their legs. A minute too late. A heavy punch hit him on the side of his head, but he struggled back up. Two men were on him, and he immediately knew why. The intruders would take him out first. He couldn't let that happen. What time was it? He thought he was in Elisa's arms just moments before or was that last night? Another punch missed when he ducked his head into the midriff of his attacker, a deep groan escaped the man's chest. The other hit him in the middle of his back with what seemed like the butt of a gun and he slumped.

Elisa screamed, and all Johnny could hear in his haze were punches and slaps. On his wife? And baby! He couldn't let it happen. He pulled himself up and wiped blood trickling from his nose. Oh no, he couldn't start bleeding from the nose now. That would slow him down faster than anything the men did. Heavy footsteps resounded down the stairs punctuated by scraps from the struggle and Elisa's screams. He found his clothing and stumbled down the staircase. He caught sight of the carriage that had brought Penny earlier a second before it pulled off. They had Elisa, and she was probably naked.

He staggered back up the stairs and grabbed her nightdress and his gun. When he got outside, he found the horse dead, shot at close range. A deep cry escaped from his chest. The carriage was gone, but he could not give up. He ran despite his bleeding nose and pounding head to the next house about a quarter of a mile away. Two horses were in a stable. He took one, thankful for it. Everywhere was still dark and he couldn't tell if this was closer to night or morning.

The horse was strong and fast, but as soon as he was at least a mile away from the house he stole from, he stopped to look for tracks. It would be easy to trace the carriage even in the poor moonlight. His instinct told him the abductors would head into town where they could easily disappear amongst others in the busyness of New York City. They would tie Elisa and keep her in a stable, so no one would suspect her, and in the early morning, ship her to wherever they pleased. Or they could kill her. This mere thought tortured him. Not after last night. She was pleading for forgiveness in her own way, in the best way. He was more in love with her now than he'd ever been.

As though they'd been partners forever, Johnny rode the horse smoothly and thanked the God of Heavens for it! What would he have done if the animal was sick or untamed? If his life wasn't on the verge of uncertainty, he would consider stealing the horse for real. Closer to the outskirts of Harlem, he thought he caught a glimpse of the evil men, but he couldn't be sure. Carriages were far slower than horses, and the mistake to bring one for this operation told him how much they underestimated his resolve to protect his wife and stay by her.

He drew closer and realized he indeed had the criminals in view, but they were approaching Harlem, a community that never slept. As soon as some went to bed, some awoke. He had to be careful to follow them to where they planned to take Elisa. He could not entertain the thought that she was dead already, so he rode on. When they got to a busy street, the carriage slowed down, and he did as well. Soon it turned into a lonely street. Johnny cocked his gun and followed at a leisurely pace. The street was narrow, but the lamps on the houses provided good illumination. The carriage driver and his passengers didn't seem to notice the rider who continued to gain distance on them. Until he was right behind, and he could see Elisa, tied and gagged, naked on the floor of the carriage. If she wasn't frozen to death. A sob escaped from his lips. How was he going to get to her?

One of the men in front noticed him and probably thinking he was just another person moving about his business, moved a little aside for him to pass. It was Johnny's chance. He drew even and pointed his gun at the driver.

"Pull over. Get down." He snarled. "On your faces."

The men hurried to do his bidding and lay on the cold stone of the cobbled street. Johnny took off the clothing of the first and when the other raised his head, he shot him in the leg. Several windows slammed shut at the ringing of the gun sound. Afraid someone would come to challenge him, he hurried to Elisa and pulled the nightgown over her head. She was cold and stiff but had a little breath in her nostrils.

Weeping and praying, Johnny put her on his horse and rode like a mad man toward the new art center down Manhattan.

"This is why I don't understand you Americans!" Henri cursed. "Get me the warmer over there instead of just standing!" He snapped.

A hot water bottle lay on a fancy dresser and Johnny picked it, clenching his teeth to keep himself from speaking. The stress of the night had finally set in and he had a hurting head and back. And his nose was still bleeding. He hated the idea that Henri asked him to lay Elisa on his bed, but there was no other bedroom in the studio. The place was warm though, and after ensuring Elisa was comfortable, Henri offered him a pot of hot French tea, which he declined.

"We'll leave her to sleep. In the morning, I will call my physician." Henri placed the hot bottle on Elisa's side, under the blanket. "She will be fine. Come in the studio and tell me what happened."

Johnny stiffened. "I will stay with her."

"I am not an American, Johnny Holt. I don't care about slavery." With the rude remark, he stomped out. "Come for tea and talk. You look awful yourself." He called from an adjacent room partitioned with a straight board.

Johnny sat at the head of the bed, and cradled Elisa. He pressed a kiss to her forehead and cried softly. "I almost lost you and our baby tonight, darling. I'm sorry." He sniffed, tasting the copper in the blood from his nose.

He knew he should take Henri's offer and get some treatment and rest, but he couldn't bear to leave Elisa alone. With all that had happened in the last few hours, who could he trust. There was only one option left. He wasn't safe in his own country and before he killed someone while trying to survive, it was best to leave. There were several options and with the one thousand Henri offered months ago, he could choose any.

Henri pushed in a couch. "If my wife was half this beautiful, I'd not want to leave her side either. But you'd be no good to her dead."

Johnny watched him march out of the room and rolled his eyes. Well, he did need a couch, but if he got on one, he'd sleep for the next two days. He remained by Elisa's side and thought of how much better he would feel lying down.

Chapter Twenty-Six

"A back brace is what he needs or he may not walk again."

Johnny stirred and opened his eyes. The lined floor of Henri's bedroom met his gaze.

He lifted himself but was constrained by weight on his back.

"Don't move or you'll crack what's left of your spine." Henri cursed in his language. "Doctor, I must leave you. Let me have your bill when you're done with him."

Johnny heard Henri's now familiar thudding footsteps on the floor recede. He worried over Elisa. Was she still asleep? And why was the doctor attending to him, and not her?

He cleared his throat. "Doctor?"

A deep soothing voice responded. "Yes, Mr. Holt?"

Johnny licked his dry lips. "My wife. Is she alright?"

"She's right here, Mr. Holt. She's fine."

Elisa squatted. "I'm here, hasband," she said softly. "I'm good."

Johnny lifted his head so he could see her face. "*Oh*, thank God. I thought I'd lose you."

She smoothed back his hair. "No. Ya won't lose me. And I won't lose ya."

The doctor cleared his throat. "I'll like you to stay flat on your belly, Mr. Holt. You may not need a back brace after all."

Johnny heaved a heavy sigh. "Thank you, Doctor."

"I should be back in the evening to check on you. There's a little basin for your convenience, and Missis Holt here has offered to be your nurse." The doctor chuckled. "No bones broken and that's what you should be grateful for."

Johnny turned to the direction of the doctor's voice but could only see him up to his knees. "Doctor, what about Elisa? Is she okay?"

"Yes, Mr. Holt. She was slapped around a little and got more cold into her body than was good, but she's doing much better than you, sir. Please excuse me."

The doctor's soft steps retreated and indicated the man had left coupled with Elisa's hungry search for his lips. He grabbed the back of her head and fed on her mouth. When they both came up for air, he chuckled.

"My love. Bruises. Bastards." He traced his finger over her face. "I thought I was watching over you."

She smiled. "Ya got on the bed."

He laughed. "Henri brought a couch–" he turned a little. "*Oh*, I'm now on it."

She sat in front of him on the floor and caressed his face. "Henri? He wanna do them paintin' on me 'gain."

Johnny groaned. "He told you?" She nodded. "The bastard. He should ask me."

"He said he told ya before."

Johnny cupped her face. "He did. But I'd hate for you to do it. He wants to paint you so he can touch you and gawk at you." He rolled his eyes. "I hate him."

"He save us."

Her words annoyed him. "Rub that in, Elisa." He let go of her face and turned away. "Tell me I'm not man enough to protect you." He jerked up, forgetting he was meant to stay on his belly and a bone in his back cracked. "*Arrgghhh*!"

She screamed. "Stop it, Massa Johnny. Ya'll 'urt yaself!"

Johnny chuckled. "I don't feel the pain anymore." He moved again. "What's on my back?"

She stood over him. "Please stop." She sobbed.

He put his hand on his back and raised himself. "It's a block or something."

"Don't remove it. Doctor, he said it goin' a set ya back."

Johnny continued to raise himself up. "That doesn't hurt so badly." He smiled at her.

She clasped her hand over her mouth and tears clouded her lovely eyes. The weight on his back shifted and as he straightened, it moved until it fell on the floor with a thud.

"I can stretch. A little at a time." He practiced and soon he was upright. "Not bad, really."

He waved at her. "Come here."

She walked closer and when she was right in front of him, he pulled her onto his lap and groaned.

"I love you." He covered her mouth with his. "Henri wants you, but I won't let him have you."

"I don't wan' him."

He took nibbles of her neck and shoulder. "Good. Only me. You'll have only me."

She moaned. "Ya, Massa."

"You know you drive me crazy when you call me Massa?" He cupped her face. "Do you know that?" He kissed her mouth. "*Hmm?*"

She kissed him back. "*Hmm*, Massa."

"Do I drive you crazy?" He held her gaze. "I, wife?"

"I don't think ya drive me mad, hasband. Mad ain't a good word to use for ya man."

Johnny threw back his head and laughed. "I thought that witch Nan taught you grammar along with sewing."

"She did, sure." She smiled. "Ya drive me crazy, Massa."

He buried his head in her chest. "We need to leave this country, I. I don't trust anyone anymore."

She combed her hand through his hair. "Me too. I taught Miz Nan was goin' a be a "mammy" to me, but she betrayed me."

"Where should we go? Europe?"

"Canada. Maybe I can see my Mama 'gain."

Johnny lifted his head and stared in her eyes. "Canada it is then."

CHAPTER TWENTY-SEVEN

Henri did not welcome Johnny's request for a loan. Not only was he not willing because he expressed fears he may never get the loan paid, he wanted to paint Elisa. The thought made Johnny so frustrated, but there were no other options. With his mother sending men after him, while he was still wanted by his father, and unable to trust Nan the informer or her dishonorable lover, escape routes had narrowed considerably. He caved in, and let Henri have his way.

"I will have five portraits of her," Henri told him.

Johnny gagged. "Five! We agreed on only one."

"When? You believe I will pay a thousand American dollars for one portrait, and a medical bill and keeping you here?" Henri cursed. "I sleep on the floor while you make love to your wife on my bed, and I keep your secrets safe?" He snapped his finger. "I should take ten portraits. And if you provoke me, I will."

Johnny stepped back as though he had been slapped. "You shall have your five portraits."

"Good. The doctor thinks she should have another few days to gain her strength back, and I need the bruises on her face to clear better. Then we start."

"Thank you," Johnny murmured.

"You're welcome. By the way, you will not be allowed inside my studio while I work!"

Every single day after the painting started was a torture for Johnny. He reluctantly admitted Henri was quite professional. After an early breakfast, Elisa would take a pose for the artist, and they would work for several hours, take a break for brunch, and resume for more long hours. Henri loved to go to town in the evening, and this was when Johnny had his wife back.

On the third day, unable to bear Elisa's lack of interest in discussing what went on during the sessions, Johnny blurted, "Does he touch you...inappropriately?"

Elisa shook her head. "Just the same way ya seen before."

"If he does anything untoward, you let me know," Johnny said. "He may be paying for this, but I'm not going to allow him cross boundaries."

Henri was finally satisfied after two weeks. Johnny suspected he had more than the five portraits they agreed to, but there was no way to know. The French man refused to show them his finished work.

"There you go, Mr. Holt." Henri folded some bills and handed them to him. "One thousand American dollars."

Johnny's heart leapt. "Thank you."

Henri clasped his hands. "I'm also pleased. The paintings look much better than I imagined."

Johnny snapped. "I bet you'll sell and earn ten times what you payed."

"You just crossed out your momentary gratitude," Henri hissed. "I should let you know you may not even be able to leave the country. Trevor Truse has joined the band of hunters looking for you."

Johnny exclaimed. "I owe him nothing!"

Henri raised an eyebrow. "*Oh*, really? He gave you a safe accommodation. Comfortable too. For you and your slave." He glared. "I do believe in a few hours you'd be telling someone you owe me nothing. What an ingrate you are, Johnny Holt."

Johnny snapped, "Trevor's lover betrayed my trust."

"But you still owe on your promise. To stick around and help their campaign. To willingly show off your slave wife–"

"He got a painting of her."

Henri snickered. "There's no winning with you. I only pity that pretty little thing stuck with you."

Johnny clenched his hands so he would not hit Henri. "We'll leave your hospitality tomorrow. You have been very kind."

Henri turned away from him. "Leave after dark. And make your inquiries from the black people. Trevor has spies planted at the harbor." He walked to the door and added before he exited. "If you were traveling alone, I'd let you fall into their hands."

Johnny felt small for his ingratitude, but these were hard times. Even with Henri's added retort, the Frenchman had been sympathetic and generous. He didn't hesitate when Johnny banged on his door those weeks ago when he was desperate for help and had nowhere to run to. New York could be no man's land, a city that accommodated everyone and everything, but the segregation here fell across all lines much the same way it did in other parts of the country. People of color were still being killed or kidnapped in broad daylight. Many people associated only within their social, racial and religious strata. It dawned on Johnny he could never have a normal life with Elisa. Not here anyway, unless he joined a band of gypsies. The mere thought made him laugh.

Elisa walked out of the room. "I hear ya speakin' with Henri. Wha'd he say?"

"He paid the money for you. We leave tomorrow evening."

She moved into his arms. "Ya not soundin' 'appy? Wha'd he say to ya?"

Johnny sighed. "Nothing too surprising. Trevor Truse's lover sends my mother after me, and now he's not happy I disappeared. What did he think I'd do?"

Elisa shrugged. "People we'd be people. Ya can ne'er please people, my Ma always said."

"I guess you're right."

She cupped his face. "Hasband, be 'appy. We'd soon be free."

Johnny frowned. "In another man's land."

He hated to leave, but what other choices did he have?

Chapter Twenty-Eight

The journey to Canada was uneventful. With the cash they had, it was easy to buy a luxury cabin in the boat and they had all their meals privately. Johnny enjoyed every bit of the trip, pushing behind the horrible experiences of the past. He discussed the possibilities of getting a job, and with Elisa's sewing skills, they could make a comfortable living.

Canada was more than they bargained for. Johnny, from his studies in school, knew it would be a cold country, but it was much colder than he imagined. Saving grace with the money they had, he bought heavy and warm clothing at exorbitant prices and found a temporary shelter for them in an inn right there at the harbor.

"We can take a day to rest, and then I'll go out and make findings."

Elisa smiled. "Yes, hasband."

"I'm hopeful things will improve. We can live here." Johnny shrugged. "It's not like I have anything back home."

He had no regrets, either. At some point, he came to the conclusion that his father would have fallen out with him anyway. If he refused to take over the plantation, or go to Law School and enter politics, or marry one particular woman…the list was endless. JJ Holt liked to think he was in charge all the time, of all the people under him, including his wife and kids. There would have come a time when Johnny would need to be a man of himself. If not over slavery or love, over career or family affiliations or business.

The following day, Johnny left their inn early. The room was warm, they had a heavy breakfast delivered, and Elisa seemed safe. He had no plans of staying long. All he needed was to find out about the boats that berthed and if he was lucky, he'd find someone who knew about Dee and Anthony. Or even the ridiculous Captain Ingrid who brought them.

Johnny was not lucky. He was blessed.

Elisa stayed in the room praying and crying, somewhat afraid things would fall apart again. By noon, Johnny returned, and he had Anthony with him. She screamed at the sight of her father and leapt on him.

"Papa." Her emotions overwhelmed her. "I'm so happy to see ya. I got so much to tell ya." She checked behind him. "Where's Mama?"

Anthony hugged her neck and sobbed. "Ya Mama ded. She go ded on me as we got 'ere."

Elisa stumbled backward. "Dead! How she dead?"

"She got the *neemoneea*! Cold got to 'er." Anthony shuddered. "She not get a month on 'er."

"Mama been dead all this time?" Elisa wept. "I wan my Mama."

Johnny held her. "Ssh, it's okay." He pressed a kiss on her forehead. "It's okay, dear."

"I wanna see her grave. She wanted me to come with her. She never goin' a forgive me."

Anthony sniffed. "She understood ya, Elisa. Said she'd 'ave gone with 'er man too."

"She did?" Elisa walked back into Anthony's arms. "I'm sorry, Papa. I shoulda come with ya."

Anthony heaved. "Ya did the best. I almost ded too. Canada ain't all that. Yes, no slavery 'ere but no job for the black man." He smiled. "So good to see ya, child. Seem like ya've got some flesh."

Elisa sighed. "Yea, Papa. I got me some flesh. But we still on the run. Massa JJ and Miz Penny want Johnny dead!"

"Tha' 'orrible there, Massa Johnny." Anthony heaved. "I gotta go now. I gotta be on the job."

Elisa gasped. "Can we visit tonight when ya get off work? I wanna see Mama's grave."

"She ain't get no grave, child. We ain't get no land so I buried 'er by the road." Anthony shook his head. "I'd be 'ere before work tomorrow."

Elisa's mouth dropped open. "Why can't we visit tonight?"

Johnny cleared his throat. "Wife, your Papa got married. And she may not be happy to have us over."

Elisa gasped. "Mama ain't dead two month, ya gat yaself another woman!" She cried. "Go! Go away." She fell into Johnny's arms. "I don' wanna live here no more, hasband!" She sobbed.

Johnny saw Anthony out, while Elisa buried her head under a pillow and wept.

Anthony moaned. "Ya gotta hep me talk to 'er, Massa Johnny. The woman I marry, she great. She hep me when Dee get sick and ded."

Johnny nodded. "I understand you, Anthony. Elisa has been through a lot and it doesn't look like things will get any better."

"Sorry to 'ear 'bout ya Papa and all because of we." Anthony bowed. "Where do ya wanna go now? Canada ain't no place. I fear I goin' a ded too. Like 'er mama."

"You don't have to be sorry. None of this is your fault in any way," Johnny sighed. "I can't go back home. I'll ask about other places. I know the movement had settlements on the islands and Africa. Maybe Europe."

Anthony's face lit up. "Africa. Back 'ome."

Johnny smiled. "Were you born there?"

"No, but my Pa was. I would go back now 'cept fer the wife."

Johnny nodded. "Well, I'm really sorry about Dee and I hope you find peace in your new life."

Anthony smiled. "My wife, she a great woman. Young too." He looked away. "Wanna 'ave a babe or two."

Johnny laughed. "Anthony, you ain't too old yourself."

"Thank ya, Massa Johnny. For everthin'."

Quite unusual for both men, they hugged spontaneously, and Anthony walked away with his shoulders slouched.

"Hey, Anthony!" Johnny followed him. "Wait."

The black man turned. "Yes, Massa Johnny?"

"Do you by any chance know anything about you know, going to Europe or Africa from here?"

Anthony nodded. "Yes, Massa Johnny. I got me a friend who gone and come back a couple times."

"Great, can you arrange for us to meet. I think it's best to take Elisa from here. At least until the baby comes."

"Ya got a babe on the way?"

Johnny smiled. "Yes. I'm sorry, I think she didn't want you to know yet."

"Tha' fine, Massa Johnny." Anthony shrugged. "I goin' a ask my friend to come see ya tomorrow."

"Thank you so much, Anthony." The two men shook hands. "And sir, please call me Johnny."

Anthony's face dropped. "Johnny."

Chapter Twenty-Nine

It took another week before they could secure accommodation aboard a ship to Africa. Because Elisa was black, she could and did apply for the transition and with Anthony's friend's help, they got on the journey without paying a lot. It would have been free if Johnny didn't request a private cabin. He had never seen his wife smile so widely. Not even when he got them a luxury cruise to Canada.

Emancipation groups had their campaigns thriving with Canadian, British and American collaboration. For years, freed slaves had been returned home and given parcels of land to cultivate and settle on, giving them a sense of belonging in what could have been their homeland. The fact that many of them had lost their languages and culture and were not even sure if their ancestors were taken away from the destination country was unimportant.

On the ship, contrary to what he expected, there were many black families, and none had to be snuck out of the country. Some of the people moved as families, and some as individuals. Johnny, for the first time, felt like an outsider as he was the only white-skinned passenger. He made friends with members of the crew, because the freed men discriminated against him.

Elisa made friends faster than anyone else and at some point, Johnny felt she was avoiding his company. Gradually, he retreated into the cabin and only came out either in the night to stare into the water from the deck, or to get his meals directly from the kitchen. The captain was sympathetic but couldn't understand why Johnny would want to go on the trip.

The ship berthed on the coast of the West African country of Liberia in late January 1860 on a sunny Thursday afternoon. It would be the most memorable day of Elisa's life, not only because she felt she was "home" but because her baby kicked for the first time. Her belly wasn't showing, but early that morning she woke up in Johnny's arms and felt the soft tremor. She moaned and turned on to her side, unsure of how she felt, and Johnny came awake.

"Are you alright, dear?"

Her hand rested on her lower abdomen. "Huh!" Then she sat up. "He moves. Yes now, Johnny. My babe move."

"What?" Johnny sat up too. "Are you sure?" His hand covered hers.

"No, here. Here!" She moved his hand. "Can ya feel it?"

He yelped. "Yes. Hahaha! He's moving a lot. Goodness." He spread his hand over her stomach and covered her mouth in a kiss. "This is grand."

Elisa laughed. "He so strong."

He smiled. "Like his daddy."

"Don' know 'bout tha'. His mammy, she be the slave."

Johnny kissed her again. "You're not a slave, Miz Holt."

They prepared and disembarked from the ship a few hours later and were taken to the resettlement shelter where they were allocated a private room. The organization was so well-done, they had self-catering options and a well-stocked pantry if they didn't want to eat in the general dining hall. A coordinator told them they could sleep in, and on Monday they would be shown to their property.

They opted to have dinner in the hall, and the meal of fries and a steak sauce was not only filling, but well-prepared. Johnny wanted to turn in early, but Elisa was restless. This was more freedom than anyone could ever have. She walked out as soon as they were done eating, despite Johnny's objection.

"I think this is not the day to explore," he said. "And the baby needs some rest."

She called out as she leapt off on light feet. "I'm fine, and my babe is fine."

The shelter had rooms on either side of a long corridor, and people moved in and out. Shelter workers dressed in neat, crisp para-military uniforms moved along the corridors answering questions and helping families settle in. On the more-than-a-month long journey from Canada, Elisa had made friends and went in search of them. Her thoughts were wild. She wanted to run and scream and hug people. The last time she felt so in touch with herself were those nights when she went swimming alone. As soon as Johnny joined her, she lost her freedom, but she could never disclose this to him.

She found a couple she'd made friends with and followed them around the settlement. Then they left the protected areas and went into a village to meet with some of the local people who flocked around them and offered them local food and clothing. Elisa returned so late, Johnny was standing outside their shelter, and making a report to one of the guards.

"There she comes," he breathed. "Thank you." He shook hands with the guard who bowed and left.

Elisa walked past as though she didn't notice him.

He followed her into their room and snapped. "Where were you, I looked everywhere?"

"I'm not ya slave no more." She took her shoes off and moaned. "Ahhh."

Johnny came around to face her. "You're my wife. And I was worried."

"I didn' get lost."

Johnny gasped. "So? You can't just go off without my knowledge. I didn't even know who you were with."

She took her clothes off and wore her nightdress, then stretched on the bed. "I have friends now, sir."

Johnny clenched his hands. "Don't call me sir. And you are not allowed to leave without my approval."

Elisa closed her eyes. She was so tired from all the walking about the village and dancing with the locals and her friends. She didn't care about Johnny's anger. She didn't belong to him or anyone anymore. This was not America. This was Africa. And she was African. She was home, on the land where her forefathers were free-born. She contemplated replying him.

"Elisa?"

"Goodnight, ol' Massa Johnny. I'm in my homeland."

Chapter Thirty

Elisa woke up sick the following day, and Johnny worried over her. At mid-day, she had thrown up everything she ate, and started running a fever. Johnny had one of the guards get a doctor, and it pleased him an American doctor was called to attend to her.

"She's with child," he blurted, before greeting the doctor.

The doctor stretched his hand to him. "Good afternoon, Mr. Holt. I am Dr. Obed."

Johnny took his hand with both of his. "Good afternoon, Doctor. We need your help."

"Let me see her." Dr. Obed moved closer to Elisa and touched her forehead. "She's hot."

Johnny came to stand beside him. "Is she going to be okay?"

"We'll see. You both came in yesterday?"

"Yes, sir."

"From New York or Pennsylvania?"

"From Canada."

"Oh, Canada." Dr. Obed opened his bag. "I was in Canada for three years after I finished up my internship over in Washington." He put a small stick in Elisa's mouth.

"She's been sleeping for over an hour, Doctor,"

"She'll be fine." The doctor opened his bag again and brought out a syringe. "How long did you live in Canada?"

Johnny leaned forward. "Just a week. Elisa didn't like it."

Dr. Obed moved to stand in front of him and blocked his view. "Canada does that to you. You either love it or hate it." He waved. "Get me some extra pillows, will you? From the Housekeeper."

"Huh, okay." Johnny hurried out.

He found a guard who directed him to the Housekeeper's office. There he found a tall, slim man seated behind a cluttered desk, in a large room with beddings and supplies on different shelves.

Johnny panted, "Good afternoon. Please I need to see the Housekeeper. We need pillows. For my wife."

The man stood. "My name is Margibi. How many pillows do you need?"

"Huh, four maybe. Please."

"Of course, Mr. Holt."

He walked to one of the shelves and pulled out four pillows, a blanket and bedding.

"You may need these as well," he called out. "I'll carry along with you."

Johnny hurried over to him, pushing aside the first thought of how the man knew his name. "Thank you." He carried the pillows and the blanket, and Margibi took the bedding.

"You can go on, I will join you after I enter this into the log."

"Thank you."

Elisa was awake when Johnny returned with the pillows. Dr. Obed helped to prop her up on two of them as Margibi entered with the extra bedding.

She murmured. "Thank ya."

Margibi exclaimed. "Ah, Dr. Obed. Good afternoon. I didn't know you were here already."

"Hello Margibi. Good to see you." Dr. Obed looked at Johnny. "She'll be fine. She needs a lot of rest, and water."

Breathing hard from running with the pillows, Johnny slouched. "Thank God. Thank you, Doctor."

"I have some medicine that will help stabilize her. Safe for her condition." Dr. Obed started to leave.

Johnny pressed a kiss on Elisa's forehead. "I'll be back." He walked Dr. Obed and Margibi out.

Outside, the doctor stopped walking. "She ate something that didn't agree with her. But she'll be fine."

Margibi arched an eyebrow. "We scrutinize the menu very diligently. I must speak with the cook."

Johnny shifted on his feet. "I don't think it's the food from the dining room. She went out last night."

"Out?" Dr. Obed sighed. "I see. Well, what I gave her will settle her stomach. You know how to reach me, but I will check on her again tomorrow."

"Thank you, Doctor."

Dr. Obed shook both men's hands and walked briskly away.

Margibi addressed Johnny. "Rule number one, ask questions before you move around."

Johnny pushed his bushy hair back. "I know. I feel awful that I let her leave like that."

"Hmm." Margibi narrowed his eyes. "Did she say where she went, what she did?"

Johnny shook his head. "I was upset. I didn't say the right things and she refused to speak to me."

"I understand, Mr. Holt. When people arrive here, there is a lot of excitement and many mistakes made."

Johnny folded his arms. "How do you know my name?"

Margibi smiled. "Besides the fact that you are here with your wife, I make it my business to know people's names."

"Well, let me get back to her. Thank you for your help."

"My name is Margibi. You know where to find me if you need a friend."

Johnny nodded. "Thanks, Margibi."

The liquid the doctor gave Elisa tasted terrible, but it made her feel better instantly. The man was professional as he asked her all the necessary questions and urged her to tell him everything she did since she arrived. His mild attitude gave her some confidence, and since Johnny was nowhere around, she could speak freely. She didn't think her American husband would be happy to hear she had started getting initiated into the cultures of the land, which meant she drank some of the awful alcoholic stuff and ate foods she had no idea what it came from. She thought she was so deprived, she wanted to soak everything in. Well, her body didn't think so. Dr. Obed didn't think so either and he told her as much.

"Please don' let Massa Johnny know," she whispered a moment before Johnny came in with the extra pillows.

Johnny returned from seeing the doctor off with the same frown on his face, which seemed to be a default expression since they arrived Africa. He sat on the edge of the bed, his gaze locked on hers. She wasn't sure what to think.

"Dr. Obed says you'll be fine."

She twisted her hands in her lap, and Johnny reached out to hold her. An apology seemed in place, but were not those traits of slavery? When you apologize for everything whether you were wrong or right?

"He said so," she mumbled.

He shifted closer. "I'm not mad at you, Elisa. I just want you to be safe. We're new here. We don't know their ways."

"I don' 'xpect ya to follo' me 'round."

Johnny held her hands in both of his. "And I won't. I just need to know you're safe."

"I safe." She looked away. "I thought I safe."

"Exactly, darling." He scooted closer. "We don't know these people yet. We don't know their food, their drinks. We just need to take things slow."

"I kno'."

Her apology hung in her throat. She wasn't a slave anymore and didn't want to act like one.

"With the baby, you need to be more careful." He moved even closer. "I nearly died of worry over you." He cupped her face and kissed her mouth. "I love you, Elisa."

She pushed down a suitable response.

Chapter Thirty-One

Elisa had to take a mild medication that purged her system of whatever her body was reacting to. The doctor placed her on light soup and fruits until she could eat properly again. On the other hand, Johnny enjoyed her company and though he noticed none of her new friends visited, he made no mention of it. He fed her and teased and laughed with her. The baby kicked more, and it was always the highlight of their day. Dr. Obed visited every day to monitor her progress, and so did Margibi, who showed himself friendlier with each day. Johnny knew he would need friends, but he was a little reluctant about being close to the locals like Margibi.

On Monday, allocations were made and Margibi offered to drive Johnny and Elisa to their new home in his cart. The house was a two-bed bungalow built on five acres of beautiful farmland, with a stream that ran across the property. It was one of several on a well-planned secured estate.

"This reminds me so much of home." Johnny came down from the cart and stood just staring out.

Margibi and Elisa came to stand with him. "It's government's plan to resettle many who had worked on plantations. Farming is what most know."

Johnny held Elisa's hand. "My wife knows how to sew."

Margibi's eyes widened. "She does? That is fantastic. She—we can get her a job immediately if she wants." He looked at her.

Elisa turned to Johnny. "Tha' if Mas—he agree."

Johnny shrugged. "Of course. Why would I not agree?"

"We have a warehouse and we have been training many women to sew. So, a trained seamstress is a blessing." Margibi laughed. "And the salary is good."

Johnny chuckled. "Good. When can she start?"

"As soon as she's settled in. I will take her papers and we can do the documentation." Margibi clapped. "Shall we go in?"

Whoever designed the house thought to replicate what the houses looked like in America. There was even a fireplace, though the climate was tropical. The house had basic furnishing and the rooms were large enough to take two beds each. The kitchen had a small pantry already stocked with dry foods and a large basin was filled with water.

"Water supply is still an issue, but we have some locals who bring water daily," Margibi said. "It gets hot and dry around this time."

"Okay, thank you." Johnny led the others back into the living room. "Will you be able to show us the market?"

"We have a central one on the estate. Also, the locals bring fresh food for a small price. You may see them walk to the front of the house."

Johnny folded his arms. "What kind of fresh food?"

"Fish from the stream. Or meat hunted. They bring fruits from their farms. And potatoes, vegetables." Margibi shrugged. "Beware of the mushrooms. Some of them are poisonous."

Johnny gasped. "No mushrooms."

Margibi walked toward the door. "I need to get back to my office."

"Yes, of course. Thank you." Johnny walked him to the door.

Outside, Margibi clasped his hands. "You know where to find me if you need me."

Johnny nodded. "Thank you for your friendship."

"I was able to get a good horse for you. But you'll have to pay for it when you start earning."

Johnny exclaimed. "That is so kind of you. I do have some money. I can pay now."

"Oh, really. It's just thirty dollars."

"Give me a minute." Johnny hurried into the house and came back with the money.

"Here. Thirty-five. Tip for your–"

"No, please." Margibi took thirty. "I cannot take more than the price." He got into his cart and waved. "So long."

"So long, my friend."

Johnny waved till he was no longer in view and went back into the house where he found Elisa in the room lying on the bed.

"He's very kind," he said. "Are you alright?"

"Yes." She nodded. "He kickin' 'gain."

Johnny joined her on the bed and spread his hand over her abdomen. He could feel the baby kick too.

He chuckled. "He will be a strong man." He wrapped his arms around her and kissed her neck. "When do you want to start work?"

Elisa arched an eyebrow. "And what ya be doin'?"

"Farming, I have a horse, a piece of land and a stream."

"And who'd be heppin' ya?"

"We'll figure that out when the time comes." He smoothed her hair back. "Margibi will surely help with getting someone for me."

"I don't wanna work for 'im."

Johnny lifted himself up to look at her. "You'll be working for government, not him."

She squared her shoulders. "Well, I don't wanna be workin' for nobody."

"That's fine. With the baby coming, you'll soon get very busy." He caressed her face. "I want what you want."

"Really?" She leaned forward. "I'm no slave no more. I fear ya be angry I tell ya what I wan'."

"I never saw you as a slave, Elisa." He gathered her into his arms. "You know that."

"I just wanna make my babe clothes. And make for me and ya."

"That will be great." He kissed her mouth. "I'll ask Margibi if he can get a sewing kit and a machine."

"Ya will?" She hugged his neck. "Thank ya."

"I will do anything for you, Elisa wife."

He kissed her deeper and lowered her onto the bed. It had been a while since they had been intimate, and he was desperate for her.

Chapter Thirty-Two

Margibi arranged for the sewing machine, solidly placing himself as a main feature in their lives, but all Elisa wanted was to move out and make acquaintances with other people. With the way she fell sick, Johnny would not hear of it, which frustrated her to no end. The only other person they saw for weeks was Margibi, who came around early in the morning before he left for his job at the settlement to help with the farm work, and also at night for dinner. Johnny did all the shopping, so Elisa only went out for walks in the evenings to step out of the house. Dr. Obed warned about mosquito bites and so she couldn't stay outside for long periods.

Despite herself, Elisa thought Margibi was a likable person. He was much older than her and Johnny, in his early thirties, and had never been married, which she thought was strange. One night, he told a story about a freed slave he fell in love with, but she died before they got married. He threw himself in his job afterward and would do anything to make sure new settlers fared better.

A month after they arrived, Elisa got her sewing machine. It was not new, but it had been ordered from New York, and the same type she used to learn. She screeched when Johnny and Margibi moved it into the spare room.

"This 'ere will be babe's room." She waited until the machine was placed against the wall. "I will sew 'ere."

Johnny smiled. "Yes, darling. It looks just like the one you had back in New York."

"We can go out tomorrow to the city to buy the fabric," Margibi said. "The main city is about eight miles away."

"That will be grand." Johnny nodded. "I think I will like to see the new stable you talked about too. An extra horse will be needed. For Elisa."

Elisa yelped. "A 'orse for me?"

"You need it, darling. I will get busy with the farm and won't always be there to go out with you."

Margibi cleared his throat. "I can always come and take her out. Going about on her own–"

Johnny shrugged. "You may be right, but she needs to be able to move around." He smiled at Elisa. "She's been home all this while. I will feel better if she starts getting around. Isn't this what you want?"

Elisa's gaze dropped. "Yes."

Margibi sighed. "Maybe a cart then. Though she will stand out even more. Some of the women use a donkey when they need to go a far distance."

"A horse." Johnny patted his shoulder. "Tomorrow, please."

Elisa couldn't contain her joy when they entered the new stables and a young brown horse was chosen for her. She could ride a horse fairly well from the lessons Johnny gave her back in New York but had never had one of her own. The mare had been half-broken, so Johnny told the manager to work on it before they took it. Then they went into the fabric store where Elisa saw so much, she could not stop running from aisle to aisle. The men followed her. Finally, she saw some soft fabrics in different colors, and touched them one by one.

"These would be good for baby's clothing?" Johnny asked.

She nodded. "Look like it. They sof' 'nof."

"Elisa!"

A deep female voice called behind her and all three of them swung around to see a smallish, elderly woman stand at the end of their aisle.

"Miz Beth!" Johnny exclaimed. "You're here?"

Beth rushed to them and hugged Elisa. "Elisa! Ya 'ere? The Lord be praised, child!" She turned to Johnny. "Missa Johnny. Margibi? Why? This 'ere is some reunion."

Elisa's mouth hung open. She didn't know what to say. She was glad to see a familiar face for once. She'd wondered where all the friends she made were, but Johnny refused to discuss this, and she couldn't blame him.

"Miz Beth." She hugged the woman back. "So good to see ya."

"What ya doin' 'ere shoppin' for cloths." Beth smiled. "I work down 'ere."

Johnny arched an eyebrow. "How long have you been here?"

"Came 'ere right after the 'scape." Beth touched the fabric Elisa was looking at. "This 'ere good cotton."

"Maybe ya can come over for dinner?" Elisa flashed a look at Johnny for approval.

"Sure. We'll be happy to have you." Johnny shrugged. "I got a lamb roast going." He smiled awkwardly.

"We be at the estate," Elisa said.

"I be there too. I'll find ya." Beth hugged her again. "Gotta get to werk." She hurried back the way she came. "See ya in the evenin'," She called.

Margibi arched his neck. "You knew her in America?"

Johnny cleared his throat. "She, ur, was my father's slave." He chuckled. "We ran off together. From the farm." He scratched his beard.

Margibi smiled. "Oh, I see."

To end the awkwardness of the moment, Johnny touched a green fabric with small patterns. "This looks like a nice one for a baby."

They all turned their attention to it. At the end of the shopping, Elisa had enough materials to fill a baby's cupboard.

"I need to start werk on all o' them," she giggled. "Be werkin' day and night on 'em."

She picked out two new fabrics for herself and two for Johnny. Margibi made sure to point out she could sew for men as well, which would have been a great asset to their dressmaking warehouse had Elisa not declined working there.

Beth arrived for dinner with three other women to Johnny's amazement. She joked about the African culture of extra guests showing up without invitation.

Margibi, who always had his dinner with the Holts, hid his embarrassment under a joke when he said, "Welcome to Africa."

"The good thing is that we have enough food to go around." Johnny shook hands with the women. "Please make yourselves comfortable." He looked around at the four available chairs.

"We men will sit on the floor." He chuckled and hurried into the room to bring the only other chair in the house for Elisa.

Margibi took to the floor immediately. Beth hugged Elisa and motioned on the ladies to do the same.

Johnny didn't feel good about this at all. The memory of how Beth had used them to escape rankled. He joined Elisa to bring more plates and the leftover lamb roast he'd thought they could have the following day. When everyone was settled with a plate of food, Beth offered prayers.

"So 'ere is Bomi, Lofa and Simba." Beth introduced. "Them all come from America 'xcept Bomi. She never been a slave." She giggled.

"But I was born and raised by slaves," Bomi said, her voice fierce. "My family came here when I was three. Fifteen years ago."

Johnny chewed on his bread as though it was stone. "You have non-American names."

"We all do. First thin' we got goin'," Beth chipped in. "My name now is Sino."

Johnny frowned. "That's interesting. What do they mean?"

"The Americans were encouraged to change their names to local ones to help them fit in faster." Margibi interrupted. "It helps quicken integration and acceptance."

"It also reminds everyone they speak different, so they don't belong." Johnny tried to control his building anger but couldn't. "So, Elisa here will soon be given a name."

Margibi took a sip of water. "She would choose a name if she wants one."

Johnny fought the urge to ask Elisa if she wanted a local name but held his tongue. He didn't think those discussions were appropriate where strangers were. Just the mere introduction had turned the atmosphere tense. He turned away and caught Bomi glaring at him. She had bright green eyes he just noticed, but her skin was darker than the average mixed black and white slave. He concluded only one of her parents may have been mixed.

He looked away from her and turned his attention to Margibi. "What was it like when—fifteen years ago?"

"Wow, beautiful question." Margibi leaned against the wall. "I was seventeen. And at the time a lot more activities were going on. Many of these houses were not built. There were a lot of things people like me could do at the harbor."

"When we first arrived, I was too young." Bomi stared into space. "But I remember my father was never happy. And then he fell sick and died. I was just five."

"Sorry for your loss." Johnny stole a glance at her direction and as he expected, her gaze was fastened on him.

"Many died of illnesses caused by change in diet, and malaria, food poisoning." Margibi sighed. "But medicine has improved as well."

"I truly am glad about that." Johnny finished his food. "Anyone care for a desert?"

"Missa Johnny, tha' kind of ya." Beth spoke again after her silence. "I missed some of the food 'ere."

Johnny left to get the pineapple pie he made from an old apple pie recipe he knew. It didn't taste as good as anything he'd had, but it sufficed. He was also glad to escape from Bomi's continuous glare. Many people stared when he walked by, and he knew there was a lot of talk about him being married to his "slave", but this girl seemed to have a lot more on her mind. Elisa remained quiet all through the evening, which made Johnny wary. She didn't talk a lot usually, but with the earlier reference to naming, he felt he'd need to have a serious discussion with her and know what she felt. He'd do whatever she wanted, but it would be up to her to make a decision.

After desert, Margibi and Beth drove the conversation around the church and the movements' efforts to totally eradicate slavery in the world. They talked about the country of their nativity and how much kept changing and more people arriving every day. Finally, Margibi stood.

"We have stayed late enough. We all have jobs to do tomorrow," he said.

Johnny, as was his habit, saw the visitors out. He waved the women off and expected Margibi would get on his cart, but his friend stood beside him until the women were out of earshot.

"I spoke with the owner of the stable again," Margibi said. "He wants the horse to be trained with Elisa."

Johnny frowned. "With her condition?"

Margibi shrugged. "I told him she was with child, and he only said the horse was mild."

"No." Johnny shook his head. "He can send the horse and I will train it myself, but not with Elisa."

"I thought you would say that." Margibi chuckled. "About the change of name, may I speak?"

Johnny didn't expect that. He shot his friend a worried glance. "Speak."

"Protect Elisa, Holt."

He moved to his cart before Johnny could respond, got in, and drove off.

Chapter Thirty-Three

February got hotter each day, but when Johnny fell on his face while working his field, it wasn't because of the heat. He had woken up with a headache but thought nothing of it. Luckily, Margibi had sent a young African boy, Gibe, to help him at the stables for a stipend, and it was Gibe who saw Johnny and rushed to get help for him.

Dr. Obed attended to him, while Elisa and Gibe loitered in the background.

"It looks like you have malaria, Johnny. I'm afraid." Dr. Obed closed his bag. "I'm going to place you on a strong medication. Or you won't come out of this, I'm sorry."

"I feel like I'm dying, Doctor," Johnny moaned.

He could feel the burning at the back of his eyes and his throat. He had never been so thirsty in his life, and yet, the water he drank tasted bitter and horrid.

"You will feel like that for the next few days." The doctor turned to Elisa. "Malaria is one of the deadliest illnesses we have to deal with. Make sure you take your supplements."

Johnny coughed, "She does."

"I will be back in the evening to check on you, Johnny. But if you feel anything different from now, send Gibe." He looked at the farmhand. "Stay here with him."

"I stay too," Elisa mumbled, and sat beside the bed.

Johnny grabbed her hand. "Thank you, darling."

Elisa gasped. "His hand so cold." She pushed the blanket around him tighter.

"I feel cold," he mumbled.

"It's all part of what ails him. It will be good if he can sleep and eat. Broth mostly," Dr. Obed sighed. "I think he'll be fine, though."

"Thank ya, Doctor." Elisa looked at the medicine man with teary eyes. "I just pray he get better."

After Dr. Obed left, Gibe continued to sit with Elisa, and they both watched Johnny drift in and out of sleep. Elisa prepared thick clear broth and fed it to him despite protests. He just could not taste food.

Elisa excused herself as soon as Johnny slept off again after eating some of the broth she prepared.

"I get to do some sewin'," she said. "Call me if he waken."

Gibe nodded. "Yes, ma'am."

Making her baby's clothes had been the best thing to do. She thanked Johnny for the opportunity to do it, though he waved off her gratitude. From the plain styles Nan taught her, she designed varieties and beautifully cut them out. Before the older woman stopped teaching her, she had noted Elisa's eye for fashion and design, and once told her she could learn to make beautiful clothes "after the war." Nan's words had seemed as though the war was inevitable. But until they left the shores of America, there was no such thing. Elisa had a feeling Nan was supposed to teach her other styles besides soldiers and nurses' uniforms. Or how could they be so sure there would be a war.

She had hardly settled to her sewing when Gibe stood on the corridor in front of the room and called in a loud whisper.

"Ma'am. Please come."

Elisa shot to her feet. "He good?"

"Mister Johnny is good, Ma'am. Still sleeping. You got a visitor."

She slumped in relief, and then stiffened. "Visitor? Who?"

"Two women from the fabric store in the city."

Elisa frowned. She thought of Beth, but why would the older woman come again. It was obvious Johnny wasn't happy having them around the other night and he made it clear to everyone in the room, especially the green-eyed witch, Bomi. Elisa hated the way she couldn't keep her eyes off Johnny.

She followed Gibe to the living room where Beth stood with another woman, who didn't come to the house for dinner the other day.

"Ah, here she come. Tonto, come meet Elisa." Beth strolled over and gave her a big hug. "My daughter, Tonto."

Elisa smiled, unsure of what to do. Tonto, a little older than her, was slim and dark-skinned with small facial features that made her look almost like a ghost because she was so slender. She hugged Elisa, and for a moment, Elisa perceived a pungent smell on the other woman.

"Ya goin' a ask how she my daughter, but she is." Beth smiled. "Moment I saw 'er, I knew."

"Ain't ya goin' a werk today, Miz Beth?" Elisa burst out. "I mean, I ain't think ya'll goin' a be 'ere at this time."

"Yes. We come this time because Massa Johnny goin' a be out in the field." Beth eyed Gibe. "Waz wonderin' what the boy doin' 'ere."

Gibe frowned. "I'm here because of–"

Elisa cut him off. "Please go inside." Gibe did her bidding.

Beth's eyes widened. "Weh-ll, my girl know better now. Some good brown skin in ya bed sure goin' a do ya good." She smiled. "We come take ya to meet new friends. This 'ere white man ain't goin' a do ya no good. Many fine men among the colored."

Elisa straightened. "He my hasband."

"Where?" Beth's eyes drifted to the corridor Gibe just disappeared through. She snickered. "Show me the marriage paper."

Elisa looked away. "We goin' a get it."

"From where? No man on earth goin' a 'gree join ya to a white man. His people won't and ya people 'ere won't," she hissed. "So, come, meet real men who goin' a make ya real 'appy. Not some poor farm boy."

Tonto spoke for the first time, her voice thin just like her face. "And Mama Beth has said you need to braid your 'air in the local way."

Elisa subconsciously touched her hair. "It don't need braid."

"Ya hasband gonna lakit!" Tonto mimicked. "Come, let's go." She pulled Elisa's hand and headed toward the door.

Elisa shot a quick glance toward the corridor, unsure of what to do.

"Ya owner ain't goin' a know ya's gone by the time he 'ead back." Beth put her small frame behind Elisa, blocking her in case she decided to stay back in the house.

Johnny woke up feeling even hotter than when he slept off.

"Water," he croaked. "Elisa."

Gibe rushed to the small pitcher with cool water kept in the room for Johnny and poured some into a cup. "Here, Mister Johnny." He tilted it toward Johnny's mouth.

The cool liquid traced a chilling path down his throat and Johnny closed his eyes to relish the feeling. Afterward, he laid his head on the pillow as the after-effect of the cool water turned hot and bitter in his mouth. Malaria, of all the deadliest diseases on earth, had to attack him. He felt miserable. His head continued to throb and pound in a way he had never experienced before, and all his joints ached.

"Elisa?"

Gibe cleared his throat. "She had to leave."

Johnny's eyes popped open. "Leave to where?" If he could stand, he'd be on his feet now, but even raising himself slightly was a huge task.

"She, ur, the ladies from the city came."

Johnny pulled himself up. A bout of nausea exploded before his eyes and he took a moment to breathe from his mouth to control himself.

"Why did you let her leave? Why didn't you call me?"

"You were fast asleep, Mister Johnny–"

"Don't Mister Johnny me, Gibe!" Johnny closed his eyes. "Oh, my goodness." He slumped back on to the pillow and broke out sweating profusely. "Oh God. Since when?"

Gibe took so long in responding, Johnny opened his eyes and glared at him. "What day is today? How long have I been sleeping?"

"You've slept a long time. She left at about noon." Gibe swallowed. "It's dinner time now."

Johnny shut his eyes. "When Margibi comes, ask use of his cart. Ask him to follow you to find my wife."

His heart heaved, but he couldn't hold back the tears that burst out of his chest.

Chapter Thirty-Four

Elisa knew her hair was soft and rubbery and easy to hold up, but she never imagined it could be braided into the beautiful locks Tonto made them into. The edges hurt, but she didn't care. She yelped in delight when Beth held up a broken mirror in front of her.

"See how beariful ya look now." Beth beamed. "All them local boyz goin' a drool just lookin' at ya."

Tonto smiled. "She's shy, Mama Beth. I'll show her the way."

Elisa squirmed. "I need a get back. Mas...Mister Johnny sick."

Beth giggled. "Best time to stay 'way from 'im."

"Please Miz Be–"

"Call me Mama Beth now, child. I ya mama, now."

Elisa stood. "I gotta go, please."

Tonto laughed. "You are not a slave anymore. You don't have to run back to anybody. You are your own woman! Live your life."

Elisa started to shake, panicked. Johnny would be terribly upset and she didn't want to have to handle it. Besides, he was sick. This was not the time to be out with some women living life. She looked around, but the shanty the women brought her had only one exit and Tonto stood right in front of it.

"We ain't have no food none." Beth grabbed Elisa's hand. "We goin' a go to Pizzi store to grab some good local food."

Elisa cried. "No, Miz Beth. Please. I ain't 'unger."

Outside was getting dark, which made her fears more real to her. In daylight, she didn't know her way home, how much more as it grew dark. Tonto and Beth pushed her along on a long walk to the village. Elisa remembered how the local food and drink upset her system and feared she'd be sick again and Johnny would be unhappy with her. Tears sprang to her eyes, but she controlled it.

Pizzi was a dark-skinned local man who stared at her with hooded eyes, and Elisa knew at once this was not a place to visit. There were other people at the store, with stools and stone-crafted benches on the front where people sat and chatted. Apart from the store where several sundry items were displayed and sold, food and drinks were served.

Beth walked toward a group of men and women seated on long benches facing each other. Food and drinks were in abundance and everybody ate from a big basin and drank from a gourd. A few people hailed as they approached and soon seats were created for them. Young children brought a flattened gourd with water and Beth washed her hand, pushing Elisa to do the same. Tonto followed suit.

The food basin was tossed toward them and Beth dipped her hand in. "Eat, child." She shoved a morsel of something with a strong smell in Elisa's face and she turned sharply away.

Some young men and women started singing and making rowdy music and dancing. Others joined in. Tonto pulled Elisa up and dragged her to the group of dancers. Elisa had never felt so weak. She thought she'd throw up if the wild moving didn't stop. Beth came to her rescue and shouting above the noise, told Tonto she couldn't dance because of her condition.

Elisa refused to eat or drink as the night wore on, she could barely hold the tears in her. Johnny would be beside himself with worry. She hinged hope on Gibe who may know of this horrid place. The darker it got, the more people arrived. The slimy snake girl, Bomi came with another girl, and even in the dim light Pizzi kept outside for the fun-seekers, Elisa could see her disdainful gaze as she walked by and joined some other people, drinking and watching the crazy entertainment. Many of the men and women were drunk and starting to misbehave.

Pizzi walked over to her, and whispered over her hair, his breath heavy with smoke and alcohol. "Come inside the store away from these mad people."

He didn't give Elisa a chance. He pulled her up and pressing himself to her backside, maneuvered her inside his store, and made her sit on a large chair with soft clothing piled on it for comfort.

"You're so beautiful," he slurred. "What are you doing with a white...white..." He pressed his face close to hers and said something in his local language before he laughed. "Beth says you need a good, rich man who can spoil hell out of you."

Elisa snapped. "I carryin' his babe."

"So? You keep the baby, what does it matter?" He laughed. "It's his baby because you say it is. It can be another man's baby."

Elisa wanted to slap his face, but fear constrained her. He touched her face and she swatted his hand away. "Leave me alone."

"What's a white man like, girl? You need a strong black man who'd make you shout for joy."

There was sudden commotion outside, and Pizzi turned to see what was going on. He'd hardly left her side when Johnny burst into the store and shoved him aside. Behind him were Margibi and Gibe, followed by Beth, Tonto, Bomi and some other people she didn't know.

Johnny pulled her up by the front of her dress and slapped her hard. She fell back over her seat. Maybe he would have pounced on her, but Margibi grabbed him by the waist and pulled back. Everything seemed to happen at once. She thought Johnny was sick. Was he well enough to come after her in this dead of the night? In a daze and through her throbbing face, she heard Beth scream foul words. There was a little commotion as Gibe helped her up and led her out to the cart.

A mob was forming because as Margibi furiously drove away, people threw sand and stones at them.

Chapter Thirty-Five

Until he saw her in the local man's store alone, Johnny could feel malaria in every inch of his body. They had nearly given up looking for her with Margibi's donkey-drawn cart getting slower and slower. They would have headed back, except Gibe who suggested they checked Pizzi's store.

Margibi had exclaimed. "They won't go there, surely!"

Johnny puffed. He was sweaty again and finding it hard to breathe. "Where is there?"

"They drink and lust after each other," Gibe had groaned. "No decent person goes there."

Johnny held his pounding head and wanted to faint, with all the adrenaline drained, he felt weak with the disease in his body and remorse. He had never raised his hand to Elisa or any other woman before. Why did he hit her? Truly, seeing her with that man hovering over her blinded him. He didn't think he could walk, not to talk of moving so fast, and hit Elisa, the love of his life. He closed his eyes. Since they squeezed into the cart, she had been quiet. Well, she was a quiet person, except when she was making him laugh, and to his consternation, he realized that since he married her, she had progressively withdrawn into her shell. The last time he could boldly say she was her bubbly self was when they were on the boat to New York. Since then, Elisa hardly had an opinion or said a word. At first, he had thought she missed her parents, but he didn't think so. He suspected she was no longer satisfied with the value of her life, and he was the main reason. Or how would anyone explain why she would go off with some women for the whole day. And then stay until so late, close to midnight. When she knew he was too sick to help himself?

Margibi assisted him to get into the house. Elisa ran in to her sewing room.

"Ask her to come to me." Johnny moaned. "Call Elisa."

Gibe followed her and stood in the corridor, but Elisa made no sounds. Margibi helped Johnny into the bedroom, but he refused to sit.

"If she's not coming, please take me to her."

"You need to rest. Dr. Obed–"

Johnny pushed weakly against Margibi. "Elisa!"

Margibi sighed. "Okay. I'll get her. If you promise me to remain on the bed."

Johnny shut his heavy eyes. "Okay. I will rest. Bring her."

After what seemed like forever, Elisa slowly walked in behind Margibi, her face down and her hands folded behind her back. The posture reminded Johnny too much of how slaves were treated on his father's farm. He rose slowly and walked to her, his chest heaving.

"I'm sorry," he mumbled and when she refused to look at him, he fell on his knees and hugged her hips. "Please. Forgive me."

Johnny remained sick for another four days but finally got his appetite back, and his strength slowly returned. There was no talk of the night at Pizzi's anymore and neither Beth nor any of the ladies came back. During the days of his sickness and recovery, Johnny did everything he could to reassure Elisa of his love. He commented on her beautiful hair and how much he'd love to see her make it again. She had nothing to say to him, but he knew something important had changed between them. She jumped when he entered a room she was in and stammered more than before. He hated the idea that she was afraid of him and tried his best to show her he was harmless. He was driven by fear and jealousy, and not anger as she seemed to believe.

On Johnny's first day back to work, Margibi drove up to the farm in the heat of the day and walked into the barn where Johnny and Gibe cleared space for the nursery they were working on. It was a busy day because there was little done in the last few days while Johnny was sick.

"Good morning, Johnny, can I have an audience with you?" He arched an eyebrow. "Alone."

"This looks serious," Johnny said, a small smile around his lips. "Is it lunchtime yet?"

Margibi drew his eyebrows together. "I needed to speak with you privately, Johnny. This is important."

The smile froze on Johnny's face. "Come into the house." He started to walk away but Margibi's voice stopped him.

Margibi shot Gibe a look. "Can he excuse us?"

Johnny motioned to Gibe. "Take Elisa's horse and go and check out the corn rows. You can take a bag of seeds with you to plant a few more."

"Okay, Mister Johnny."

The men watched Gibe leave.

"Why don't we go into the house? It's such a hot day, Elisa made this really nice local pineapple juice–"

"I don't want Elisa to hear us."

Johnny turned. "Is this about her?"

Margibi started to pace. "When I met you for the first time, Johnny, I feared you will get into trouble, I didn't know it will be this soon."

"What happened?"

"The blacks who come from your country have a lot of baggage, and I don't mean clothes and shoes. They hate whites and with good reason. And they hate us."

Johnny frowned. "Hate you? You're their brother."

"Who sold them to slavery." Margibi cursed in his language. "Whoever thought sending freed slaves back here didn't think it through or did not care."

Johnny nodded. "I see your point."

"We locals don't see or accept them, and we can't be blamed." Margibi sighed. "We have been neglected by the chiefs and government for so long, yet the American blacks come and are given preferential treatment."

Johnny groaned. "What happened, Margibi? Please do tell."

Margibi stopped pacing and held Johnny's gaze. "You shouldn't have come here with Elisa. You both send such a wrong, strong message."

"She's my wife."

Margibi snickered. "You said so."

"What do you mean by that? I married Elisa."

"Where? How? When?"

Johnny went quiet.

"My thinking." He walked over to his friend and grabbed his shoulders. "Marry her. If you love her, marry her here."

Johnny heaved. "I love her."

"Then go to the local chief and ask for her hand in marriage. Perform the rites and everyone will respect you for it." Margibi turned his back. "You don't have to take my advice, of course. You are a white man."

Johnny swung him around and punched his shoulder. "What do you mean by that?" He laughed. "That is a great idea." He pulled Margibi into a rough hug. "Thank you, my friend!"

Chapter Thirty-Six

The drummers wore masks and beat the drum so viciously, if it wasn't his traditional wedding day, Johnny would cringe. But the only expression on his face since the day four weeks earlier when Margibi gave him the idea about marrying Elisa the local way, was a grin. He couldn't not smile at the slightest thought or matter.

Margibi proved to be a friend indeed, instigating meetings with the local chiefs. The chiefs gave Johnny an exorbitant list of items he knew he could not afford. Margibi again took him to an American missionary who rallied some other foreigners around and they were able to procure the items and the African attire needed for the ceremony.

At first, Elisa took the news all in stride but as the preparations gained momentum, she caught the excitement. It pleased Johnny she didn't jump at the sight of him like before. Margibi brought his mother into the picture to make preparations with the bride and they discussed colors and outfits for the three different times Elisa had to wear something new. They helped get Johnny's outfit as well. Members of Margibi's family had a local woman make Elisa's hair into an elaborate heap tucked in with local bead, corals, and cowries.

Margibi's uncle led Johnny's "family" and was spokesman. At the edge of the property which belonged to the local chief, fifteen people of different races and nationalities danced to the local drumbeat and waited for someone to come out and attend to them. They sang fun folklores and happy songs, and after several minutes, some local women all beautifully dressed came to meet them. A man assigned by the local chief to represent Elisa's "uncle" responded.

Johnny watched in pure amazement as both sides spoke with songs and haggled over the purpose of the occasion in the African language, he decided he had to learn. It was fun, he sweated profusely under the heavy local fabrics and beads he wore, but he didn't think he had ever done anything so fulfilling in his life. Margibi's uncle presented kola nuts and gifts, and after bringing three other disguised women to Johnny, Elisa was brought to him as his bride. She was the most beautiful creature he had ever seen. She smiled at him, and he knew everything he had ever done to have her was worth it.

The dowry was presented, and the bride handed over to the groom. Villagers were served with food in abundance and drinks. The drummers drummed furiously, and everyone took to the dance floor. Johnny and his bride were surrounded by local women who taught them dance steps.

As night descended and the dancing continued, Johnny snuck away with his bride on his horse, back home to consummate his marriage.

The days following the wedding ceremony were the best days of Elisa's life. Johnny took a week off his farm work and refused to see anyone. Even Margibi was begged away. They did everything together, reliving the first few weeks after they met when the highlight of each day was their time together. Johnny pampered her like the new bride that she was, despite her slightly bulging belly. In the cool of the evening when they were sure no one was on their property, they went for walks, kissing and touching, and enjoying the liberty that came with having each other.

On the last evening of Johnny's "leave" they went for a long walk along the bank of their little stream. Johnny took a blanket and they sat down, talking and teasing, making fun and love. The moon was full and for a moment, Johnny noticed the reflection on the water.

"It's so beautiful out here," he said. "The way the water moves on this side is so lovely."

"It don't look like water a lot." Elisa tucked her head in his chest. "Just like some gold."

Johnny chuckled. "You're so funny, Elisa. It's just the moon shining on water."

"Hmm." Elisa giggled. "Moon shine on the river on Creek View, it don't look like that."

Johnny raised his head for a minute and stared out. "You are right."

She lifted herself off the blanket and pointed. "This 'ere look like it goin' a stick to my body or som'un if I try to swim init." She walked to the bank and put her hand in the water.

"This 'ere ain't no water." She returned to the blanket with a stone in her hand. "Look at this?"

Johnny touched the stone. "It's beautiful." He pulled her to lay back with him and caressed her back. "The water does glisten. I wonder why. The other side doesn't look like this. Skipper won't even drink this water over here."

He pushed his hand through the elaborate hairstyle she wore for her wedding.

She giggled, the soothing massage of her head made her sleepy. "If ya 'orse won't, I won't too."

"Elisa?"

"Hmm?"

"Darling, do you remember our last night at our house in New York?"

She tried to keep her eyes open. "Hmm. My mama said a good girl ne'er goes to a man."

"Not the same for a husband." His hand dropped to her hip. "I never thanked you for that night. Thank you."

"Hmm."

"I want to thank you in my special way."

He slid down her body and ducked his head under her skirt within seconds.

Elisa yelped. "Johnny!" But her protest was soon drowned in loud moans.

Chapter Thirty-Seven

Elisa wanted to get some more fabrics for her baby. She had so many already but was obsessed with the designs. The baby kicked so strongly now at seven months, making its presence real in her life, and Johnny encouraged her to make as many clothes as she pleased. His positive attitude, coupled with the gifts she got from her wedding, which included some money, made her leave for the city with Margibi's borrowed cart. It took some convincing, but Johnny reluctantly let her go by herself after she protested, she'd one day have to run errands on her own and it was better to do so when he wasn't too busy at the farm and the baby hadn't come yet. She won.

To move faster, Johnny hitched Skipper to the cart and put a bit in his mouth. He placed a kiss on Elisa's forehead. "I can ride your horse if I need to come to your rescue, Miz Holt."

She rolled her eyes. "I ain't goin' a need it, Mister Holt."

The ride was smooth and short. She enjoyed the hot breeze, though she made Skipper walk all the way. She didn't want to make a fool of herself with a galloping horse. At the fabric store, a small local boy helped her secure the cart for a cent. She remembered Beth worked here and after the trouble going to Pizzi's, she just wanted to steer clear. She entered the store and walked the opposite direction from where they went the other time, where she suspected Beth would be. There were several beautiful lacy fabrics, a little expensive for her budget, but she indulged in a few yards of different ones. She found a soft cotton material she could use for a long shirt for Johnny and got it too. By the time she stepped out into the open, the sun was high up and she was hungry. The boy who took care of her cart appeared out of nowhere with it.

Elisa smiled and found another cent. "Thank ya so much."

She gave him the money and he jumped for joy. She understood his feeling. She only started seeing money after she escaped from Creek View with Johnny. The boy started to leave.

"Huh, boy ya know where a 'ungry woman can eat?"

"Pizzi's just behind the store, ma'am."

"Oh. Thank ya."

Elisa got on the cart and had Skipper gallop back to the farm.

She stayed longer than he expected, which got Johnny cold with fear, despite the heightening temperature. He stood at the entrance of the barn and re-stacked hay Gibe did previously because it had the best view of the road. The dust created by Skipper's furious galloping made him run out to meet her. Was something wrong? He crossed the horse's path as Elisa pulled the reins. His fears dissipated when she stepped out of the cart, laughing.

"I did it! Ya see, Mister Holt?"

Johnny laughed, feeling silly about his fears. "Of course, you did, Miz Elisa Holt! You are a great woman." He covered her face with kisses. "I'm going to leave this cart here and carry you inside." He bent and picked her up quite easily.

She squealed. "Mister Holt!"

Johnny laughed and took her into the house. Gibe waved from a distance off.

"Take the cart." Johnny shouted to Gibe. "Bring the fabrics!"

He took Elisa into the house and put her on the bed laughing over her. She gasped and sat up, pushing him off playfully.

"Ya need to get back to work. I need to eat."

He saluted and straightened. "Yes, ma'am."

Gibe came into the house. "I dropped the fabrics on the chair, Mister Johnny."

"Thank you. Get on back to the farm. Be right there with you." He turned to Elisa. "Better get some food. I don't want you or my baby starving." He gave her a peck on her mouth. "See you at dinner, wife."

She nodded weakly. "Yea, hasband."

Johnny hurried back to the farm because he had done little since Elisa left. The rains would soon start, and he wanted to be sure they had all the crops planted. Out of the five acres allocated to Elisa, he had succeeded in cultivating less than two and he knew he would need more than only Gibe's hand during harvest. The corn rows were now filled with young stalks, which made him happy. Next, he had focused on cassava, but he knew little or nothing about the crop and wanted to proceed cautiously with it. This left him buying only a hundred stalks, which he planted next to the corn. He had some fruits and vegetables too.

Margibi had told him selling food crops may not bring a lot, and he should consider cash crops like cocoa or rubber. Johnny knew these would definitely do better, but he was new to these crops and didn't want to take on something so cash-intensive with his baby so close to arrival.

Elisa didn't enjoy cooking and cleaning as much as sewing, but these were chores a woman had to do. She couldn't be angry with Johnny in any way, in fact, he did more than his share of work around the house. Some days when she wasn't up to any task, he did everything for her. She felt blessed to have a man like him. As a farmer's wife, she got much of her produce fresh, and about a month earlier, just before the wedding, Johnny started a poultry. And tonight, she wanted to roast one of the first chickens to come from the old layers they started with.

She dragged her feet into her kitchen and prepared the meal. Then, she found left over pies and had some with her home-made mango juice. This was a fruit she just had for the first time in Liberia and was so much in love with. It pleased her tremendously they had several trees of the fruit on the farm, and it was in season. With the chicken roasting slowly in her local oven, Elisa brought out pieces of her old sewing and put her feet up on a stool to finish the stitches.

Someone knocked on the front door.

After the last incident with Beth coming to drag her out of her home, Johnny had a plank drilled on to the door and he locked this with welded iron so Elisa could not open the door from inside and whoever came around would have to stand outside and speak. If Elisa had any reason to leave the house, she used the back-door Johnny carved out by himself, but this door was so hidden from view, no outsider could have access unless they were shown where it was. In this way, Johnny protected himself and his wife.

Elisa stood, unsure of what to do. She had no friends, no visitors. Though the house was on an estate with similar properties, most of the other occupants kept to themselves. They would wave when they passed one another but nothing more, which was fine with Elisa.

"Who'z there?" she said softly.

"Pizzi. Your man."

Elisa clasped trembling hands. "Ya not welcome 'ere. Please go."

"I brin' 'im, Elisa." Beth's voice came across. "I brin' 'im coz only 'im can save ya from ya slave massa!"

Elisa exclaimed. "I ain't got no slave massa!"

Beth hit on the wooden door with what sounded like a stone. "Yea, ya do. Massa Johnny Pa bought ya and ya ma and ya pa. And he still got ya."

"I married."

Pizzi laughed. "That nonsense he did to make a jest of you in the village? And the village chiefs allowed, just to get money from him? Listen here, you're a beautiful woman, and I'm ready to take you and the bastard in your stomach." His voice hardened. "Now, open this door."

Elisa went silent. She thought of escaping through the hidden back door, but she feared they would see her when she got outside unless she remained pressed to the door. She'd never bothered to use it before. Johnny had put off another hidden door long enough, one which would open directly to the main road.

"Ya can't open, can ya? He locked ya in like a slave." Beth snickered. "He was my massa too and I werked inside tha' 'ouse. They 'ate us, Elisa, why would ya let 'im treat ya like this?"

Pizzi raised his voice. "Well, know this, woman. I've got my eyes on you. And who Pizzi wants, Pizzi gets." He drew in a noisy breath. "Let's go, Beth."

Beth made a sound as though she was sobbing. "I know ya thinks he love ya, but he don't. He just usin' ya. He a looser. His pa was goin' a throw 'im out. Please my babe, ya the only thin' I got on 'ere in Africa."

Elisa clasped her hands over her ears and slid to the floor, sobbing, as a minute later the kitchen door opened, and Johnny walked in.

The farmer and his helper worked until sundown and as was customary, Gibe walked through a bush path to his home in the village. Johnny walked into his house through the back door. The sweet aroma of roasted chicken filled his nostrils and he smiled until he walked into the living room where Elisa sat on the floor, weeping.

He rushed to her side and shouted. "Elisa!" Something like a big stone hit the door. He stood but Elisa pulled him down.

She whispered, "Pizzi and Miz Beth, they been–"

"Elisa! We saw you today. You came by and couldn't say hello? He wants to separate you from us and we won't let him," Pizzi yelled. "Beth! I will fight for you. I will get her for you! And for me. No white bastard can take our children from us anymore!"

Johnny held Elisa in his arms and massaged her back.

More stones hit on the door. "Go back to where you came from and leave my *wife*, Elisa, alone!"

"I'm not goin' a give up on ya, babe Elisa. I ain't goin a–" Beth sobbed aloud.

"See how the bastard came into my store and assaulted her. He is an animal." Pizzi seemed to kick the door from this new sound. "Come Beth, tomorrow is another day."

Johnny held Elisa until it was obvious they were gone.

"Maybe ya need to open the door so Margibi can come in for dinner?" Elisa mumbled.

"Margibi isn't coming tonight. A new ship arrived," Johnny sighed. "He's busy. That's why I didn't come through the front." He pressed his face to the crown of her head. "I was testing another route as though I knew and didn't see our frontage at all."

"What we goin' a do?"

Johnny pressed a kiss on her head. "Live our lives. They can't hurt us. They. Can't. Hurt. Us. And now we can come in and out of our house without anyone knowing unless they surround the house."

Merely saying "surround the house" made him shudder.

CHAPTER THIRTY-EIGHT

Margibi was busy the following day as well, so Johnny went in search of Dr. Obed. Though he reassured Elisa they could come to no harm, he didn't want to take any chances. After the horrible incidence in Pizzi's store, he'd learned a little more about the man. Pizzi was not only one of the wealthiest amongst the locals, he was influential. The chiefs did his bidding; he ran an evening show every day at his store where all manner of business was done. If Pizzi set his mind on something, he usually got it.

Dr. Obed was attending to a patient when Johnny got to his clinic at the harbor. He took the opportunity to watch the recently docked ship from the lobby window in the doctor's office, reminding himself of their first day over two months earlier. He saw the excitement in the air. Most of the passengers were not in the harbor anymore, but the captain and sailors laughed with locals and chatted as they worked.

"Johnny, good morning." Dr. Obed walked up behind him.

He turned. "Good morning, Doctor. Thanks for seeing me."

"How's Elisa?"

"She's fine. We are." Johnny swallowed. "Can we speak privately?" He looked around the small lobby. Though no one was present, it was still early, and he knew the doctor had people working for him. Besides, he had many patients.

"My office is small and shared by my nurses. Will this take long?"

Johnny frowned. "I suppose not."

Dr. Obed shrugged and led the way through a tight corridor with two rooms on either side. He opened the one on the right, and they entered a small stuffy room with two desks and wooden chairs. Dr. Obed drew one of the chairs behind a second desk closer and waved Johnny into it.

"I don't feel safe on the estate, Doctor. I need accommodation near you and the missionaries," Johnny said.

"What happened?"

Johnny explained his challenge in detail. "I don't want to take any risks."

Dr. Obed shoved his hands in his pockets. "Can I be candid with you, Johnny?"

"I just need your help, sir."

"How old are you, Johnny?"

"Twenty-one."

The doctor paced. "My son was twenty-one when I lost him to a slave-rising. I vowed I would do everything to get rid of those people from our land. That's why I came here. Working for the cause." He sniffed. "My wife was, still is, in an asylum back home. But I have come to love these people and appreciate their struggle, too. That's why I'm still here."

Johnny scratched his head. "Sorry for your loss, sir."

"The truth is that everyone is still so wary. You came here innocently without knowing the problems you would face," Dr. Obed sighed. "Marrying Elisa...huh, I don't know. Our ways never change, you know."

"I just need to move away from–" Johnny swallowed. "To where we can feel more secure."

"The Reverend Michaels is in charge of the residences where I live."

"Not the consulate?"

"No. It's a missions' settlement. The movement got it through the church." Dr. Obed stared above Johnny's head. "We have armed security."

Johnny heaved a heavy sigh. "We need a place, sir. Please. Even if it's just a room." *And a gun*, he thought, but that request would have to come later. He'd lost his gun in Henri's accommodation and hadn't the mind to accuse the French man of stealing.

Dr. Obed squared his shoulders. "If you can wait until one of the nurses arrive, we can see the reverend before he leaves for work."

Reverend Michaels was much older than Johnny expected. He thought the clergy would be in his middle-age, a stereotypical mindset, probably because he had never gotten to worship in his assembly. The first time he and Elisa attended the church, she had refused to enter because she felt intimidated by the racial coloration. Johnny had opted they returned home, because he understood her plight. He hadn't been able to attend the small chapel in the estate either. The old reverend had a small pouch belly and a head full of white hair. His eyes were sharp though and Johnny noticed immediately he did not wear eye glasses or walk with a stick, despite his slightly bent frame. He received the duo in the small study at his house.

"Hello, Doctor," Reverend Michaels said, gruffly. "What brings you so early? Hello, Mister?"

Dr. Obed made the introductions, and something changed in Reverend Michaels' eyes. A small smile touched his lips or it could have been Johnny's imagination.

"Johnny needs accommodation at the shelter," Dr. Obed said.

"I can do that easily." The reverend walked to his desk and picked a sheet of paper. "Fill this out, will you?"

"Thank you, sir."

Johnny took the paper and pen provided and leaning over the desk, filled it rapidly. Reverend Michaels offered him a seat, but he didn't care for one. When he was done, he gave the paper and pen back.

Reverend looked through and frowned. "You are married?"

"Yes, sir."

"We have to give at least two rooms." He kept the form on his desk. "You need to show me a copy of your marriage document. When do you want the accommodation?" He picked the form again. "Immediately."

Dr. Obed looked at Johnny. "There may be a problem with getting space immediately, Johnny."

"I do have two rooms to spare."

Johnny smiled. "Thank you, Reverend."

Reverend Michaels nodded. "You're welcome, son. I will be at the church office and you can bring your marriage document."

Johnny frowned. "They didn't give us one."

Dr. Obed raised an eyebrow. "He had a local one with the, ur, locals."

Reverend Michaels shrugged. "Well, I don't know why I would do that, but we can conduct one for you. If you bring your fiancée for counseling at the–"

Dr. Obed cleared his throat. "She's with child."

Johnny had to give credit to the old clergy. His face remained stoic. The old man would have had such instances if he was a clergy of many years. People err.

He shrugged again. "As soon as she gives birth to a baby, you can come with her. No white dress for the bride, is all."

Dr. Obed arched an eyebrow. "Three months left?"

"Two." Johnny heaved. "Please, is there nothing you can do to–?"

The doctor cut in. "Thank you, Reverend Michaels, sir. We have taken enough of your time this morning. Johnny?"

Reverend Michaels sighed. "I would go ahead and give you the space, but you must understand these are laid down rules I must abide by."

"Thank you, sir." Johnny breathed hard. "I will come back when she's had the baby."

Reverend nodded. "Good. I wish you the best."

The men shook hands, and Dr. Obed and Johnny left. Outside as he mounted his horse, feeling upset with the whole situation, and particularly the doctor who seemed to have antagonized him, Johnny felt a nudge on his shoulder. He stiffened because he didn't want the doctor to see the anger he could imagine brimmed through his eyes.

"I'm glad you didn't tell the reverend Elisa's skin color or where you live." Dr. Obed got on his horse and rode away.

Johnny bit down on his lips. Two options came to his mind. He could ask Margibi to help with the temporary shelter for newcomers where he worked. It felt safer there and Elisa could have their baby without fear. The other option was to move again. Go to Europe. But with the baby coming so soon, he didn't want to take that risk. He decided to find Margibi.

The storeroom brimmed with activity. It seemed the shelter had more than they could handle. Johnny saw Margibi but he had at least five newcomers around him. There was no way to get the housekeeper's attention, so he decided to return to the farm. He would wait for Margibi to come for dinner as he usually did, and if he didn't, then he'd have to go and find him. One thing for sure though, he wasn't going to take any chances with Beth and Pizzi's threats.

Gibe had the farm going by the time he returned in the late morning hours. Together they worked for another several hours. As dusk descended, the two parted as usual. Johnny rode his horse to the front of the house as he did except for days Margibi wasn't expected for dinner, and stopped Skipper so abruptly, the horse jerked. The barricade on the door was broken down with what looked like a heavy impact.

Johnny jumped down, his heart beating hard against his chest. Immediately, he regretted his decision not to take Elisa to stay in the barn at the farm. It had occurred to him, but he didn't want to scare her. He got to the door and pushed it open slowly, fearing the worst. He peeped before entering. There was no one in the living area but he could smell a dish was cooking in the kitchen. He heaved a heavy sigh and dragged in a deep breath. *They had only come to scare her, and him*, he thought.

"Elisa, dear. I'm home." He strolled into his kitchen and again stopped short.

Right at his stove, Bomi, the girl with the green eyes, stirred something in the pot.

Chapter Thirty-Nine

"Where's my wife?"

Bomi smiled, her eyes a daunting bright green, her voice husky. "She left."

"Left. To where?" Johnny closed up on her. "What did you do to my wife?"

She turned into his arms and placed her lips on his before he could avoid it. Her lips were soft and firm, determined. It took a few seconds before Johnny could free himself of her.

"What's wrong with you?" He ran from the room, shouting, "Elisa! Elisa!"

He entered her sewing room, and the emptiness hit him faster than if there were a hundred people inside. He turned and bumped into Bomi.

"She said I should give you this." She stretched her hand to him. In it was the clear stone Elisa found on the bank of the stream the week after their wedding, wrapped in lace. "She seemed to think it will send you the right message."

Johnny breathed hard. "Please, where did she go?"

"Come and eat, and I will tell you everything."

"No! I am not hungry." Johnny trembled. "Please tell me where Elisa went."

Bomi rolled her eyes. "She doesn't want you, Johnny. She still sees you as her slave master." She reached out to hold him, but he jerked his hand back. "I want you. I am not American. I have never been a slave." She pressed into his arms. "I will make you very happy."

He shoved her aside. "I will find her on my own." He stomped out of the room.

"She's with Pizzi," Bomi called out. "If you go near–"

He spun around. "Pizzi."

She sneered. "If you go near his house, his thugs and mad dogs will kill you."

Johnny stood still, unable to control his shaking. "How do you know this?"

"That his thugs and dogs will kill you?"

"No!" Johnny yelled. "That my wife is with him."

Bomi smirked. "Because we all came here early this morning, and watched you ride away." She stood with her arms akimbo. "And as soon as you were gone, we broke your barrier and entered the house." She folded her arms across her chest. "Do you want to hear more?"

Johnny swallowed. "Go on."

She smiled. "And we conducted a wedding between Elisa and Pizzi. And watched the marriage consummated."

Johnny fell on his knees. "Oh, Elisa." He covered his face. "I'm sorry, darling."

"You don't have to be sorry. She was happy. She left without being forced. Packed all of her things on to Pizzi's buggy."

Johnny pushed himself to his feet and headed toward the front door.

Bomi followed him. "You will never find her. And if you do, two things will happen. She will refuse to follow you, and Pizzi will kill you."

Johnny stomped off through the broken door.

His first port of call was Margibi's. He didn't go to the shelter, but his mother's house where he lived with his family. Margibi wasn't back from work and Johnny decided to wait for him. Again, he rejected a corn meal offered by his friend's mother. Instead, he paced for what seemed like hours, outside the big house and waited for however long it took.

Margibi pulled up after it was pitch dark and lanterns were placed in front of the house. He got off his cart and ushered Johnny in.

Johnny started. "I need your help–"

"I heard of it. Elisa and Pizzi." He pulled one of several cane chairs in the room closer to Johnny. "Sit."

Johnny screamed. "You heard? When? Why didn't you inform me immediately?"

"You saw how busy it was today at the shelter." Margibi shrugged. "She had gone with him, anyway."

Johnny pushed his hair back so tightly the veins on his forehead stood. "Gone with him, anyway. What does that mean, Margibi? Why would my wife go with a brute?"

"I went straight to your house when I closed from work." Margibi sat. "I saw Bomi there and she also confirmed what I heard."

"What did you hear exactly?"

"Elisa left you, Johnny. I know it's tough to accept but–"

"Elisa would never leave me! Why would she?" Despite himself, he sank into the cane chair and burst into tears. "Why? I love her. She loves me," he sobbed.

"Johnny, Johnny!" Margibi snapped. "She doesn't love you."

Johnny's head shot up. "She does."

"Look at you. Look at her. What do you two have in common? You run away with your father's slave, and you think that is love?"

Johnny gasped. "What are you saying?"

"You two don't belong together. Get a life, go back home."

Johnny stood. "You won't help me bring her back?"

"I can't." Margibi stood too. "Let me explain this to you, Johnny. You are white, she's black."

"So? I was born white. Is that a curse?" Johnny yelled. "I love her. She's my wife. She's expecting my child." He headed for the door.

Margibi rushed and blocked his exit. "Will you listen?" When Johnny stared at him, he continued. "There is a lot happening every day. You came to add color to an ongoing conflict. It's not your fault. Neither is it theirs."

"Is that why I should suffer for what is not my fault?" Johnny said softly. "They took my wife."

"They didn't, she left."

Johnny stamped his feet. "And I don't believe you. Elisa would not leave me." He inhaled. "I will go and find her by myself if you won't help me."

"The only way I can help you is to tell you the truth. Go back to your house."

"Where another woman cooks as though I have anything to do with her?"

"That woman has successfully removed herself from the conflicts of the locals versus the American blacks. In this country, she is in the best position to give you a decent existence–"

"To hell with her. And with you!" Johnny pushed Margibi out of his way and left.

For the rest of the night, he rode his horse within the estate at first, and then he went into the city. Nothing moved. He had no idea where Pizzi lived, and no one to ask. Tired and unsure of what to do, he rode to Dr. Obed's clinic, tied his horse to the front, and slept off. In the morning, the doctor woke him and let him in.

"What do you plan to do?" Dr. Obed said after he told his tale.

"I thought Margibi was my friend and now I know." Johnny moaned. "I just have to find Elisa. I don't believe she left me."

"Well, Margibi is a local so he's probably right." Dr. Obed shrugged. "I don't know. He's a powerful person in their circles. He is educated."

Johnny frowned. "So, he can help, he just doesn't want to?"

Dr. Obed shook his head. "I don't know a lot about him. If he says you should leave the matter though, I would take his advice."

"I definitely won't take such a piece of advice." Johnny snapped. "I have to find my wife."

Dr. Obed sighed. "She's not missing. They've told you she left. She's with Pizzi."

Johnny exclaimed, "I don't believe that. She would never leave me!"

"Well, I don't advise this, but the only way to find out is to go to Pizzi's and ask her."

Johnny heaved. "Can you come with me?"

Dr. Obed laughed. "Don't be ridiculous. I shouldn't even be having this conversation with you." He poked Johnny's chest. "The slave you brought has found her way home. You go find yours. Excuse me."

He left Johnny gaping in his lobby.

Chapter Forty

"You look awful."

"Thank you."

Margibi opened the door wide. "Come in. You need a bath and those insect bites on your face…it's not a good thing."

Johnny walked in. "Can you please come with me to find Elisa?"

Margibi halted in his tracks. "You–are you out of your mind?"

"If you won't, then I'd better be going." Johnny turned around.

"You really love her?"

He sniffed, fighting the urge to cry. "I do."

"I'll follow you," Margibi sighed. "Well, clean up first, and I'll get some balm for those angry welts. Come with me."

"Thank you."

Johnny followed Margibi through the house to a small out-bath. It had been one full day since he found Bomi in his house and never had his life been so miserable. Not even through those months of uncertainty and escape had he felt so afraid and forlorn. He had no appetite for food. All he just wanted was to see Elisa and to have her back. He was ready to do anything required.

Margibi insisted they go in his cart. "I don't want your horse to come to harm."

Whether this was just to scare him or not, he didn't know. He didn't care either. Though Pizzi had his business in the heart of the city, his house was on the outskirts and bordered a small village. Johnny could understand part of why everyone warned him off Pizzi. The sun just set, and daylight would soon vanish, so he had a good view of the big house, which sat on massive land. Several young men carrying locally-made knives and axes loitered the premises casually, but Johnny did not think they were there by coincidence.

"I will get one of his men to let him know we're here," Margibi said. "Don't speak unless I ask you to."

"Okay." Johnny nodded. "But I want to speak with Elisa privately."

Margibi arched an eyebrow. "If he permits."

He raised his voice and called to one of the men in the language. Three men approached and circled the cart.

"It's Margibi," one said.

"I need to see Pizzi. It's an urgent matter," Margibi said.

"Pizzi just got married. He's busy," another of the men said, and all laughed.

"She's my wife!" Johnny shouted. "He has no right to my wife."

"You'll get hurt," Margibi mumbled. Out loud he said, "Tell him I am here."

Pizzi stepped out instead, and right beside him was Elisa, holding hands. "Ah Margibi, the untouchable. America's toy. Why are you making noise in front of my house seeing I just got a new wife?"

Johnny jumped down from the cart. "You bastard! She's my wife. She–"

One of the guards formed a band with his arms and ran it into Johnny's stomach. Johnny doubled over.

"That makes the sixth, and I am happy for you." Margibi arched an eyebrow. "But this one already belongs to another man."

Pizzi walked closer to the cart, Elisa's hand firmly in his. "An American rat? Come on, Margibi. You know better. I think eating their food so long has turned your intestines around."

Johnny moaned on the ground. He could feel the tangy taste of copper in his throat. He closed his eyes and prayed to God he would not have a nose-bleeding here. He needed to be able to speak with Elisa. Tears sprang to his eyes. The look on her face. She didn't look down or at her hands. She stared directly at him, not a trace of emotion to detect.

"No need for insults, Pizzi," Margibi said. "We are African."

"Exactly, brother. And our sister is home."

Johnny pushed himself to his feet. A drop of blood trickled from his nose, but he didn't care. "Elisa. Elisa, please."

Pizzi's man who hit him the first time drew closer, but his boss raised a hand to stop him. Johnny took it as a sign to plead with his wife.

"Please, wife. You know what we have–"

"We got nothin'."

Elisa's voice was clear as day and cold as the sea. Johnny could not recognize it.

"Darling, I love you. We–"

"I don't love ya. Please go."

She turned to leave but Pizzi held her hand firmly. "Margibi, what are we still waiting for?"

Margibi sneered. "You rubbed your charms on her face, didn't you, Pizzi? How bad can you get?"

"Now who is trading insults? She's too little to rub anything on." He waved his hands and ten men appeared from the shadows. "See our visitors off."

Margibi lowered his voice. "Let's go, Johnny."

"No. No! I won't leave Elisa here. I won't–"

Dr. Obed walked into the room and stood beside his bed. Sensing a presence, Johnny opened the only eye he could. Recovering his feelings, he realized there was a lot more going on than the doctor in the room and a bandage over half of his face. His legs were up in the air, and one hand as well.

He opened his mouth to test it. "Water."

Dr. Obed put a small cup to his mouth, and he sipped. "I'm glad you woke up, Johnny."

He wanted to sit up, but it seemed he had been strapped to the bed. "What happened?"

"You got a mad dog angry. He bit you."

The voice was Margibi's, but he spoke from the bandaged side of Johnny's face.

"Did you make a report to the local authorities?" Dr. Obed said.

"No. I reported to the estate security and they said it wasn't their duty. Pizzi is feared by everyone–"

"What happened?" Johnny whispered.

Margibi groaned. "They moved so fast. You had hardly finished speaking when they pounced on us. Four men held me and made me watch them beat you to pulp." Margibi paused. When he continued, his voice was thick with emotion. "I thought they had killed you."

A tear slid down Johnny's eye. "And Elisa?"

Margibi cried, "She watched too. Emotionless."

Johnny sobbed, "How long have I been here?"

"Four days," Dr. Obed said.

"Four horrible days with doctor fighting for your life," Margibi moaned. "Once you get better, you need to leave this country. Go back to America. There's nothing for you here!"

"I have news," Dr. Obed heaved a heavy sigh. "You have broken ribs, Johnny. I can't fix them. I have booked a cabin on the next ship to Europe. My sister is a nurse, she'll go with you and they will take care of you."

Chapter Forty-One

Winter in the early months of 1860 was vicious. Coming from the tropical climate of West Africa, sick as he was, his caregivers were quite concerned about his health. Instead of taking him to a general hospital, a private doctor agreed to take him in and Dr. Obed's older sister, Margareta, fondly called Nurse Marge, took care of him. Through the rest of March and part of April, it continued to snow. Johnny wasn't too bothered anyway. He was bedridden almost all of the time, and when he could stand, he had to be taught to walk again.

During the day, he had company. Nurse Marge gave him books to read, and when he was not in the mood, kept him busy with small talk. She reminded him of one of his mother's sisters in Creek View. There was also the noble doctor and a member of the King's inner chamber, Lord William, who came to see him every day and talk about world news after he learned of Johnny's travels. The baron had been involved in the movements to eradicate slavery, often attending to freed slaves and "commoners" despite having a long list of "royalty" on his patients' accounts. William's visits were enjoyable, and Johnny looked forward to them.

Spring came and went quite fast and Johnny started to walk with a stick. His ribs were healed but his left hand, broken at the wrist, wasn't well-set yet. Nurse Marge was kind but strict on the regimens, and as the sun came out and the snow melted, Johnny could take short walks. It had been two months of unbearable physical and emotional pain. Dr. Obed stayed in touch, only to get reports about his health. Not even Margibi sent a letter.

On the first day of summer, Lord William walked into Johnny's room with great news. "I feel confident to release you into the world, Mr. Johnny Holt!" He said elaborately. "I have your discharge document here. You can walk out, with your stick of course, a free man!" He waved a sheet of paper in the air.

Johnny smiled. "I wish I could be so enthusiastic, sir."

"Well, why not?" William stood at the edge of Johnny's bed. "I will allow you to stay at my expense in a wing of my apartment in Oxford Street, with a view of the train station. And you have my beautiful daughter, Cynthia, to keep you company." He turned, and behind him stood a tall, slim young woman. "Come and meet Johnny Holt."

Cynthia stretched a slim hand to him, her voice soft and soothing. "Hello, Johnny."

Johnny sat up. "Hello, Cynthia." He took her hand and noticed how small and soft it was. "Nice to meet you."

"Nice to meet you as well," Cynthia said.

"Cynthia is home for the summer. She has been a student at the prestigious University of Cambridge studying a rare field of neurology." William patted her hand. "She's only twenty and doing so well already."

Cynthia giggled. "My father seems to think I am remarkable. I wonder why?"

William laughed. "She says that every time she wants me to sing her praises."

The father and daughter bantered for a few minutes and Johnny watched them totally amused.

"Well, well," William clapped. "I must be on my way. Your rooms are prepared, and I will have my carriage ready whenever you are."

"You are very kind and generous, sir." Johnny reached for his cane and stood. "I am ready when Nurse Marge is."

"Very well. I hope you find your new abode habitable."

Johnny laughed. "I know I will."

"Cynthia is coming with me to see the Viscount Gabriel of York." William winked. "The young royal wants to meet my Cynthia. She will return to Oxford street afterward, before dinner, if the Viscount does not invite us to stay on."

Cynthia rolled her eyes and Johnny noticed how deeply blue they were and complementary of her soft brown hair. "He's so full of himself, Father."

"You would be. I would be. So, would Johnny if at twenty-five he stands to inherit an estate worth over a hundred thousand pounds!" William waved his index finger. "And remember, he is royal."

"Aren't we all," Cynthia gasped. "He's not the only royal. He's at least fifty people away from the throne."

William bobbed his head. "He's still in line to the throne, my dear. That is something."

Johnny winked at William. "A lot, if you ask me, sir."

"Exactly. A worthy American with a good mind." William walked to the door. "Come on now, Cynthia. We do not want to keep His Majesty waiting."

Cynthia heaved an exaggerated sigh. "See you later on, Johnny."

"Thank you, see you later."

The two left and Johnny continued to smile. It had been a while since he engaged in simple-life conversation. He couldn't. Most days he missed Elisa, and wondered what she was up to, and if she was happy. The mere thought broke his heart, besides the fact that he still wanted her so much, loved her.

Her voice rang out "I don't love ya!"

Johnny shut his eyes. "I don't believe it. She loves me."

He walked to the single wardrobe where all of his life's possessions occupied one shelf and pulled out the small wrap the girl with the green eyes gave him. The clear stone Elisa found by the river bank with a few strands of her hair, wrapped in one of the pieces of the lace fabric she bought.

"She loves me," he whispered and put the treasure back into safe-keeping.

Nurse Marge knocked once and opened the door. "I see you are up and about. The carriage is here."

"Thank you, Nurse Marge. I will be ready in a minute." He headed toward the private room.

Marge walked to his wardrobe and placed the items in a bag. "I will not go with you to your apartment."

Johnny turned. "Why?"

Marge chuckled. "Who's going to pay?"

"Huh," Johnny gasped. "Well, I didn't think of it. I'm sorry."

"You don't have to be, Johnny. It was great working with you."

"Well, thank you, Nurse Marge." Johnny frowned. "Who paid all this time? For my treatment too?"

"The taxpayers, boy. And don't you worry yourself about it. But now you are recovered, and the payment is no longer justified." Marge moved the bag to the floor beside the bed. "You look terrified. I'll get you settled in, and then I have to leave."

"That's very kind of you, Nurse Marge." Johnny nodded. "Thank you."

"You're blessed those evil men didn't do any permanent damage to you." Marge smiled. "You are a good person."

Johnny pressed his lips together to get his emotion in place. "Thank you, Nurse Marge. I was blessed to have you." He escaped to wash up and prepare.

The apartment on Oxford Street was a luxurious one with two en-suite rooms. The living room was tastefully furnished with feminine colors; a clear indication the owner was a woman or liked floral themes. Johnny's room indeed overlooked the busy Oxford station, and what a view; men and women of different races and color moved with purpose in and out of the station, which got Johnny yearning again for Elisa. They had been through many journeys and he wished she was here with him.

"I have all your things arranged, Johnny," Marge said behind him. "This is where we part ways."

Johnny turned but before he could say a word, quite unlike Nurse Marge, she hugged him. Johnny hugged back and swallowed the tears that threatened to fall.

"I will never forget you, Nurse Marge."

"Me neither." She pulled back. "Take care of yourself."

It was after she was gone Johnny realized she never spoke about her plans or her brother, Dr. Obed.

CHAPTER FORTY-TWO

***D**ear Johnny,*

This is my first letter to you. It is my first time of writing anything apart from measurements for sewing. I got a book of ~~speelings~~ spellings and I use it now to write to you.

How are you?

Where do I start from?

Jane Johnny Holt was born two weeks ago. She looks just like you. She came with a lot of hair. And she's so fair. White, like you. Her eyes are so blue and beautiful, like yours.

Johnny, I have to go. Please forgive me and reply my letter.

I love you.

Your wife,

Elisa Johnny Holt.

Elisa tucked the letter into her skirt and carrying Jane in a pouch the same way the locals did, walked out of the house. One of the men walked up to her.

She snapped, "I *gotta* get my babe some milk."

"Good women feed their babies from their breasts." The man stood on her way. "You're American. Just black."

Elisa had learned never to respond to the men's insults. She ducked and would have continued to walk. It would be a long one because Pizzi's house was so removed from everywhere. The man followed her.

"You're just beautiful. Look at your round backside, like that of our local women, even better. For nothing. A weak American shouldn't have you. Pizzi should."

Elisa swallowed the hard words she had for him because she could get beaten up. She'd seen the way Pizzi's men treated his wives, except the first one, who was as mean-hearted as the men. She controlled everything Pizzi shared from food to money to favors. Elisa still could not crack the secret code to get friendly with that woman. She'd thought being Beth's friend would do the trick, but the women were full of suspicion and hatred for each other. And speaking of Beth, she couldn't understand why Beth did all of this, setting her up with Pizzi, and then treating her like trash afterward.

"You can't walk all the way to Pizzi's to get milk, shaking your backside like that," the man said.

Elisa stopped short and faced him. "I can. I been a slave all my life. Walkin' is what we do."

Her simple answer must have gotten to the man. He turned and walked back to his guard post. Another man showed up in front but let her go without a word. Since that night she almost died watching Johnny beat up for her, she hadn't stepped out of Pizzi's house during the day. Part of it was because she feared what the outside world held. She only wanted to have her baby and then kill herself, but with the safe and smooth delivery of such a beautiful baby who reminded her so much of the only man she ever loved, she decided to stay alive. And if Johnny didn't live after that brutal beating he took, then she still had a part of him to herself.

The mid-May sun beat with fury on the back of her neck. The local slippers she wore became slippery from sweat under her feet. Thankfully, Jane slept. She was mostly a good baby. Elisa lied about getting milk; Jane fed only on breast milk because she feared any of the other women would poison her baby if she gave her water from the house. Sweat poured down Elisa's face and by the time she reached her destination, she was almost bent with fatigue.

Margibi sat behind his desk and wrote in a long ledger.

"Water, please."

His head shot up. "Elisa! What do you want?"

"Water."

She sank on to the wooden bench kept for visitors. Her throat was so dry, she didn't know how many drinks before she would feel better. She gazed down at her hands and prayed he would have mercy on her. A tin cup was pushed into her hand and she drank greedily until the water finished.

For a moment, the silence around her was crippling. She feared to look at Margibi. After all, he was there, had always been. He must hate her as much as Johnny now did, but she needed his help and she would take any anger he had to give to achieve her purpose.

"I said what do you want?"

Elisa raised her head. "Take me to Johnny."

Margibi bared his teeth. "You must be a fool to think I will ever let you near him again. After being that criminal's prostitute all these months. Has he taken another wife and dumped you?"

Elisa pulled the letter from inside her waist knowing she deserved any harsh words the man had for her. "Then give this to him if ya will not take me to him. Please."

Margibi shared an equally ferocious glance between her face and the letter in her hand. "You wrote? Who taught you?"

"Johnny. And Miz Nan. And the small book of *speelings* I stole from Pizzi."

He took the letter and openly read, not caring for her presence or permission. "Let me see the child."

She took Jane out of her wrap and the baby opened her eyes.

"She's so beautiful," Margibi said softly. "I see her father's soul in her eyes."

Elisa clasped her hand over her mouth. "Please, take me to him."

"I will never. How could you do that? How could you let Pizzi do this?"

"I thought Johnny will go away if–" She sobbed so hard Jane started to whimper. "Ssh, okay, okay Jane babe."

"Leave here, please Elisa. I don't want any more trouble from you or your husband."

Margibi pointed to the exit and when Elisa hesitated, he shouted. "Leave!"

She stood and re-wrapped her baby in her pouch. "I will come and ask again."

Elisa did not expect him to indulge or help her. This was just a first. She only prayed Margibi would deliver the letter. She had great faith Johnny would reply and they could plan a way to escape together. There definitely had to be a safe place for them and she was ready to go anywhere Johnny wanted. Even back to America. Never in her life had she imagined she could be in this low estate. This was worse than the slavery she knew. Pizzi was a brute and treated everyone around with disrespect and hate. She should never have gone with him when he came for her. Her intention to protect Johnny had gotten him almost killed...if he wasn't dead already. She couldn't bear that thought. And if he was dead, surely Margibi would have told her so.

She continued on her path to her next destination. The distance was not too far away but she'd have to cross the fabric store or walk behind Pizzi's and both options were not favorable. In the nights following the last time she saw Johnny, she had come out when even his guards were asleep, and scoured the city center, looking for her husband. Though she didn't find him, she discovered several ways to get to many places. At the time she didn't think she would need those alternative routes, because she was going to stab herself to death after her baby was born, but now she was happy she knew those other back roads.

Dr. Obed's nurse received her at the reception area. "Is the baby sick?"

"No. I want to see doctor."

The nurse arched an eyebrow. "For yourself?"

"No." She swallowed. "Yes."

"Your name, please?"

Elisa provided the details the nurse needed.

"Please take a seat. I will call you when the doctor is available."

"Thank ya," Elisa murmured and sat.

The wait was long but finally, Dr. Obed walked into the reception area. Elisa stood.

"Is the baby alright?"

The doctor's voice was cold, nothing like she remembered and his face bland of any emotion. She knew Dr. Obed would know where Johnny was. Margibi would have brought him to the doctor and he would have treated him. If he was alive.

Elisa's voice trembled. "Jane Johnny Holt is two weeks old, and she is fine, sir. I want to see ya."

"What about?"

"Please take me to Johnny."

Dr. Obed's eyes widened. "Johnny? You came to find Johnny?"

"Yes, Doctor. I love him. I want to find him."

The doctor frowned. "Johnny–is not here. I'm sorry."

"Where is he?"

"You can't find him where he is," Dr. Obed sneered. "Is this all? I have other patients."

Elisa wept. "Is he dead?!"

"Johnny–please. Yes. He is dead. To you."

She bent her head and cried. "I'm sorry. Please, doctor."

"You have to excuse me, Elisa." Dr. Obed turned to leave.

"Doctor. Doctor." She sniffed and pulled out her letter from her skirt. "Please give this to him."

Dr. Obed hesitated. "Who is it from?"

"Me."

"You write?" He took the letter and opened it. "May I?" But he didn't wait for her approval. He read the letter quickly and folded it. "If I have any opportunity to give it to him, I will. I have to go, Elisa, I wish you luck." He left her standing there.

Dr. Obed had not even taken one look at Johnny's baby.

CHAPTER FORTY-THREE

Dear Johnny,

How are you today?

Jane is three months now. I have written a letter every week since she was two weeks.

Did you get them?

Writing to you makes me happy. My master allows me to work at the fabric shop now. He can see me from his store so I can't run away. I take Jane with me everywhere. She is very big and beautiful. She has your big blue eyes. And they shine when she is happy just the way yours do.

I send the letters to Margibi and Dr. Obed, and Gibe. Gibe keeps the farm. He also hopes you will come back home one day.

I have to go.

I love you.

Your wife,

Elisa Johnny Holt.

Pizzi walked into the small room she used since giving birth to Jane, and Elisa tucked the letter under her hip. She guessed he'd seen it but couldn't help herself. He pulled her by her hair and flung her against the wall. By some stroke of luck, the letter was stuck to her sweaty hip, and Pizzi didn't find it.

He snarled. "What are you hiding from your husband?"

"Nothing."

"Where did you go from work last week?"

Elisa whimpered. "Last week?"

He hit her face with his fist. A scream escaped from her throat and she slid to the floor. Jane stirred and Elisa crawled toward her but Pizzi grabbed her head and pushed her back.

"When will you start being a wife and come to me on your own?" He shouted. "You foolish woman. I will deal with you."

"No, please. My baby is awake. Please."

He did not heed her pleas. He tore her dress off her back, and brutally raped her while Jane cried until she turned pink.

Leaving when everyone was in bed had become difficult with Pizzi's continuous suspicions and she needed to get the letters out. After his brutality the night before, she had been so sore she couldn't even stand. She'd spent the rest of the time nursing Jane. The poor baby was so big now and her milk wasn't enough anymore, so Jane made more demands and cried more. Elisa realized she needed to do something, or she'd go mad. Or just kill Jane and then herself. The fabric store had rodent poison. If she fed Jane with some and drank enough of it at night, they'd both be dead before anyone noticed they were missing in the morning.

She tiptoed to the side of the house. Morning had yet to break but she knew this path like the back of her hand. A loud scream froze her progress. It was followed by soft whimpering and deep female voices chanting a song in the local language. Elisa knew she should just continue on her way, but she needed to find out if she would be in danger of any sort, so she followed the sounds until she got to the back of the house. Her mouth dropped open at the sight she beheld, and she quickly clasped her hand over it so she would not scream.

Three elder women held the one-year-old daughter of one of Pizzi's wives while her mother stood holding a brightly lit lamp, crying and screaming at intervals. Elisa pressed closer so she could see what they did to the baby. Two of the women chanting held her legs wide apart; her hands were tied above her head. The baby's mouth was gagged with what looked like rags, and for a moment, Elisa saw the terror in the poor child's wide eyes. The third woman cut small pieces of flesh off the girl's private part. Elisa couldn't watch anymore and turned around. She ran as fast as she could, as quietly as she could. She had to get to Gibe and back before everyone woke up.

Since Johnny was gone, Gibe started to live in the barn so he would have access to the animals any time of the day. Bomi refused to leave the house, so Elisa tried to go to the farm and leave undetected by the other woman. She hated how she was suddenly removed from the life she so loved without the ability to fight for herself. She only now realized whatever next steps she took had to be well-thought out, because she was surrounded by enemies worse than the ones she left in slavery.

Gibe was still asleep in the barn when Elisa banged on the door. He opened to her, a little disoriented.

Elisa panted, "I'm sorry. I—they took the child."

Gibe shook her. "Your child?"

"No. I'm sorry." Elisa wept. "My baby good."

Gibe led her to a bench and made her sit. He got a cup of water and after she drank, told him what she just saw.

"I was coming to give ya Johnny's letter when I hear them." She heaved. "What are they doing to the child?"

Gibe sighed, "It's our culture. To protect our female children from being immoral and to ensure they are fertile when they grow."

Elisa gaped. "No. No one did that to me. They goin' a kill that babe."

Gibe arched an eyebrow. "You have a female child too. This is our culture. If the baby dies, then she wasn't meant to live."

"No!" Elisa jumped to her feet. "I will never let 'em do that to my babe."

Gibe smirked. "You can't stop them. Those three women come to your house when it is time. Unless, your baby is dead. And they won't even show up at all."

Elisa grabbed his hand. "You have to help me, Gibe. This is Johnny's baby. She's an American child. This will not happen if she in America."

"Then take her back to America." Gibe pushed her hand away. "This has been our culture and you despise it."

Elisa covered her face with trembling hands. She needed to calm down. She couldn't lose Gibe's respect and help at this time. She took deep breaths and smiled.

"I'm sorry. Of course, I can't go back to America, where I be as a slave." She shuddered. "I just get carried by the surprise."

"It's alright," Gibe mumbled.

She scratched her scalp. "Huh, here the letters. Pizzi think I go somewhere...can ya please help me give one to Margibi and one to Dr. Obed?"

"Alright. I will."

She wanted to ask him what he did with all the letters she gave him for Johnny but thought this wasn't the right day or time.

"I need to get back. Thank ya so much, Gibe."

"Alright."

She headed for the exit.

Gibe called after her. "If you're going to gather stones at the stream, be fast. Bomi now takes a lot of walks in the mornings."

Elisa nodded. "Thank ya, Gibe. God bless ya."

She hurried away. Sitting at the stream and picking the clear stones made her happy and hopeful. It reminded her of Johnny and what she had with him, how much she missed him. How much she loved him and will forever love him. She prayed at the stream to God, to forgive her foolishness and bring her husband back to her. Those stones were few and she didn't find any sometimes, but it gave her joy, the one she left for Johnny was the biggest she ever found. Did the evil Bomi deliver the message? She just had to assume the girl did.

Remembering Gibe's warning, she lifted herself. She didn't find any stones, but it didn't matter. She would be back next week. She ran across the field as fast as she could with a big baby tied to her body, and again considered her options – escape or death – but cutting off any parts would never be an alternative for Jane.

Chapter Forty-Four

Cynthia returned late and though Johnny heard her move around the house, he did not leave his room. The house indeed was luxurious, and better equipped than any he'd been to. Not Trevor Truse's or Henri Jean, even though those two men lived well.

The following morning, he got up later than usual and recalled too late Nurse Marge was no longer at his beck and call. He missed her already with hot tea first thing in the morning. Unsure of what the routine was, he made himself presentable before he stepped out into the living room. The sound of soft footsteps led him into the kitchen where he found Cynthia boiling water in a kettle. She turned when he entered.

Cynthia smiled. "Good morning. You are a late riser like me, then."

"Good morning." Johnny smiled back. "I got spoiled by Nurse Marge. Back in Liberia and back home, I wake up early."

Cynthia arched an eyebrow. "Good. So, tea-making is on you, Mister."

"Sure, I can do that." He walked to stand beside her. "I just need to know where everything is."

"Everything is easy to find."

The water boiled and Cynthia poured some into a teapot. Johnny opened a cupboard randomly and found teacups, which he placed on the tray Cynthia was setting.

"Works."

"I don't live here a lot. Only in summer actually," Cynthia said.

"Really? Where do you spend the rest of the year?"

"We do a lot of our tours in winter and researches in spring." She poured tea in the two cups. "Milk, sugar?"

"No, thanks. I like my tea plain."

"It's not coffee," she rolled her eyes. "At least a teaspoon of sugar? And a pinch of salt takes you to heaven."

Johnny chuckled. "I've never had tea with a pinch of salt."

She passed a fancy golden cellar to him. "Try it. You may never take tea without salt again."

"I doubt. I may never take tea again." He added a pinch of salt and took a sip. "No, never again."

She laughed. "Why would I trust an American with tea?"

He laughed too. "So, during summer, what do you do?"

"Go for boring dinners with my father and his friends. He seems to think I will get into a relationship with the Viscount Gabriel of York." She rolled her eyes again. "Much like having a relationship with a piece of wood."

"He's royal, so I guess he will be serious a lot of time." Johnny sipped his tea. "It doesn't taste so bad on the second sip."

"If you add a little sugar."

"No, please." He shook his head. "I can't handle another taste shift."

She snickered. "I don't imagine you could. So, what do you do besides get into fights? My father said you were brought to him with broken ribs."

"Isn't that patient confidentiality?" Johnny smirked. "If Lord William had not been so generous, I would sue him immediately."

"You have a great sense of humor. So what do you do?"

"I… huh, I was a farmer before some man tried…well, to take what's mine." Johnny frowned. "Very hard to talk about."

"I understand that. If my life was not so regimented, I'd probably not know what to do with it." Cynthia giggled. "And now it's going to get worse."

"The relationship with the Viscount?"

She rolled her eyes again and Johnny giggled. They were the bluest eyes he'd ever seen, and he couldn't help but notice them.

"You have beautiful eyes," he murmured. "Bluer than mine."

"Oh, thank you." She paused. "Now to the subject of my disapproval, Viscount Gabriel. He thinks he's the only royal. In fact, he's more pompous than the king!"

"I haven't met him, so I can't make a comment."

"And you soon will." Cynthia yelped. "Father wants him to meet everyone I know. It's maddening."

"I have never met a royal before, so I look forward to it."

"I'm royal if you want to count like the two-hundredth to the throne."

Johnny bowed. "Your Majesty."

They finished the pot of tea and Cynthia noticed. "You've had three cups of tea already. With salt."

Johnny winked. "I hate it."

She smiled and straightened. "Well, the day is almost all gone. I want to do some shopping. What are you doing today?"

"Moping."

"You can come shopping with me if you're that type."

Johnny smiled. "I will get to see your beautiful city."

"Warning. The weather changes without telling, and I like to walk."

Johnny kicked the air before him. "I can walk."

The walk was long, but Johnny seemed to enjoy it. They entered several shops and Cynthia got him measured at an exclusive tailor shop. They later had lunch in the open sun until the clouds changed and it rained heavily. Though they ran into the restaurant, they still got soaked. Cynthia wasn't ready to go home yet, so they took a train to the park close to the apartment and walked aimlessly shivering in their wet clothes and laughing at stupid jokes. Johnny enjoyed every minute of the outing and didn't feel a lot of pain from walking so much as he had envisaged.

The coming days followed the same pattern. Cynthia seemed to have an insatiable appetite for new clothes and in the evening, modeled them. For Johnny, it was just a way to unwind. Lord William came to have dinner once every other day, but never stayed long afterward. He would give news from around the world, and this Johnny started to look forward to.

CHAPTER FORTY-FIVE

The hunting season officially opened, and Johnny got to meet Lord Gabriel of York for the first time in August, when he invited Lord William and Cynthia to join his hunting party at his castle.

"I hate hunting," Cynthia moaned. "Why must life be so difficult?"

"I don't have anything suitable, to wear," Johnny gasped. "Can I be excused?"

"No. You are the reason why I won't fall ill on this awful date," Cynthia screamed. "I will take you shopping."

"It's the only thing we did all summer." Johnny smiled. "Thank you so much."

"You enjoyed it too." She hit his shoulder. "Well, we have to leave you, Father." She grabbed a sweater and her umbrella and headed for the door. "Are you coming or not, Mister Holt?"

Johnny faked a bow. "At your service, Your Ladyship."

Lord William smiled. "I need to leave as well. We shall meet at Lord Gabriel's party tomorrow then?"

Cynthia rolled her eyes. "You sound so pleased saying this. Come on, Johnny."

Shopping went well and the following afternoon, they attended the hunting party. The Viscount was handsome and as noble as Johnny expected him to be. The ladies clustered and gossiped, and Johnny understood why Cynthia could not enjoy this company. Many did nothing but chit-chat all day. The men were assembled and divided into four groups. A marksman announced the competition was about to begin and the group with the best hunt, who returned first won the prize.

As a Southerner, Johnny knew a great deal about hunting. From a young age, his father took him and he could handle a gun quite well, but he'd never had to use a bow and arrow, and this was what was shoved into his hand. He followed his group of four men all strangers. A man closed upon him and in a heavily accented voice introduced himself. Johnny didn't hear a word of what he said and only the handshake gave him a clue.

"I'm Johnny."

"Huh, Johnny o-i." The rest was just a jumble of fast words pronounced differently.

After about an hour and a half, his group returned third with a buck. Johnny felt proud, though Cynthia couldn't stop laughing. They had dinner afterward with the viscount and after the dessert, which was served in an ante-chamber, he walked up to Johnny and Cynthia.

Cynthia curtseyed and Johnny followed suit and bowed.

Gabriel smiled. "She does this all the time to embarrass me." He stretched his hand to Johnny. "Pleased to meet you, at last, Mister Holt."

"The honor is mine, Viscount."

Gabriel clasped his hand in front of him. "How do you find our country? Lord William says you may decide to stay."

Johnny cleared his throat. "Well, I haven't given it much of a thought. I must decide what to do at first."

"Johnny is a farmer. I have asked him to come to Cambridge with me," Cynthia said. "We have great research programs for agriculture."

"I dare say the best in the world," Gabriel said.

"I have heard a lot about it." Johnny smiled. "Cynthia makes it clear her college has everything I need."

"Especially now your country may go into war?" The viscount arched an eyebrow. "I say, send all the slaves out." Johnny's face hardened, and Gabriel noticed. "Forgive me, that is a politically insensitive thing to say."

Johnny stole a glance at Cynthia who had her lovely blue eyes rolled to the back without any attempt to hide it from Gabriel.

Gabriel sighed, "She hates my outbursts most of the time."

"Uncouth. For a royal," Cynthia muttered.

Gabriel laughed. "It alarms me how she displays all of this rudeness and still curtseys." He smiled. "Makes me adore her even more."

"I was about to pinch her into respectful submission, Viscount," John teased.

"Why don't you come tomorrow. Alone. I can teach you how to use a bow and arrow," Gabriel said suddenly.

Johnny gasped. "That will be very kind of you, sir."

"Noon and we can have a late lunch afterward." Gabriel started to walk away. "Alone," he called back.

"He's so rude, Johnny." Cynthia cringed. "He makes me want to strangle him."

Johnny chuckled. "I didn't know you could call a royal, uncouth."

"If he is." Cynthia pulled him. "Let's leave. I'm tired."

They said their goodbyes and left the castle.

"Can we walk?"

"Of course."

Johnny would have loved to take a carriage, but he knew how much Cynthia loved to walk.

"The night is so beautiful." She looked up. "I couldn't resist."

"I hope it doesn't pour tonight." Johnny snickered. "The weather changes so abruptly."

Cynthia danced. "Then we'll dance in the rain."

Johnny didn't think that would be funny at all. They walked quietly for a while, then Cynthia took his hand in hers.

"Johnny?" she said, softly.

His heart skipped a beat. It had been so long since he had any physical contact with a woman and despite himself, Cynthia had really gotten close. He liked those deep blue eyes of hers, and the way she rolled them turned him on. And her long, soft, brown hair had gotten in his eyes more often than not, several strands of which he had to move out of his mouth. She was also feminine about many things and would have him lift things she could well lift by herself.

These gestures made them do nearly everything together, from their waking hours to bedtime.

He croaked. "Yes?"

"Why won't you come to Cambridge?"

Johnny nearly let out a long sigh of relief. "Well, I don't want to study farming. For sure."

She pressed a little closer. "What do you want to study?"

He cleared his throat. "I know I never talked about this. I was once a student of law."

Cynthia shrieked. "Law. Why would you never mention this?"

"It was such a long time ago."

She jumped in front of him. "And what happened? You must tell me, Johnny Holt."

Her excitement amused him. "It didn't end the way I wished."

She stopped walking right in front of him. "You have to tell me. How long ago?"

It dawned on Johnny it wasn't all that long ago. This time last year, he was on the run with Elisa. A few months earlier, he had been a student of law at a prestigious college. He closed his eyes and told her everything. He had no intention to upset her when he sobbed during part of his story, but he apparently did because Cynthia didn't say a word. She resumed holding his hand and they walked to her apartment in silence.

Inside though, she pulled him into a hug and kissed him passionately.

And he kissed her back.

Chapter Forty-Six

For two days, all Elisa heard was crying and wailing from mother and child. None of the old women who cut up the child showed up again. They told the mother to pack a lot of salt on the wound which made the baby cry so hard, day and night, day and night. It was unbearable but she didn't know what to do. She thought of running to Dr. Obed, but Pizzi detested the whites so much, he may beat her to death for involving any. So, she cried along with the mother and child in the privacy of her room, and because she cried, Jane cried.

On the third day, the child died. Pizzi carried her on his back in the morning time and walked into the deeper part of the forest behind the house with some of his men. The women held the mother and followed behind. It was a taboo for the mother to see the baby's grave, but no one must remain in the house. At a safe distance, the women waited, and the men dug a shallow grave and put the child in it, wrapped in a white blanket. The mother fainted. The day was bright, with the sun up early. Not a day to bury a child murdered in cold blood.

The men returned to the house and Pizzi's first wife served locally made beer and dried meat with cassava pudding. There wasn't any rejoicing, but Elisa could not eat. A woman she could not recognize noticed her sitting in the corner, Jane tied in her pouch, thankfully asleep.

"Come and eat. So, your baby will live when it is her turn," the woman snapped. "The other one is gone. She is an evil child."

Elisa's gaze shot to the mother of the dead child. The woman seemed resigned and ate the food along with others. Elisa realized there was no way to escape this. She took the food and pushed it through. The eating seemed a part of the ritual because once everyone was done, Pizzi stood and announced the "gods" of the land had accepted the soul of the dead child, and everyone should go about their daily chores. A woman led the mother of the dead child away, and one by one people went about their business. Elisa made a decision without further delay. She knew she'd die if anyone touched Jane.

She entered her room and packed all the stones she'd been gathering in the past months into Jane's small sack which contained her change of clothes and dried fruits. Then she tucked in extra clothing for herself and her daughter. Her sewing machine would have to be left behind, as much as this prized possession was important to her. Beside this, she had nothing. She breast-fed Jane, who now sucked as a mere snack, and tied her securely on her back. Everyone expected her to go to work at the fabric store, and that was where she went.

Pizzi and the others who worked at his store trekked behind her. When Elisa got to her place of work, she told Beth, knowing the older woman would be the first to report to Pizzi when they discovered her gone, she had a sick stomach and would want to buy some of the locally-made bitters down the road.

Beth frowned. "Ya told ya Pizzi first? Ya go tell 'im."

"I thought ya could help me, but–" She shrugged. "Thank ya, never mind. I'll go tell him."

Beth called after her. "Pizzi got anythin' ya need!"

Pizzi's was at the back of the store but taking the front could get her there too. The front exit also led to the dock area, close to the whites' church, near Dr. Obed's. Elisa stepped out of the fabric store, knowing Pizzi would soon come around to find her because Beth would go and tell him she was leaving. She ran as fast as she could. A long road separated her from her destination. She only needed to get past it, and she'd be okay. Away for good from murderers of children. She didn't care she was trying to escape in broad daylight with a big baby and a bigger bundle.

"Elisa!"

Pizzi's voice echoed to her. She knew he would come after her as soon as Beth told him she wanted to go somewhere. She breathed hard, willing her feet to move faster. The dead weight of Jane's sleeping form in her pouch made things more difficult. As she got to the end of the road, he grabbed her shoulder and jerked her back.

Pizzi snarled. "Where do you think you're going?"

"Please, let me go. I don't want my baby to die. Please," she wept.

Pizzi slapped her hard and she staggered back, but he caught hold of her before she fell. He pulled her as she wept and pleaded. Jane woke up and wailed. A woman from across the street yelled.

"Let go of her, you!"

Pizzi did not even act as though he heard anything. Elisa mistakenly dropped her bag and he turned to slap her again, but a hand stopped him. That was an abomination. People milled around but no one dared intervene so for someone to hold Pizzi... Elisa raised her head. It was an old white man who challenged him. She knew Pizzi could be a terror to every black, but he dared not resist an old white man. He let go of her. Elisa did not care what happened afterward.

She picked her bag and ran in the direction she was headed. In his focus on her, Pizzi may have forgotten they had entered the white-zone where he was not boss.

Chapter Forty-Seven

The old white man who challenged Pizzi was none other than the Reverend Michaels, the pastor of the white church. Elisa didn't know this until she ran into Dr. Obed's clinic, panting and weeping. The nurse and another older woman had seen the assault from within and it was the older woman who spoke.

"God saved you today, child. My name is Marge. I shouted for him to leave you."

Elisa sank to her knees, shaking all over, unable to breathe. She had never been so scared in her life. Dr. Obed came out of his office to see what the fuss was about and asked his nurse to take the baby from Elisa and attend to her, then she was led into a room and given water.

Dr. Obed sat across from her. "What happened?"

She panted and in between tears, related the events. She fell on her knees. "Help me, Doctor. Please don't make me go back."

The old man walked in. Dr. Obed stood.

"Good morning, Rev. Michaels."

"Good morning, Dr. Obed. I wanted to be sure the young woman was safe." Rev. Michaels shook the doctor's hand. "These rough locals need to be controlled. I don't care if she's his wife or not."

Dr. Obed cleared his throat. "You remember Johnny Holt? The young man who wanted accommodation."

Rev. Michaels frowned. "Of course. He got killed in a beating, right?"

Elisa bent her head, the truth of what happened to Johnny hitting harder than she ever expected. To think they took her letters making her believe Johnny lived! A wave of anger rose within her and she screamed.

Rev. Michaels gasped. "Did I say anything wrong?"

"Elisa was his pregnant wife," Dr. Obed mumbled. "The one–"

"I remember," Rev. Michaels cut in. "I'm sorry about his demise."

She covered her head and wept.

Elisa was given a small room on the top of the building. Next to her room were Dr. Obed's private living quarters where he and Marge stayed. A clinic was downstairs, but this wasn't the one close to the harbor. She suspected the doctor attended to foreigners and the missionaries here and to everyone else in the clinic by the harbor. It was in the secured estate managed by Reverend Michaels. In the evening, she was invited to dinner with her hosts. She ate hungrily the potato pie served to her. She hadn't had a taste of the food she grew up eating in more than six months since Pizzi took her hostage.

After dinner, Marge served chilled tomato juice, a most appropriate drink for the hot evening, and the three sat in soft cushion seats in the living room. Jane slept peacefully in her arms after crying half of the day.

"Do you want to talk about what you want?" Dr. Obed said. "By the way, Marge is my sister. She's a nurse."

Elisa acknowledged the older woman with a nod and dragged in a deep breath. "Johnny died. And ya never told me. Got me writin' all those letters."

Marge frowned. "Johnny?"

Dr. Obed stood. "Johnny Holt, the same one. Elisa is his wife. Or should I say, was." He walked to a desk pushed against the wall and opened a drawer in it. Elisa's letters were tied with a red ribbon. "I thought you would want them back."

Elisa worked her throat to get a sound, but nothing came out.

He handed them to her. "At least I saved them for you. Margibi tore up the ones you gave him."

Elisa heaved a heavy sigh. "I had hope writin' them at least."

"Wait a minute, Obed. Which Johnny?" Nurse Marge stuttered. "Johnny is not dead. I nursed him."

Elisa caught a quick glance from the doctor to Marge, but the woman didn't see it. "You lied to me?" Her lips trembled and she pressed them together to try and keep from tearing up. "Johnny is alive?"

Obed sighed. "We spread that lie to protect you. And your baby. And Johnny."

"Where is he? Please take me to him. I was wrong, I made mistakes but please–"

Obed folded his arms. "He's not here, Elisa."

She turned to look at Marge, who she trusted already. The woman had saved her twice today without knowing who she was.

"He's in Europe," Marge said. "He was in a bad state and taking him back to America was too far."

"Europe!" Elisa slouched. "How will I ever get there?"

"It's almost impossible," Dr. Obed said. "First off, you can't afford it. Who will pay your fare? Secondly, I don't think he wants to see you. And third, he may want to come back, so you will miss him if you leave."

Elisa knew the doctor was lying to her but didn't know what else to do. "I can sew. I will sew if I can get a job. I make hair for the local women too and got good at it."

Marge leaned over and touched the braids on her head. "They look good."

"I make this on my own. And I make for Jane too. And the women in the village and in Pizzi house. I don't think I will want to leave here." She bowed her head. "I can make my own money and care for Jane and me."

"I will ask Rev. Michaels for advice. He may know someone who can give you a job. Margibi can too, but that will expose you to the tyrant."

Elisa looked at her toes. "Thank ya, sir."

"You can stay here for as long as you want." Dr. Obed walked to the door. "I need to attend to some business. Excuse me, ladies."

As soon as he was gone, Elisa turned to Marge. "Please, tell me where Johnny is. This is his babe. He'd want to see his babe."

"Johnny is in Europe, Elisa." Marge's voice softened. "So, you are his Elisa? Never thought I'd meet you."

"Please how's he?"

Marge smiled. "Strong. I nursed him back to health."

"I so sorry," Elisa sobbed. "Pizzi said he would kill him if I didn't disown him. And I know he would. He evil."

"I know, dear. I would do the same if I was in your shoes."

Elisa, carrying Jane to her bosom, knelt in front of Marge. "Please, help me. I love Johnny. I want my hasband back. I want him to see his babe."

"I understand, Elisa. Johnny really loves you too. He talked about you all the time." Marge sighed. "But it is so expensive to travel these days. And we need to find out if he has gone to America or not." She ran her hand over the neat rows of Elisa's woven hair. "Your hair is beautiful. The white ladies may not want to do this, but many of the black ones in the church would. What is this called?"

Elisa smiled for the first time. "Weave. They have plait and braid, and thread too. Many styles. And I know them all."

"You are so gifted, Elisa, and you will make money making hair."

"Yes, Miz Marge."

"But I will help you. We will get you a job and then you can save some money. And we can send messages to Europe to know if Johnny left." Marge squeezed her hands. "And you will be fine."

Elisa bent over and wept with relief.

Chapter Forty-Eight

It took Johnny a moment or two to realize where he was. A lot of hair lied across his face and it was its sweet scent that triggered his memory. Cynthia lay cuddled in the crook of his arm. He shut his eyes, struggling to deal with the sense of guilt that overwhelmed him. He really liked her, but he was still married to Elisa regardless of the fact that she no longer belonged to him. He continued to have these guilty feelings, yet it would be unfair to Cynthia to show it. She had brought him more happiness than he had had in a long time.

She stirred and pushed the hair out of her face, pushing more of it into his.

He chuckled. "Are you trying to feed me with hair?"

She lifted her head and placed a kiss on his mouth. "Hmm."

He moaned. "Good morning, darling."

"What's today? I have been sleeping forever."

He pressed a kiss to her forehead. "It's Sunday morning and Viscount wants us to go rabbit-hunting."

"I'm going shopping then." She stretched. "Oh, the shops will not open. I may go and see Father about your admission."

"You do that."

He lifted himself, thereby pushing her up too. She slid off his side with a yelp and kicked him.

"I'll get you breakfast before I leave," he called to her as he walked through the door.

"It's too early to go out," she called back.

He shouted, "It's almost noon. You overslept."

She shouted louder, "You too!"

Johnny smiled to himself and put the kettle on the stove. She was so much fun, day in day out. He proceeded to prepare a simple breakfast of bread rolls, eggs, and sausages, and when the water was boiled, placed the teapot and cups on the tray. Cynthia was asleep when he returned, and he nudged her.

"I'll take a cup and then leave."

"Okay," she mumbled. "I love you."

He poured himself a cup and left her to return to the kitchen. He didn't know if she noticed he had never said those three emotional words to her, couldn't bring himself to. There was no doubt she loved him. It showed in her words and deeds. Did he love her? He knew he loved Elisa and what he felt for Cynthia was just so different. Could he live with her? Definitely. Commit to her? He wasn't sure. He heaved a heavy sigh and finished his tea. Cynthia had told him she understood he needed time to get over Elisa, but how much longer before she made a well-deserved demand on his heart?

The viscount was all set when Johnny got to the castle. They took off, just the two of them and rode deep into the woods on two powerful horses. Gabriel loved to ride, and each time Johnny went with him, he had commended his prowess on a horse. Somehow, the two seemed to have a bond Johnny respected. Especially now Cynthia was in some sort of relationship with him. It made him feel uncomfortable and he had pleaded with Cynthia to keep the relationship secret until they both could face her father and the viscount.

Gabriel pulled up in a clearing with a massive cottage and Johnny beside him.

"This is where I come when I want real game. The rabbits here know no sense." Gabriel smiled. "Give them a few more minutes."

Johnny gazed around. The trees were full and green. There was no autumn in this place. It could be a bright sunny day in summer and not a few months away from winter.

"Where is this, Lord Gabriel? It's so beautiful."

"My hideout." He chuckled. Then exclaimed. "It's time. Do you see the one over there?"

He set his arrow and gave a perfect shot. A brown rabbit dropped off a tall tree. Gabriel smirked.

Johnny smiled. "You are perfect."

"Now your turn, Johnny." He circled and stayed aside.

"I don't see any rabbits, Your Lordship."

"I see at least three in the trees." He pointed. "That way."

Finally, Johnny got a shot, but it didn't hit the mark, and it was Gabriel who shot the second one. They made a fire, which Johnny could do quite well, and roasted the rabbits. Then with sweet red wine from Gabriel's rich collection, sat in the cottage and ate like old friends. The two had a lot in common already and laughed at jokes they found mutually amusing.

"Lord William said you plan to take up an offer in Cambridge." Gabriel leaned back on a fluffy cushion. "I think that is indeed a noble decision."

"I changed my mind." Johnny blurted, surprising even himself. "I'm sorry, sir."

Gabriel leaned forward. "Did you want to discuss something. I've never seen you so pale." Then he chuckled. "Not that I see a lot of you, my friend."

The atmosphere seemed different with his outburst and for the first time in a long while, Johnny felt safe and wanted to talk. Over the months, he had admired the young royal, and at times even wished he had his life.

"I think I should go back to America." He swallowed. "I miss home, and–"

"Your country is on the verge of a war." Gabriel narrowed his eyes. "This is the time to return if you want. But if you choose to stay, I will support you." He sighed, "You strike me as a man who has a need."

Johnny turned away from Gabriel's searching eyes. "I have nothing here. I am nothing."

"You have a good soul."

Johnny let out a shuddering breath. "Well, thank you, sir. So kind of you to say so."

"If you will drop the sir, and the lord, I can make you into–something. A friend."

Johnny laughed despite himself. "I am not worthy, Lord Gabriel." He stood and pushed his hair away from his face.

"Is there a woman in America?" Gabriel said softly.

"I wish." Johnny gasped. "I was married once."

Gabriel misunderstood him. "Then you must go by all means. Leave and find her. And I will ensure you are granted royal passage."

Johnny staggered forward, fell on his knees and wept.

Johnny just folded the letter and would have walked out of the room to place it on the mantle place where he was sure Cynthia would find it, when the front door burst open. The letter dropped from his shaky hand. He didn't waste time with it. He hurried out and met her in the living room bent over the sofa.

She startled. "You are back! I didn't expect you until night. Gabriel bored you to hell with dead rabbits?" She jumped on him and rained his face with kisses. "There's good news and I love you. I love you. I–"

Johnny laughed and lifted her. "I love you, too. What's the good news?"

"Father got you a provisional admission to study law." She screamed, "I am so in love with my father."

Johnny froze inside. "Oh my. What does that mean?"

"There is an exam to write. You have the admission if you pass."

"Will I pass?"

Cynthia rolled her eyes. "Of course, you will." She jumped on the spot. "You are going to have the best law degree in the world." She grabbed his face and kissed his lips. "Father is coming for dinner in an hour. I must get his favorite wine. Will be back before you know it." She picked her tossed umbrella and ran off.

What had she come back for?

Johnny stood at the window, watched her exit and skip down the street, and a tear dropped from his eye. But he had to do what he had to do. The longer he stayed, the tougher it would be. He returned to the room and picked the letter from the floor where it had dropped. If only Cynthia had entered the bedroom, she'd have seen his packed bag and his farewell note. This was for the best and she would one day realize it. His heart belonged to Elisa and as long as she lived somewhere, he would feel attached to her.

Many times, he considered going to Liberia. She would have his child by now. He longed to see the baby, his first blood. He longed for the life he had with Elisa, even in the turbulent times. But going back to America would be the closest he would be to her again. He could be able to send letters to her through the emancipation movement. Maybe, just maybe he could build a decent life and bring her and their child, someday. Was it a boy or a girl? They wanted to name it Jacob or Janet. Did Elisa honor that?

He picked up his luggage and placed the note on the mantle. It would not be the first thing she'd find when she returned, that would be cruel. But when she looked around the room for him, she'd see it.

Chapter Forty-Nine

Johnny dozed on and off on the train ride to France because it was the only way to leave that night. With the royal booking Gabriel made, he could get on a ship in a luxurious cabin the following night. Not until he was settled into the cabin did the extent of his actions dawn on him. He had broken a beautiful girl's heart, just as his had been broken by Elisa. He had many regrets. Had he done the right thing, or was he now on a self-destructive path? Deep down, he could not feel any regret, he only hoped he had said the right things as he reminisced on his words.

Dear Cynthia,

You won't believe I just left. I find it hard to believe too. The prospects of living here, being loved by you, getting back a future career in law, surrounded by loves and friendships. I must be out of my mind to throw it all away. But I have to.

Not because I don't love you, or I am not grateful, but because I am too involved in the mess my life became. Don't say it is because of Elisa. It is, though. It will be unfair to you, loving you while still loving her.

I make no sense. Forgive me.

I have returned to my country. Thank you for your care and kindness and love.

Please extend my apologies to your dear father.

So long, my love.

Johnny Holt.

NB: Lord Gabriel of York is a great man, and I greatly respect him. He loves you. Please give him a chance.

The ship docked on a frosty December morning. Johnny could not believe the journey of a month had taken almost four due to bad weather. The fact that his accommodation on the ship was royal, only made it a little easier and he used the opportunity to write speeches and letters. It gave him the chance to plan out his next steps as well. He intended to seek asylum against the charges on his head and plead his case. With the heated-up rumors of war, he hoped he could return to college. More than ever before, he wanted to be a lawyer. He wanted to get into the Senate as his father had desired for him, but not for the same reasons. He wanted to fight for the weak and speak for the ones who could not speak for themselves. He even planned to set up a foundation called The Elisa Holt Foundation.

Sure his college would be closed for the holidays, Johnny found his way there first. He made sure it was dark and any form of recognition would be difficult, and then he went through the faculty building in search of posters. It had been a year and some, but he had to be certain. With nothing in sight, he headed for his old room. Cole hated to live with his father, so he opted to keep his board on campus. After several knocks on the door, he realized no one was available.

Without hesitation, he headed to the Art House. The last person who helped him was Henri Jean. He needed help again, though now he was armed with a plan for his future, and besides ensuring a royal passage to America, Gabriel gave him currency. He did not return empty. The exhibition halls were closed, but a doorman told him Henri returned to France a month earlier. Only the hotel in the building was open. Johnny took a room.

Despite himself, he went in search of Trevor Truse the following day, a little more. confident he wasn't wanted, at least by his father again. Nothing had changed much in the city but when Johnny entered Trevor's store, it was buzzing with activity. None of the faces he saw was familiar. There weren't any gun sales going on either, but a lot of paperwork. Nobody gave him any attention and he strayed into one of the inner rooms Trevor used for storage. Here, he saw cases of ammunition being moved by three men.

Johnny cleared his throat. "Excuse me, good morning." No answer. "Trevor Truse here?"

One of the men responded without looking at him. "Third door down the passage."

"Thank you."

Johnny found the door ajar and pushed a little. Everyone in the room turned to look at him. He recognized only Quaker Peter who stood and ushered him to join the roundtable.

"The prodigal returns," Quaker Peter laughed. "Get him a chair."

"Thank you," Johnny mumbled. Someone pulled up a chair and he sat.

"Trevor will be here in a minute. And the meeting can start."

Johnny cleared his throat. "I didn't come for a meeting. I thought—"

"Well," Peter clasped his hands. "You're here now. So, where have you been?"

Johnny stiffened, his gaze on Peter. He was unsure of the answer he could give. He shrugged. "Around the world."

A snicker went around the room and Johnny stole glances at the eight-to-ten strangers with him. A side door opened, and Trevor Truse walked in. Everyone stood, which surprised Johnny. What was this?

"Please sit, thank you." Trevor took the seat at the head of the table and fixed his gaze on Johnny. "There is a reason to believe at least five southern states will secede in the next few weeks. When this happens, America will go into war. We have work to do. We need to collaborate to ensure this happens. The south must be forced to bow."

"I don't believe this country will go into war," Johnny blurted, irritated at the way Trevor looked past him. "We have a republic we love, respect and protect."

Trevor waved at him. "Permit me to welcome a wanted fugitive who is enjoying our protection from the same people we challenge every day. Johnny Holt."

"Johnny Holt," a rotund man gasped. "The same one?"

Trevor nodded. "The very same." He snickered. "Now, to important matters before I was rudely interrupted." He held Johnny's gaze for a split second. "We are preparing for war. We want it. We will do everything to get it." He opened a big book on the table right in front of him. "We will do everything to provoke the south to stop slavery or fight for their right to keep it."

After a meeting that spanned over two hours, Trevor adjourned and continuing to ignore Johnny, walked into his private office. Quaker Peter and two other men followed him. Johnny realized he had to seek his attention and help. And an apology was appropriate too. He entered the office and Trevor stopped talking mid-sentence.

"I will attend to you later, Gregory." The two men left. "What do you want?" Trevor snapped.

"I'm back," Johnny sighed. "I'm sorry for the way I left but your...but Miz Nan almost got us killed."

Trevor arched an eyebrow. "What are you talking about?"

"My mother came with men to take us to an unknown place. She said Miz Nan gave her our address—"

Trevor pushed his desk aside and stomped out of the room before Johnny could finish speaking.

Quaker Peter sighed, "He's going to give her the pounding of her life."

"I'm sorry, I shouldn't have said anything."

"Oh, she's had it coming. Messing with a lot lately." The Quaker sat. "Her son is back from Europe. She thinks that's a good reason for Trevor to marry her now."

"Well," Johnny sat too. "I don't know what to say to that. Just I'm sorry."

"So, how's your wife?"

Johnny stood and gave the Quaker his back. "Can we talk about something else?"

Chapter Fifty

The rooms behind the church hall were used for the schoolhouse, but Reverend Michaels let Elisa use the one converted to a storeroom to do her sewing. With her machine left in Pizzi's house, she could only work with her hands and though she was slow, she did a good job. The mothers at the church supported her, and soon she was busy. As the end of the year approached, she hardly had time for herself because her work was so good, and she had a long list of clients. She didn't want to spend the little money she made, though the mothers' union came together and promised to get her a sewing machine she could lease from one of the ladies. The offer was great, and she'd be able to work faster.

Her Jane started to sit properly and even made attempts to crawl, so Elisa created a small space on the side of the store where she could roll a little when she was awake. She was now so big, putting her in the pouch was no longer possible and Elisa had to carry her on her shoulder. This exposed Jane's coloring as a mixed-race baby, and sometimes, they got stares from the people coming to the schoolhouse.

Close to Christmas, while Elisa put finishing touches to a pretty dress she had made for a young mother, a man walked into the store. She didn't know him, but he was well-dressed and took off his hat when he stepped inside. His hair was thick and curly and combed out.

"Miz Holt?"

Elisa shot toward the corner where Jane played with a small wooden bowl she ate from. She stood protectively in front of her baby, knowing she had not much for defense, but the pastor's office was just across the hall, and she could scream if she needed.

The man took a step backward. "I'm sorry to come in uninvited. My name is Richard Alvin Allen."

"Yes, sir?"

"I–Miz Beth told me about you." He swallowed. "I'm sorry. You're so beautiful. I didn't expect–"

"I don't know her. Please go."

He smiled and Elisa noticed his face relaxed immediately. He pushed his hair back, though the thick clump didn't move a bit. He couldn't be all that much taller than her and his skin seemed light enough to suggest mixed race, but she couldn't be sure. She couldn't put him anywhere near her age. Maybe ten or more years older.

"She did say you may not want to hear her name." He shrugged. "She does have a change of heart. I guess she sees clearly now."

"She sees clearly now," Elisa grunted. "Oh."

"Your anger toward her is justified. She told me everything, right from back in Kentucky."

Elisa felt Jane's hand on her skirt, and she picked her baby. "What do ya want, sir?"

"Like I said, my name is Richard. I came into Liberia five years ago from America." He folded his hands to the back. "I have been in and around for a while and been working with the government on a smooth resettlement of our brothers and sisters."

He moved a step back again putting more space between them, which made Elisa feel a little better.

"Recently, I have had a lot more complaints than I want to hear, and I wanted to meet you and talk about your experiences since you arrived."

"I'm sorry, sir. I have to finish the dress." Elisa darted her eyes toward her seat and the pile of work she had. "I can't talk."

"Can we fix a time for me to come back?" He shrugged again. "Anytime will be suitable. I was told you lived in Creek View? Well, I lived in Kentucky for several years before I was sold to a plantation owner in Mississippi. Later on, I bought my freedom and traveled to Pennsylvania where I joined the movement." He smiled. "And here I am still working for the good of our people."

Elisa rocked Jane who was getting restless. "What do ya want to talk about?"

"What happened to your husband, Johnny Holt."

Elisa sat in her chair with her hands folded in her lap, Jane had been fed and was asleep. Richard Alvin Allen paced while Elisa related her story. He did not interrupt her until she stopped talking.

"I am not interested in the locals," Richard said. "Some of them sold some of us. We are still alive and the ones who sold us are too." He seemed to have a habitual shrugging gesture. "I am really not interested in them or their progress. But I did not come here to be treated like an outcast. This is my country. My home. I am just as entitled. Maybe more."

Elisa watched him with hooded eyes. She still knew not to speak unless she was asked. And this man may have the color of her skin and speak like her, but he was a stranger and she didn't know the powers he possessed, or what his true motives were.

"Miz Beth told me, you and she served under your husband–"

"Miz Beth left my hasband and me cold in the 'ands of 'unters," Elisa cut in. "I don't blame her. She a slave." She slowed her speech so she could use better grammar. "But she come-came here. And she still treat us bad."

"As a revenge to your husband?"

"I don't know. I don't want to know. She got her revenge now. My has...husband is not here anymore." She swallowed. "Please, is this all ya want to talk?"

"Can you come to the consulate and speak at a congress meeting?"

"No. Please. I just want my peace. No!"

"I understand, Elisa." He shrugged. "I know I have taken a lot of your time, and I do apologize. Whenever you feel up to it, you can find me in the government office at the harbor." He straightened. "Thank you, dear."

Elisa watched him leave through the window, he put his hat on and got on a horse-driven cart. The air about him spoke wealth of some sort. She felt he had a good plan to help the slaves who came from America, but she didn't want to be a part of it. She had suffered enough.

For the past few months, she had found stability. She worked hard in both her trades and Marge helped her save her money. In another few months, she would have enough to pay her way to Europe to find Johnny. The mere thought of it got her so excited and it was all she wanted to focus on.

She spent the rest of the day finishing her sewing and waited for the daily evening church service to end, before she joined Marge to return home. She had been welcome in the evening services and to church altogether, but she sometimes felt self-conscious taking Jane with her, so some days she waited the service out.

Dear Johnny,

I miss you so much.

How are you?

After the shock of getting all my letters back, I decided to continue writing, just to keep in touch with you in my own way. Gibe told me the letters I gave him got soaked up when the barn leaked, and rain fell and destroyed in the barn. I don't believe him. I still go to the farm to pick my white stones. I stay at our spot on the stream and remember you, and I tell Jane stories about you. She's a big girl now. She started crawling. I have to sneak there because Pizzi's woman, Bomi, still lives in our house. Yes, she's Pizzi's woman after all. He married her the same way you married me in the village...

Miz Marge has been a mother to me and Jane. She's very kind. She agrees Jane looks just like you. I work in the schoolhouse now, and the school teacher lets me sit at the back for a few hours. I read and write well now.

I have started saving and I will find you, Johnny. I will find you.

I love you, my husband.

Your wife,

Elisa Johnny Holt.

Chapter Fifty-One

Richard Alvin Allen visited the next day and had with him a bag of apples. His gesture reminded her of the first few times with Johnny on Holt Land, and she recoiled from it.

"The captain of the ship is very generous." He hugged the apples like a child. "I thought you might want some."

"No, thank ya." Elisa pressed her lips together. "I am good."

Richard smiled. "A proper lady, indeed." He placed the apples on a small area on her workspace. "How's your baby? I forgot to ask her name."

"Jane John Holt."

"She's a very pretty girl, like her mother."

"How may I help ya, sir?"

"Please call me Richard." He folded his hands behind. "I was walking by the school-house, had the apples, and I wanted to say hello."

Elisa didn't know how to reply to him. She was wary of any man; the only one she had any affection for was her husband.

She drew in a short breath. "Well, thank ya. I will need to join the class soon."

He arched an eyebrow. "You take classes?"

"Yes."

"That's wonderful, Elisa. Growth. This is what I try to tell our young women. They need to desire growth." He shrugged. "I would love for you to come to our center, really. Your story is so strong. You need to help our people."

"I don't have a story and I can't help anybody."

"We all have beautiful stories and yours will help people." He frowned. "A little girl came on the ship a month ago. She, huh, had been raped several times by her master and his sons. On the escape route, her mother committed suicide at a time they almost got caught. But she escaped."

He stole a glance at her, and she knew he was saying this all to convince her, but she couldn't help but listen. If not for Pizzi, she could have said no one ever raped her. She knew how awful that experience was and could not imagine having it with more than one person.

"What happened to her?"

"She's at the center. We could not give her accommodation because she's still so young." Richard shrugged. "If you talk to her about learning to sew, or coming to the school–"

"The school house is only for the whites," Elisa blurted. "They only let me."

"But if you ask, they might let her too."

Richard's soft voice had a hypnotizing effect. Elisa did not want to ask any more favors from Reverend Michaels, but a child too young to be given a house of her own would need someone.

"I can come to the center. Tomorrow in the early morning before the school opens."

He bowed. "I will be here, Elisa, to take you there. Thank you."

The center scared the hell out of Elisa, for reasons she could not understand. It was at the same address with the consulate, the courthouse and the jailhouse, which probably was the reason she feared it. All the same, Richard led her into a small hall where some thick mats had been arranged against the wall. They stood outside the hall and peeped in through a large window. It was a bit early and the residents had only just woken up. Elisa counted six occupied mats.

"I'd like you to meet her now, but we can't have a talk yet. There are morning routines they do." Richard looked at her. "We can wait in my office."

Elisa shifted Jane's weight from one shoulder to the other. The baby was still asleep. "How long?"

"Maybe an hour." Richard reached out. "I can help you hold her."

"No, thank ya." She swallowed. "One hour is long."

He shrugged. "I will excuse her from the morning drill. Please come with me."

Elisa followed him, already regretting her visit. Maybe she should have asked him to bring the girl to the schoolhouse instead.

Richard's office had more space than he needed and gave Elisa the first true impression about him. *He must be important,* she thought. Behind a large table were two chairs and a bench. He pointed her to it, and she sat on the bench. Another small table was cluttered and had a single chair behind it. Richard went to it and took a small book with him to sit with her. Nothing else was in the big room but space.

"I'm sorry I don't have a place for you to keep Baby Jane."

"It's fine."

"Give me a minute to ask for Mary. The girl." He left.

She adjusted Jane and sat straight. If this took longer than she planned, she'd have to ask him to bring Mary to her. Coming to the government offices already seemed like leaving her comfort area. She didn't tell Marge about this visit either, so she wanted it to be done with as fast as possible.

Richard returned almost immediately with a girl who could be a year or two younger than her. Her hair had been cut short and there were whip marks all over her body. She wasn't pretty, but she had a strong cheekbone and remarkable eyes. Elisa's heart went out to her immediately.

"This is Mary, Elisa." Richard made the introduction. "Can you help her?"

They spent half of the morning talking. Afterward Richard offered a rich breakfast of bread rolls and eggs, bacon, sausages and sweet butter with apples on the side, and hot chocolate. Jane fed on the eggs and licked her lips noisily on the hot chocolate, which made everyone laugh, even Mary. After the meal, Richard offered to walk Elisa back to the schoolhouse, and without thinking, she invited Mary.

"The teacher is really kind. She may let ya sit in class." Elisa heaved. "And if not, ya can sit with me and learn to sew."

Richard gasped, "Thank you, Elisa dear."

"Can I carry her?" Mary held her hand to Jane.

"Yes." Elisa gave her baby to the young woman, and Jane gladly went with her.

Richard smirked. "I'm jealous."

Chapter Fifty-Two

Dear Johnny,

How are you?

Things have moved on so well with Jane and me. We were offered a small house of our own in the government building. Richard Allen has been so kind. I let Mary live with me too, so she helps with Jane. Mary can read and write now too and she helps with sewing. She's a gift from God. Richard is so so kind. He comes to see us every day and buys all our food. I try to stop him, but it also saves me money. Richard doesn't think it is safe to travel yet. I'll wait for him to tell me when is good. I know he doesn't want me to go at all. He lets me talk to the blacks who arrive on how to survive. I tell them about us. How wonderful you were.

Jane is so big now. I made her a Christmas dress and Richard helped me to get a sticky gum to use on the dress with my white stones. It is so beautiful. Some of the mothers had me make for their daughters.

I have enough to travel to Europe now. I am happy it's getting closer.

Your wife,

Elisa.

Elisa folded the letter and placed it in her special box in her drawer. She hadn't written in a month and she chided herself at how busy she'd let herself become, though with the Christmas and New Year's celebrations behind, and her sewing reduced, she wanted to write every week as she did before. Richard kept her busy with the work she did helping to resettle young women, and families as well. In less than two months of meeting Mary, she had gotten three other children accepted in the schoolhouse, which Richard greatly applauded her for. He was also able to make enough progress to get the government to start a small schoolhouse in the city where other children would have the opportunity to go to school, though they needed a teacher, and this was scarce.

Mary knocked on the door. "Mister Richard is here, Miz Elisa."

Elisa straightened. "Please give me a second. Thank you."

She heard Mary's receding footsteps and wondered what could have brought Richard so late in the evening. He saw her every day, sometimes all day, and today, he had informed her a new ship arrived, which meant he would be very busy in the next few days. She peeped into Jane's cot, which had been a Christmas gift from Richard. The baby was fast asleep, her thick curly hair framing her beautiful oval-shaped face. Elisa pressed a kiss on her forehead and closed the door behind her.

Mary was already retired to her room and so Richard was alone in the living room. He took his hat off and smiled.

Elisa smiled back. "Good evening, Mister Richard. I didn't expect to see ya this evening." She sighed, "Is everything alright?"

"Everything is fine, my dear Elisa." He shrugged. "I wanted to see you."

She exclaimed. "Ya see me every day."

"I know." He bowed his head for a second. "It just seemed heavy on my mind that I wanted to discuss something important."

She looked around. "Shall we sit then?"

He shook his head at first, then sat on the edge of one of her three wooden chairs. "Thank you."

Elisa clasped her hands in her skirt. *What did he want?* She couldn't guess. When he didn't say anything for another few seconds, she prompted him. "Is this about the new people on the ship that arrived?"

He frowned. "No, not at all." Then he stood. "You have no idea why I'm here?"

"No. Should I?"

He started to pace. "I was born a slave, but I bought my freedom when I was only twenty. It was hard labor, but I did it. And five years later, I left for Pennsylvania. Another five years, I came here. Another five years, and I'm standing in front of you."

Elisa tried to calculate his age but lost the addition after twenty-five.

"You have been a very strong force in my life, Elisa. I have never met a woman more beautiful, or more intelligent than you."

Oh, dear. No.

"And I can't keep my attraction for you away any longer. I have tried." He stopped pacing. "I want more from our relationship. I love you, Elisa."

His words seemed to jerk her off her seat and it was her turn to pace.

"Ya know I have a babe. For another man."

"He won't come back for you." Richard shrugged. "I'm not trying to be disrespectful. But he left you."

"No." Elisa shook her head. "I left him. I was foolish, and I lost him. And I will go back and find him."

He moved closer and held her shoulders. "Look at me. You are grasping at wind, and you know it."

Despite herself, Elisa looked into his eyes and his passion and the softness in them broke her down. She slumped into him, and he held her tightly.

"Oh, my love." He pressed kisses on her forehead. "I've wanted to tell you from the first day I met you."

"I still love my husband," she said, feebly.

"I know. I understand and I respect that." He cupped her face. "But he's not here. And he won't come back. He has gone back to his farm, and he will continue to own slaves. And he is not the kind of person you should worry your sweet head about."

Elisa didn't want to agree with him, though his words made sense. It would be easy for Johnny to forget her, and he could go back to his Holt Land, and his father would forgive him.

She moaned. "He was a good man."

"He's no longer here, my dear. I am here with you, and I will protect you from anyone." He pressed a kiss on her lips. "I love you and I won't let anybody take you from me."

She stiffened. Nobody had ever kissed her on her mouth except Johnny, not even the rapist Pizzi, and it felt so strange. She didn't think she wanted to be intimate with anyone. Richard would provide the stability she needed, but she'd have to take her time to trust him.

She pulled back a little. "Give me time."

He nodded. "I know, darling. Thank you."

Chapter Fifty-Three

Cole Truse maintained a cold silence all through the ranting noise from within his father's house, which went on for more than thirty minutes between Trevor and Nan. The moment there was silence though, he started to speak.

"We need to stop them, Johnny. Or they will kill each other, soon."

Johnny arched an eyebrow toward the exit to the bedrooms. It was too early to fight but since he moved in to live with the Truses, he'd learned no time was too late or too early. The banging and throwing sounds had woken him up and brought him to the living room in his pajamas, only to find Cole, apparently woken by the same noise.

"It doesn't sound like this is new."

"So, we should let them kill themselves? Johnny?" He pushed at his thinning hair. "I've had enough. They are cat and mouse. It's disgusting the wayward paths their passions ply. This is why I stay on campus, but he still won't let me anymore. I am not a child!"

Trevor walked into the living room and glared at the two young men. "We are going to war."

Cole gasped. "You and Nan?"

Trevor snapped. "Don't be daft."

"America," Johnny mumbled. "I got the news last night."

Cole shot to his feet from the couch where he had lazily lounged and assessed his father's love-life. "Finally." He frowned. "So, what got them out of their heads to decide?"

Johnny sighed. "The south attacked. We have no choice."

"Well-said. I need to get to the store immediately." Trevor headed for the door. "Are you men coming?"

Johnny stood. Cole shook his head.

Trevor made to speak, but instead took his coat and hat and slammed the door behind him.

Johnny smirked. "You do not cease to amaze me, Cole."

"He is in this just for the money," Cole cursed. "He doesn't think I'm going to go to war, does he?"

Johnny shook his head and went out the door as well. He'd been at Trevor's beck and call since he returned home but made progress with his plan, which was most important. He could return to college as soon as the fall if the war would not stop him.

He knew it would.

The battle of Logan's Cross Roads was Johnny's last. Trevor, heavy into the arms supplies got Cole to work as his assistant, and hence not enrolled. Otherwise, it seemed every young man in the northern side of America went to the war of the rebellion. At least, those he knew. It perplexed Johnny to return to Kentucky for the first time to fight, after all of his troubles and escape with Elisa. But this war had gone too far to be sentimental. Friends he knew from college wore the enemy's uniform and died by his side. The whole war had begun to have no meaning to him, even though it hadn't lasted even a year.

Johnny's brigade marched a long distance in the rain to get to the cross roads. He didn't care much about staying alive except to achieve his goal of becoming a lawyer and a senator so he could through American might propose laws that would frustrate the country called Liberia. Over the months, his desire to save had turned sour and now all he just wanted was to punish the African country that stole his wife.

After waiting two days, there was finally some combat. He knew he was tired before the battle began, but the feisty attack on his army and adrenaline kept him going. As night approached, confusion mounted. He feared he would kill someone in his army, or he'd get killed himself.

There was nothing brave about hitting the enemy in the face, but Johnny soon recognized a general in the enemies' camp and swung his musket at him. He should have shot the man if he wasn't suddenly so close. With darkness and smoke from the guns blinding him and causing him to choke, he realized his nose was about to bleed. He swung his gun again forcing the general to side-step or get hit on the head. Stepping aside however, put the enemy in the direct line of fire of his brigade. A gunshot rang and the leader fell. For a moment, Johnny and all the soldiers stopped. But then combat resumed. Three soldiers aimed at him, but his troops were more, and the fierce battle had the enemy retreat.

His brigade, joined by three others, pushed hard until the Southern soldiers retreated. It couldn't have been a worse coincidence when one of the other soldiers took aim at a fleeing enemy. Johnny had seen the young man earlier when the battle was tilted in the opposition's favor, and he had hoped his old friend did not see him. Gilbert. It was bad enough he had to return home only in war, he could not watch someone he knew get killed fleeing. He threw himself in the line of the fire sideways and took the bullets meant for his friend.

The last thought in Johnny's mind was that Gilbert Goodling would never know what he did for him, and would never thank him, but he had absolved himself.

Chapter Fifty-Four

A soft but frantic knock on the door got Elisa to open it without asking who. She lived in a safe complex. She stepped back, shocked when a trembling Beth stood at her doorstep, half of her face swollen and her lip split and bleeding. Elisa's first instinct was for her daughter.

"Mary! Take Jane inside," she yelled.

Mary who had been playing numbers with the toddler Jane picked up the toddler and the bag of white stones they counted and hurried inside.

"Miz Beth? Why are you here?"

Elisa hadn't seen the older woman in years, which was good for everyone. She didn't care for what the woman did, and she believed the feeling was mutual.

Beth did not say a word but Pizzi stepped up from beside her and in Elisa's full view. Fear gripped Elisa's heart and she made to close the door but Pizzi put his foot forward and pushed Beth into Elisa, forcing the younger woman back. Elisa stumbled but got a grip of herself before she fell.

"So, this is where you were hiding all these years? Sheltered by whites who love to keep you as their slave." He sneered. "And the black stooge they use to cover up their evil! Well, I have come to take you home." Pizzi pushed Beth further, and the woman fell with a thud.

Elisa screeched.

"Pack your things. You're going with me." He took hold of Elisa's hair. "You are mine."

Elisa wished she had a man living with her. Richard had tried several times to move her to his house, marry her, but she continued to hesitate. She liked him a lot better than when they met, but the freedom she enjoyed being her own woman for the first time in her life, hindered her from making the decision. Her sewing and hairdressing businesses had taken off so well, she now had a training school for young women. She could well survive on her own. And she had more than enough money to return to America if she wished, though with the war going on, she couldn't. Besides, she considered Jane. Being a single mother with a colored child got her more sympathy from the whites than she expected, and Jane was such an adorable child. Becoming Richard's wife, she felt, would affect Jane's growth, she just wasn't sure how yet.

Pizzi pushed her toward the inner room and she resisted. She couldn't let him take her. It seemed he was alone, none of his men with him, but she couldn't conclude. They could be out in the street waiting. Her house was in an exclusive government reserved area, and none of the locals had access. Why was Pizzi here? Elisa could imagine the security granted Beth access because of her recent involvement with the movement. She had heard the older woman had finally learned some hard lessons in the hands of the locals and wanted to align herself with Richard's group. Elisa had shown no interest because of her inability to trust Beth yet. Now this. Leading Pizzi to her home was perhaps the biggest betrayal yet.

Elisa screamed. "Why did you bring him here you wicked old woman! I knew you couldn't be trusted but Richard wants to include everyone!"

Pizzi twisted her locks. "Shut up!"

If only Richard would decide to pay her one of his surprise visits.

"No. Please. No!" She turned, hoping to get a release but his fist had a firm hold on her hair. "Please!"

He opened the inner door and found Mary and Jane crouching in a corner.

Pizzi laughed. "Stand up, carry everything. You are leaving here."

Mary sobbed and carried Jane, whose large blue eyes widened when they connected with Elisa's.

"Mammy!" Jane screamed and tried to free herself from Mary.

"Stay with Mary." Elisa sobbed and looked away. She needed to do something. "Pizzi, I will come to you, please. Just don't take my child."

"Shut up!" Pizzi snarled in his characteristic manner. "If I didn't finally get that stupid old woman, I will never find you."

"I'm sorry I ran away from you, but please, if you take me from here, they will come and find you." She sniffed, "Why do you still want me after all this time?"

"Who? That idiot Richard who thinks he has the government behind him? Are you so foolish?" Pizzi pushed her into her room. "In fact, why would I not want my wife. It's been so long."

He used one hand to push at his trouser. Elisa could not imagine this happening. She would die first. She struggled and screamed with all her strength and Mary ran in with Jane, both wailing.

"No, go. Mary! Run, leave!"

But Mary dropped Jane, took a wooden stool and raised it to hit Pizzi. Before she could, the man threw a punch and it hit her square on her eye. Mary fell back screaming, and tumbled Jane out. Pizzi kicked her in the side, effectively pushing her out as well, and slammed the door behind her. His solid grip on Elisa's hair made her dizzy and no matter how she tried to grasp at him, she couldn't.

With the door shut, Pizzi pushed her hard on to the bed and tore off his trousers. She had never seen anything so vicious. She rolled but he caught her by her long hair again and this time, dealt her a blinding slap. Elisa decided to let him have his way, rather than get beaten and then raped.

The door opened again, and Elisa didn't even bother to open her tightly shut eyes. Whoever would get what they had coming. If the newcomer had come to save her, she wished them luck. If it was Mary or Jane...she couldn't bear the thought.

"Let 'er go!" Beth shouted with a husky voice.

Elisa's eyes popped open when she heard a sound like the breaking of coconut. It seemed Pizzi had broken the old woman's skull somehow. She sat up and saw Beth's body slide down against the wall with a splash of blood. She screamed. Through the now open door, Jane stood in the middle of the hallway, crying. Pizzi stood panting over Beth.

Without any sane thought, Elisa dashed toward Jane and snatched her up. Mary was nowhere in sight.

"We are leaving." Pizzi rushed after her and grabbed her arm with one hand while gripping his torn trouser with the other. "Now!"

She didn't care as long as Jane was with her. Pizzi kicked her front door open and stepped into the street. Two of his men approached him and he shouted orders at them in his local language. Another man who stood afar shouted suddenly and took off running. A gunshot rang out followed by horse hooves approaching and the man fell. Pizzi let go of Elisa and dove to the side of the house.

A man jumped off a horse before it stopped and ran to her.

"Elisa!"

"Richard," she breathed. "Oh-oh."

"Mary came to inform us. We came as soon as we could." He wrapped his arm around her Jane, and led her back inside. "Are you alright?"

"He killed Miz Beth. Inside," she sobbed. "I can't stay here. I can't go inside. Please."

Richard cooed. "It's okay. You can come to my house later, but now you need to stay here. The streets are not safe right now."

Elisa gasped. "Why?"

"Pizzi has his gang firing at the police." He led her to a seat. "Wait for me to return."

"Don't leave, please!"

But he was gone.

Gunshots rang out through the night in the neighborhood. Elisa hid with Jane under the bed in Mary's room until morning when Richard returned to assist her to move. The only way she got through the night was to shut the events of the evening out and to pretend Beth's cooling body was not in the next room, her bedroom.

When Richard came for them, she told him she'd rather return to Dr. Obed's house temporarily and stay with Marge where she felt more secure. Mary had to find short-term accommodation at the government center because the doctor could give only a room. In the evening, Richard returned to give an update. It wasn't pretty. They entertained him in the living room.

"A policeman was killed today when they went to arrest Pizzi. He resisted and became aggressive." Richard shrugged. "He has guns. Nobody knew."

"I always knew those local people would rebel one day." Dr. Obed took his glasses off and cleaned it absently. "There was always the anger against the emancipation."

"Which I don't understand." Marge gushed. "Some of their old people were the ones who sold off their sons and daughters for bottles of gin."

Dr. Obed grunted. "Some still do in other parts of this continent. The emancipation is fighting hard against this."

"Part of their problem is guilt." Richard rubbed his forehead. "But this new aggression has to be quelled."

"I just don't know why Miz Beth brought him to my house," Elisa sniffed. "He tried to rape me. And Mary left my baby and ran away."

Richard walked over and patted her back. "Don't think like that. Mary panicked. And she came to call us. She would not have been able to reach help so fast if she had Jane with her. And Beth..." He sighed. "Beth had been entangled with them too long. She thought making friends with Pizzi would establish her as a local."

Dr. Obed shook his head. "I don't think that can happen in a hundred years."

Chapter Fifty-Five

Margibi walked into Elisa's cabin after a soft knock. Jane played on the bed with cloth-dolls her mother made for her, and Elisa out of habit snatched her up and held her in her arms at the sound of someone on the other side of the door. The toddler struggled out of her hold, moaning, "Mammy!"

"I'm sorry, she–"

"Don't apologize, Elisa." Margibi clasped his hands. "Dr. Obed told me you decided to leave. And the captain let me come in to say goodbye."

Elisa sighed. "I... he told me you were coming."

Margibi stared for a second at Jane's wriggling frame as she continued to seek freedom. "She's so beautiful. She reminds me of Johnny."

"Very restless like him too." Her voice hitched. "Would never take no for an answer." Elisa let her go and she rushed back to her dolls with a squeal.

"You have done so well with her, Elisa. I pray you find Johnny and your family can be together again." Margibi heaved a heavy sigh. "So, what are your plans? With the war, you can't get into America."

"Miz Marge made plans for me to stay in Europe for a brief period. Hopefully a couple months and the war will end." She shuddered. "I just can't live here anymore."

"I understand that, Elisa. More than you can believe me." Margibi frowned. "The emancipation is a good plan, but we as a people are not ready for it."

"With Pizzi still at large, I can never feel safe." She shuddered. "I still don't know why he came after me."

"He knew how important you were to the movement. Everyone saw how successful your training school was in just such a short time," Margibi said. "Malice, jealousy? And just plain evil."

"Well, was that not a good thing for me to do for the society? To have local children trained free?" She moaned, "His concubines and children all came in without a charge."

"Evil people don't want good for the society. Even if it is for their gain," Margibi sighed. "But the most important reason I believe, is that he was in trouble and he figured getting you will give him advantage. You will be his bargaining power. His criminal structures had cracks and the law was upon him."

"And I would be his pawn."

"Besides, Beth had been talking a lot with Richard who had always wanted to rehabilitate the old woman," Margibi said. "For reasons best known to him, he could not let Beth go."

"And he's got her killed," Elisa snapped. "I never could understand why Richard was so keen on her."

"Richard has a heart for his people." Margibi raised an eyebrow. "I understand, well, Dr. Obed told me you rejected a marriage offer?"

"To Richard Alvin Allen." She smirked, "I don't love him."

"You don't need to explain yourself, Elisa dear. You have done what you think is best for you and your daughter." He heaved. "I have to get back." He dipped his hand in his pocket.

"Gibe told me you love collecting the beautiful white stones, and he went in search of some for you from your stream."

He removed a small pouch full of the beautiful stones in different shapes and sizes and Elisa smiled for the first time since Margibi walked in.

"Oh! They are so many."

Margibi chuckled. "Yes, he said he spent the whole day searching. Even went further downstream."

Elisa collected it. "Please thank him for me."

"I will. He also wishes you the best of luck."

"Thank you."

"I must return now." Margibi turned, his voice emotion-laden. "Stay well, Elisa."

"Margibi." Elisa stopped him. "Why did you tear up my letters?"

He turned to face her. "Tear up your letters? I did not. You stopped writing them."

"Then what did you do to the ones I gave you?"

He swallowed. "I confess I didn't send them every week because I was not sure why you wrote them, but I sent them later. To Johnny in Europe."

"Oh." She didn't expect to hear this. "Well, thank you. I thought...I'm sorry." Her throat clogged. "Thank you, for everything."

"The captain of this ship is a friend. Please write and let me know if you find Johnny. And if you are safe. Okay? If you get the letter to the harbor to him, it will get to me."

Elisa nodded. "I will."

He walked out without another word, and she sank on to the bed beside Jane. Johnny got her letters, or at least, they were sent. She felt a sudden emptiness. She had not written in over two years, consumed by her work, and Richard's relationship. She would feel she was cheating on Johnny, pick up her pen and then push it away. She covered her face and cried softly.

The country was more beautiful than anything Elisa had ever seen before. It was spring and the flowers blossomed, the air fresh and sweet. Men and women holding hands, of different races and religions, filled the streets. There was laughter in the air and as the carriage which took her and Jane wound its way through the streets, Jane laughed and jumped, making it hard for her to control.

Elisa wrote a letter for Margibi on the ship and gave it to the captain, with a promise that she'd write again when she was settled. America was still at war, and unpredictably scary the war didn't seem anywhere near coming to an end. Analysts of both sides had thought it would be a quick war that would end within months, but running to two years already, there were speculations no end was in sight. At some point, Elisa had feared she made a mistake, but she didn't think she was safer in Liberia than in Europe. At least, here, there was no one particularly interested in whether she was white or black, slave or freed. She had been issued travel documents that allowed her to visit Europe, and with Marge's contacts, promised one that would allow her to set up her business again.

Contrary to the way she traveled to Liberia with Johnny, from Creek View to Pennsylvania, to New York and Canada before going to her "supposed" homeland, she had a lot of luggage. Two full portmanteaus contained her and Jane's personal items. She also had several hundred yards of fabrics specially woven by the locals in Africa along with other cotton materials. She had her a new sewing machine with her, which gave her a great advantage to set up her business.

Lord William, her host, received her in his grand country home outside of London. A uniformed maid, who couldn't be any older than her, took her to her room with large windows that overlooked a pond. The scenery reminded her of Creek View and her farm in Liberia, though nothing so grand. The bed was huge like she had never seen before and the draping were of blue and purple. Elisa looked at everything with her jaws dropping.

"Madam, your daughter will use the next room." The maid reached out to take Jane from her.

Elisa shook her head. "No, this bed is bigger than what we need."

"Lord William will protest, Madam."

"She's still a baby."

The maid sighed. "I will ask the butler to have a small bed moved in for her. Is this better, Madam?"

Elisa knew Jane would have a hard time sleeping in it. She hated to admit she had spoilt Jane by having her sleep in her arms out of fear.

She nodded. "That will be a very kind gesture. Thank you."

"Yes, Madam." The maid opened the curtains and more light came in. Then she opened the wardrobe and started to arrange Elisa's clothes.

"Um, please, I will take care of this myself. Thank you."

Maid hesitated. "I will be very delighted to do this."

"No but thank you."

The maid straightened. "If you need anything, please use the bell pull at the head of the bedchamber, and I will come to you."

"Very kind of you. Please, what's your name?"

"Fanny, Madam."

"Fanny. Thank you very much for your help." Elisa smiled. "And when do you think Lord William will be home? I will like to thank him too."

"At dinner time, Madam."

"Okay, thank you, Fanny. I don't believe I need anything until dinner time." Elisa giggled nervously. "Please come and get me. I may not be able to find my way."

Fanny smiled, nodded and exited.

Elisa yelped and Jane copied the sound and struggled to drop from her mother's arms. "No, no, Jane. You will behave yourself."

But Elisa wanted so badly to drop on the inviting bed, and she did, and her daughter rolled over her, squealing. The silkiness of the fabric enveloped her, and she sighed.

For the first time since the beginning of the journey, she felt she had done the right thing.

Chapter Fifty-Six

Lord William lived alone after he lost his wife in a riding accident. With his only daughter living in the city, Elisa found she would often be alone in the baron's grand country home with the servants and Jane. She loved it. Jane enjoyed running freely in the garden and kept Fanny busier than all expected. She was only turning three, but could talk and play like a six-year-old.

The spring air helped Elisa to conceive great ideas for her work. Because she did not have any clients, she decided to make beautiful dresses for the maids, and a couple villagers at no cost to them. Though Lord William had business with his lands and in the king's court daily, and his private medical practice, he made sure he got home in time for dinner, and he would make small talk with Elisa. When the first set of four dresses were ready, Elisa presented them to Fanny, who was more than delighted to deliver them to the owners. Elisa decided to give herself a few days to rest and sketch her next designs since she had brought so many yards of beautiful fabrics with her from Africa.

Over dinner in the evening, the three maids she made dresses for, and a woman from the village all came in to thank her in the presence of Lord William, wearing their fancy dresses.

"I can't believe this, Elisa. I was never told you make such gorgeous outfits." Lord William clapped. "We must host a grand opening for you. Madam Elisa, an American dressmaker in London."

Elisa giggled. "That will expose all my flaws, Lord William."

"So says the best dressmaker in all of Europe." He pointed at the blushing maids. "And behold your models."

Lord William had Elisa meet an elderly woman who had been a successful dressmaker, and a new type of training ensued. The older woman taught Elisa manners, how to speak, and behave in civilized society. Soon, Fanny became Jane's nanny, and this gave Elisa much more time to devote to her training and her work.

One day, as she told Lord William exciting news about her just-concluded training over dinner, he narrowed his eyes.

"I have been thinking about all of this," Lord William said. "An American Dressmaker in London is beautiful but when they see you, they may snub you. And I don't mean any offense, Elisa."

"I don't understand, Lord William, sir."

"You are black and American. It means you are a slave who is being emancipated. And no matter how long we argue, that is the stereotype society will place you in."

Elisa bowed her head. "You are right, sir."

"But we can change that." He took a noisy sip of his French wine and stared at the glass.

Elisa raised her head. "How?"

"A French Dressmaker in London? France has a great number of influential black people."

Elisa gasped. "I would need to speak the language."

"And you will," Lord William laughed. "You will be great, my dear."

"Thank you, Lord William. I will love to learn French."

"You may not even want to go to America anymore, Madame Elisa." He stood. "When you become the pride of society and speak English with a French slur, America will worship you when they are finished with their war."

Elisa thought she did want to go back to America.

Dear Johnny,

How are you? Are you still alive?

It gets harder to write my letters unsure of what is happening to you. The war seems to go on forever and Lord William thinks it will never end. Each time he mentions it, I am tempted to argue with him to change his mind. Is there still any hope for us? Do you remember me?

Jane is a very big girl, now. She turned four some weeks ago and speaks like true English. I wish I had her accent. But what I am learning now is the French language and accent.

I have made some progress. Lord William has been very kind to me. He says we are hosting the first dressmaking show this year. He just wants everything to be done right. I have many beautiful ideas for dresses and undergarments. I made some I can't wait to wear for you. I feel shy talking about them - the undergarments, I mean. Fanny wore one for me and told me to do a private showing for women alone. I hope Lord William will let me. Though, I think proper ladies will find it too exposing.

I will pray a lot more for God to save America. But if you can leave, please do. Come to Europe. We will have a good life here. Better than anywhere else.

God bless you, Johnny Holt.

I love you.

Your wife,

Elisa Johnny Holt

Chapter Fifty-Seven

In preparation for the party showcasing of Elisa's dresses, Lord William decided to take her out for some end-of-summer parties. There he planned to present her to society. She had learned to speak French and could be mistaken for a Frenchwoman so easily; she was proud of herself. The parties made her realize Lord William was not only a rich noble, he was a respected one. Being on his arm gave her a superiority she couldn't imagine existed.

Murmurs at some of the parties portrayed her as French royalty, a bastard born to the king by a black woman and sent to London society to cover up the scandal. Elisa couldn't imagine anyone would believe such a farce but going by the way she was invited to garden tea parties afterward, she realized some believed it.

As a smart business woman, she steered every conversation toward the dresses she made, which she wore. She even hinted at the underclothing, which she convinced her company were worn by fashion-forward French women. Elisa's stories of how men gave up their mistresses after their wives wore her undergarments elicited so much interest, Lord William permitted a private exhibition for the women, based on requests.

At the private showing, she sold all she had made and received orders to last a year. And so she launched her line of undergarments she called "Voque."

At the start of fall, and as the summer parties ended, Elisa organized an exclusive showing of her scanty undergarments, which defied anything anyone could imagine. One of the ladies in attendance, who was betrothed to the "spare" prince, exclaimed when Fanny walked out in the daring lingerie.

Afterward, she approached Elisa. "Madame Elize Voque? I would plead with you to take these sinful undergarments away from England."

Elisa shared the joke with Lord William over dinner. "But I sold out all the ones I have. Her distinguished mother ordered a full set of ten toward her wedding!"

Lord William laughed. "That is very interesting. You have done well, my dear. You are going to be very rich."

"Thank you, Lord William. You gave all of this to me. I don't know why I deserve it."

"You deserve to be happy. And you are very talented," he smiled. "Marge spoke highly of you in her letter and I am not disappointed."

Elisa swallowed, caught in the emotion of the moment. "Thank you, sir."

"Madame Elize Voque?"

Elisa laughed. "I was shocked when she referred to me so."

"Well, that is your new name, Elisa."

The Elize Voque Fashion Show became the talk of society for several weeks before and after the event. Elisa spoke with local dressmakers who wanted to leverage on the platform she had, and Lord William advised her to charge a small fee for it. This helped to reduce the number of requests to reflect class, which was the main point of the whole event. Royals would be in attendance and the quality of work had to indicate this.

Special guests were invited to a feast after the show. Elisa moved through the tables ensuring everyone was comfortable. Overwhelmed by all of the excitement of the night, she stepped into the garden for a moment and saw a shadow behind her. She startled and turned.

"Elisa!"

For a minute, she didn't recognize the man in his heavy fashionable outfit, then he spoke French.

"Henri." She clasped her hand over her mouth. "I never imagined you were here!"

"I fought my way into getting an invitation," he exclaimed. "Your name did not...I did not imagine it was you." He heaved. "As soon as I saw you, though...you're even more beautiful than you have ever been."

"Henri, it's so good to see you." Her heart thudded. "When did you arrive London?"

"I came to do some exhibitions. I've been here for two years. It's tough to get the right crowd." He looked back into the hall. "You've done well for yourself, Elisa. Unbelievable."

There was an awkward silence and she knew what he was thinking, probably because she was thinking of the same.

"Johnny, did he pass on?"

Elisa did not know the mention of Johnny would make her feel so upset, and tears sprang to her eyes. Henri took her reaction for confirmation.

"I'm sorry, Elisa. He was such a great man. He will be very proud of you."

"Elize!" Lord William called. "There you are. I need you to meet someone."

Elisa straightened. "I have to go."

"Please find me. At the royal art gallery in Piccadilly!" Henri called as she hurried away.

Elisa still felt shaken by the meeting with Henri, but she smiled at Lord William. "I'm sorry, I just wanted to take a breath."

"Cynthia is here," Lord William said with a glint in his eyes. "I did not expect her. She's been so removed from society and everything since–" He swallowed. "I told you she was heartbroken by an American gentleman."

"Oh yes, you did. So kind of her to attend tonight."

Cynthia had long brown hair brushed all the way down to her hip, and wore a long peasant gown, most unsuitable for such an occasion. Beside her was the handsome Viscount Gabriel Elisa had had the pleasure of meeting earlier, and for a moment, she wondered why he would even give Cynthia a second look. Cynthia was beautiful though, and Elisa was taken by her blue eyes.

Lord William made the introductions.

"I am so pleased to meet you, Mademoiselle Cynthia," Elisa smiled. "Lord William talks about you at least ten times a day."

Cynthia's eyes could freeze hell. "He never mentions you."

Elisa was taken aback by this hostility. "That's because he spends the whole time talking about you."

Cynthia's unfriendliness made no sense to Elisa. The viscount broke the ice.

"Come with me, Cynthia. I want you to meet Princess Amanda. The Queen Mother's sister."

Cynthia frowned. "Boring. So boring."

Gabriel led her away. Lord William shook his head. "The viscount has proposed to her six times. She won't marry him."

"I'll be praying for her."

"She needs it." Lord William clapped. "Now, continue to enjoy yourself and don't allow Cynthia to mar this beautiful evening."

Out of character, Elisa hugged Lord William. He placed a chaste kiss on her cheek but when they separated, Cynthia was right there behind him, her cold eyes on her.

Elisa smiled shakily at the baron. "Don't mind me." And walked quickly away to find other guests.

Chapter Fifty-Eight

After the last guest left, Elisa stood in the hall, smiling to herself. She had officially stepped into London high society. Lord William had made her into an important personality. She thought of the two young girls who helped with her work now. She needed to get a showroom in the city. The baron had told her it would soon happen and now she could envision it, a hall full of sewing machines, and girls working and learning under her.

All the years she spent growing and experimenting would now be actualized. Her training school resuscitated, but this time not for confused and under-privileged young women, but society's best who would serve kings and queens, princes and princesses. She thanked God she did not despise Nan's tutelage.

She heard footsteps behind her and turned.

Cynthia stood in the long peasant dress she wore to the party, a shawl flung across her shoulder, barefooted, her deep blue eyes icy. In her hand, she held a pile of sheets, tied with a brown string.

For several seconds, she said nothing.

Elisa took a step forward. "Thank you for coming to the show."

Cynthia reached out with the bundle in her hand. "You are no longer welcome here," she said slowly. "Take the letters you sent to Johnny. And leave my country."

Her words hit Elisa in the bottom of her stomach. It took several seconds for the words to come together. "Which Johnny?"

"You cannot have my father and my man. You took one from me, I won't let you take the other. Go back to where you came from."

Elisa opened her mouth to speak, but Cynthia continued to talk as though she was speaking to a wall.

"If you do not leave, I will kill your child. I will destroy you–"

"Please," Elisa cried. "Stop. I don't know what you speak of."

"You do! You witch." Cynthia's lips hardly moved. She did not blink either. "Take your letters. I kept them from Johnny, but you still twisted his mind."

Elisa's lips trembled. "You are...my... Johnny was the American who broke your heart."

"And you have come to steal my father too. I won't let you."

"I'm sorry Johnny broke your heart." Tears slipped down Elisa's cheeks. "But I don't want to steal your father."

"You do. He told me he plans to propose to you. I won't let you have him too."

Elisa swallowed hard. "I won't accept the proposal if–"

Cynthia flung the letters at her and screamed. "Take your letters and go where you came from!"

Elisa picked the bundle that dropped less than half a yard away from her. She hugged it and wept. Her hopes dashed. Johnny had never heard from her all these years. Hatred roiled her stomach and she wanted to fight Cynthia, but she held back. She needed this woman who had loved Johnny when she was nowhere in sight. She needed her father more.

Elisa hiccupped. "I have worked very hard to be where I am today. Please, don't take it away from me."

"You took Johnny from me!" She held a squashed piece of paper in her hand and now held it up to Elisa. "It's your fault. It's because of you he left me! Because of you! He wrote it in his letter to me. You! Elisa!" She shrieked. "I hate you!"

Lord William hurried into the hall wearing only his night garments. "Cynthia."

Cynthia burst into tears. "She took Johnny from me, and now she wants to take you."

Elisa sobbed. "It's not true."

"She has to go, Father. Choose." Her blue eyes lit up bright like party lights. "Choose between her and me."

"Cynthia, you are not well. Go back into your room. I will–"

"No, Father! Choose now. Now!" She stomped her feet. "Now, Father. I will kill her child. The bastard she wants to make yours."

Lord William hugged Cynthia. "I choose you. I will always choose you."

Elisa ran from the room.

All the rooms on the second floor of the castle had been converted to workrooms in preparation for the fashion show. Four rooms altogether had dresses and undergarments in different fashionable designs and colors laid out and hung. Elisa's bedroom was just one of the rooms, and Jane lay on her cot, fast asleep.

She leaned over her and smoothed her daughter's tangled curly hair back. "I always choose you too, Jane. I will never let any harm come to you." She sobbed for a few seconds, then straightened.

She needed to make plans to leave. She had a lot of money but wasn't sure what a store or salon would cost her. She had never had to pay for her own space, but it seemed she had to do so now. There was a lot to do. A lot of packing and arranging. She probably could find a cheap place in the village, but the villagers would not want to wear her dresses. They were too fancy and expensive. The city made her feel intimidated. All the times she visited, she had been invited as a distinguished guest and conveyed with Lord William's beautiful carriage.

How would she survive on her own? The huge buildings and narrow streets with throngs going up and down scared her. She walked to her wardrobe and looked in at how filled it was. She couldn't take all of this with her. Where would she get enough space to keep them? She'd have to give most away to Fanny and the other maids, and the village women. What they did with such beautiful gowns was none of her business. It took her to the thought of living again without servants waiting on her hand and foot.

Lord William's hospitality had spoiled her.

Elisa placed the bundle of letters Cynthia flung at her on her dresser and stared at them. Now, she had her two sets of letters with her. She would never destroy them. They were evidence of her undying love for Johnny and how much she regretted ever falling for Pizzi's threat. She should have run to Gibe or Margibi or Dr. Obed for help. She could be in Liberia now, having a second or third baby for Johnny instead of being here, and despite her success in sewing, facing a downturn she had no idea how to handle.

Someone knocked on the door and her heart skipped. "Who is it?"

He cleared his throat. "Lord William."

Elisa dragged in a shuddering breath and went to open the door. The baron never entered her room. Once he'd visited one of her other rooms to look at her gowns, but nothing more. She opened the door and stepped back but didn't walk away from it. Lord William pulled the door shut.

"She's back in her bed." He sighed. "She's not well, Elisa, please understand that."

"She'll kill Jane, and I will never forgive myself, and all she will get is to be sent to an asylum." Elisa hugged her sides. "I can never live with that."

"I want you, Elisa. Don't leave."

She shook her head. "No. You chose Cynthia."

Lord William snickered. "Come on, my dear. She is ill."

"I choose Jane too. I have to protect her."

Chapter Fifty-Nine

Elisa didn't sleep all night. After Lord William assured her she could stay, she decided on two things. Stay. But plan on how to do so without inciting Cynthia or endangering Jane.

In the morning, Fanny called in to take care of Jane.

"Lord William wants to go to the village today to sit with the people," Fanny gushed. "I thought it'd be good to take Jane along to–"

Elisa snapped, "No!"

Fanny jumped. "I'm sorry. I thought the weather was beautiful and she would like the countryside." She held Jane who grabbed her favorite doll and walked toward the exit. "I will only serve her breakfast and walk in the garden."

After Fanny left, Elisa paced. She needed to get her emotions together and think. Think. This was the dawn of success in her business, but it was all hinged on her connection with the baron. If she left, she would be back to zero. She might as well need to leave London. With her fluency in French, could she go to that country? But she knew no one there. Her head ached, from her lack of sleep and fear. Besides, Lord William had issued a subtle threat the night before.

"Things can get really rough for you, Elisa, all alone. If you leave me."

He didn't emphasize a deeper relationship as Cynthia insinuated or as spoken in his, *"I want you..."* statement. But Elisa could not bank on this. What would be her fate? She was so afraid to step out. She had never been on her own. There were her parents, then Johnny. Even Pizzi provided some form of safety, howbeit, abusive. Then Marge and Dr. Obed, later Richard, and now Lord William.

Jane walked in with Fanny, dressed and ready for the day. The maid quietly picked up her dolls and playthings and, made to leave.

"Fanny?"

"Yes, Madam?"

Elisa took in a deep breath. "I'm sorry I snapped."

"It's alright, Madam." Fanny smiled. "After breakfast, Jane and I will visit the stables and–"

"I'm sorry, Fanny." Elisa rubbed her temple. "I'd prefer if you just bring her back here and stay with her."

Jane yelled. "No, Mammy! I want to play in the stable."

Elisa rolled her eyes. "I'm so confused." She covered her face with both hands.

"Is everything alright, Madam?"

What did it matter, she thought? Fanny was the closest to a friend and a sister. And she needed to talk to someone. Elisa struggled to keep tears at bay as she restated everything that happened the night before. When she was done, she drew in a quivering breath and asked Fanny's opinion.

Fanny gasped. "I'm sorry, Madam. You...Lady Cynthia has been very ill." She paused. "But can she harm anyone, and indeed, little Jane?"

"That's why I'm so afraid. But Lord William will be offended if I leave." A tear slipped through her eyes and she swatted it off. "What do I do, dear Lord?"

Fanny uncharacteristically clasped Elisa's hands. "I can go into the city. Give me some money to buy some lace. I will come back to you with information."

Elisa blinked. "Information?"

"Yes, Madam. On what you can do with your business. On your own, in the city!"

"Oh." Elisa frowned, unsure. "Thank you. I will care for Jane while you are away."

Cynthia stayed in her room all through the day, but Elisa didn't know this because she was too afraid to leave hers until Fanny returned and gave her the news. Panting and excited, she laid out pieces of lace on the bed, set in line with their bold colors of red, purple, orange and yellow. There were several pieces of white and black too.

Elisa exclaimed, "No lady will buy a red undergarment!"

"I could only learn anything from the shops that sold them." Fanny smiled. "And I learned a lot."

Elisa sighed, her heart thudding. "Please, can you get Jane a snack? I was too confused about staying in the room because I didn't want to be seen. So, she's had only a roll all day."

Fanny nodded and hurried off. She returned shortly with a tray of food. "I reckoned you didn't eat too, Madam."

She placed the tray on the dresser and took some to Jane who was busy arranging more than ten dolls in a row on her bed and giving them instructions one by one.

"I can't eat, Fanny," Elisa sighed. "What did you learn?"

"You can get a small store in the East End. I found out about that." Fanny clasped her hands. "I just got to know in the kitchen now the Lord of the Manor will be going away for a while."

Elisa rolled her eyes. "How will I survive with a store? I have never–" She covered her face and sniffed. "Where is the East End? How will I set up? Who will patronize me?"

"We can move a little at a time."

Elisa's head shot up. "No. I can't." She sobbed, "I can't."

Chapter Sixty

The East End was not a place she thought she could survive. First off, her fancy gown drew attention and soon she saw the dirty, little street waifs lurking around her. Fanny walked freely ahead, and Elisa had a hard time keeping up with her. One child attempted to snatch her small pouch, though she clutched it to her chest. When they arrived at their destination, Fanny knocked on the door.

"Let's leave here, now. Please," Elisa snapped. "Now."

Fanny gasped and nodded. She continued to walk down the street, though the door she knocked on opened. Elisa followed quickly. They found a coach, and Elisa asked the driver to leave the area as fast as he could.

The coach driver slurred. "Where do we head to, Miss?"

"To–"

"Anywhere but home, Fanny. Anywhere."

Fanny swallowed. "The...to Trafalgar Square."

The jolly carriage driver whistled. "Trafalgar Square, we go!"

Elisa's head pounded. This was the pressure she felt when Pizzi asked her to leave Johnny and threatened to kill him. She always made the wrong decision when under pressure and she feared she would make mistakes again. Something would go wrong and this time, her fate would be sealed. Maybe she would be returned to slavery or Jane would die. She didn't know what, but her premonition pushed her toward a cliff-end. Her end.

"Where is this?"

Fanny lowered her voice. "A lot of traders meet there. We may see someone who has a store to give in a better area."

Elisa nodded. "Oh."

Trafalgar square was a huge open space and many people milled about. Some sat in clusters and spoke to one another, almost as though they were oblivious of their surroundings. Some strolled about, their faces happy.

The coach stopped, and Elisa paid the fare.

Elisa regarded the environment. "How do we know who to speak with?"

Fanny's eyes widened. "Look, look at the portrait." She pointed and Elisa followed her gaze. "Is that you, Madam?"

Elisa's mouth dropped open. Right beside one of the beautiful fountains, a man held a big poster and turned here and there so people could see on every side. It was one of the paintings she posed for with Henri Jean at his studio. He never showed her or Johnny the final portraits or the number of paintings. Some information was presented on the artwork inviting people to an exhibition. Fanny could not read, but that was her, quite surely, naked as a freshly born baby, her hands holding her hair up away from her face. The poster got little attention at close range but like her, people gawked from a safe distance.

"I loved a–slave," Elisa read out loud. "An exhibition of never-seen portraits of the elegant Madame Elize–Voque." Elisa turned her back.

Fanny agreed. "Let us leave, Madam. People are gathering."

They walked hurriedly away as the man with the poster began to call out and try to draw attention to himself. Elisa feared what would happen next. She had Jane to think about, and now this was no longer a decision between staying and leaving. Henri had sealed her fate. The artist had used her in the worst possible way, without her consent. If Lord William saw this, he would throw her out in a hurry.

She had to leave somehow. Anyhow.

Afraid someone would notice her, Elisa chose to leave the square through another direction and when they were safely at a side-street, she paused to catch her breath.

"I'm sorry to ask, Madam, but how did–when...who did–"

Elisa rolled her eyes. "I know who did this." She breathed hard. "Take me to–Piccadilly. Please."

It wasn't difficult to find Henri Jean in Piccadilly. The long busy street was lined with a lot of activity, but small posters much like the one they found at the square were pasted on any public space available with an address for where the tickets could be purchased. No date was set for the exhibition.

Henri used a small room in a pawn store and had told the owner he did not want to be disturbed, but the moment Elisa walked in, she knew she had been expected. The owner beamed and shouted to Henri.

The artist came out in work clothes, covered in paint. "The beautiful Madame Elize Voque! Welcome."

She could punch him in the face. If this was not important, she would not be here. Seeing him at her event had totally thrown her off and she had never intended to find him. They belonged to different societies now and she didn't think she owed him anything.

Elisa took calming breaths. "We need to talk."

"Of course," Henri spoke in French. "Come with me."

He led the two ladies into a small studio much like the one he used in New York, but so much smaller. As soon as they were inside, he turned to face Elisa, a big smile on his face. Overwhelmed by her anger, she slapped him, hard.

"You bastard," she spoke in Henri's language. "How could you do such a thing to me?"

Henri clasped his hand over his assaulted cheek. "If you hit me again, I will hit you back." Elisa raised her hand and would have, but he caught it just in time. "Stop it!"

"You have ruined me," she sobbed. "You have turned me into a woman of low morals."

"Your black skin and deceptive French heritage turned you into anything you call it." He dropped her hand as though it burned him. "You think decent ladies will buy your garments? With all those colors that provoke men?"

"Lord William will kick me out once he sees those portraits. Please, take them off the streets!"

"Why? I will make a lot of money. Your name is in the corridors of royalty. Such a scandal will get all of London talking about my art!"

Elisa breathed hard. She could kill him. She thought of coming at night to take the posters off but how many would she remove? How would she be able to know where they all were? She looked at Fanny, whose drawn eyebrows showed as much concern.

"How much?" Elisa sniffed. "How much will you take to remove all of them, please?"

Henri laughed. "Remove all of them?"

"I will pay a thousand pounds." Elisa cried. "Two thousand."

"From the night of the party, I have painted non-stop, making copies. They are all over the city."

"Lord William will be so embarrassed." Elisa trembled, ignoring the tears streaming down her face. "Please, help me. I have come such a long way to get here."

Fanny moved closer and held Elisa's side. "What's he saying, Madam?"

Elisa shook with her sobs and Fanny raised her voice at Henri. "You cannot do this to her!"

"I can, my dear mademoiselle. I have." He clasped his hands together. "It will make me a name in all of society. I will be a trusted, wanted artist!"

Elisa swallowed. "Let us leave, Fanny." She walked to the door and Fanny followed her.

"Elisa." Henri took a step toward her. "I have an idea."

She rolled her eyes and wanted to walk through the door and call his bluff, but she knew she may regret it forever.

"What?"

"Move here with me. We can make a lot of money together." Henri lowered his voice. "*Je t'aime, ma cherie.*"

CHAPTER SIXTY-ONE

With Cynthia still in the castle, Elisa kept Jane by her side and used this as an excuse to stay away from dinner, though Lord William continued to assure her Cynthia was just a little sick and would not carry out her threats. For a week, Elisa chose to stay away. Her solitude gave her the opportunity to think about her life because her continued inaction meant she was willing to accept her status, which was not predictable. The moment Lord William got to know about her nude portraits, she'd be finished.

One morning, the baron summoned her into his study. She was uncomfortable being alone with him. First, she feared he knew about the artwork and was about to send her away without warning. Then she thought of Cynthia's accusation of his profession of love. He hadn't said anything of it and she would hate to turn him down. He smiled when she walked in, and her stomach sank.

"Elisa, my dear."

"Good morning, sir."

"I wanted you to know I will be off on a visit of the countryside, on the King's assignment." He arched an eyebrow. "I know the past two weeks have been hard, but Cynthia will not harm you. Believe me."

"Thank you, Lord William." Elisa nodded. "Do you know when you will return?"

"A month. New territories will be surveyed. Negotiations." He sighed. "That takes time."

"I will be here when you return."

"Excellent. When I do, we will make new plans for your fashion house." Lord William beamed. "Now leave me to write some letters in preparation."

She smiled and nodded. With a small curtsy, she hurried back to her room. One more month to decide her own fate. She couldn't ask for more. With Henri bent on continuing with his treachery, she had no choice but to take a decision best for her and Jane. She didn't ask when the baron would leave on his journey, but he usually did the day he informed her. So, she spent the rest of the day by her window, watching for the departure.

It did not happen until early the following morning. The sound of the coach and horses neighing got her up from her bed and she discreetly watched a host assemble and then leave.

Shortly afterward, Fanny ran to her door and knocked several times. "Madam! Lady Cynthia leaves," she whispered harshly.

Elisa opened the door and she rushed in.

"Lady Cynthia leaves. She will move to her house on Oxford Street until Lord William returns."

Elisa lit up. That made a lot of sense to her. "Thank you for bringing this news to me."

"I thought you would want to know, since you don't want to encounter her in the hallway."

"Yes, thank you," Elisa sighed. "I can move about freely. When does she leave, do you know?"

"Right now." She hurried to the window. "See."

Elisa went to stand beside her just in time to see Cynthia get on a carriage. Her baggage was loaded in and the coach-driver pulled off.

"Makes me feel a lot better." Elisa looked at Fanny. "Thank you."

Fanny curtsied shyly. "I must finish up my morning chores before Jane awakes, Madam." She walked to the door.

"Fanny."

She turned. "Yes, Madam?"

"You have been my friend. Please call me Elisa."

Elisa knew she could not leave Lord William's castle unnoticed unless she did not take a horse, her daughter, and her wares, so she organized a meet-party at the Trafalgar Square to advertise her new styles for undergarments. Fanny told her it would infuriate Lord

William to learn of such a thing being done and especially in his absence, but there was no other way she could convince anyone to pack all her gowns and designs into carriages and drive to town. She knew she would never return once she left. Her plan was to escape without detection. It was a herculean task, but without anyone's knowledge she went to the harbor and booked a boarding for two, a nice private cabin cost a whole lot more than she imagined. But she could afford it.

Then she got a stall at the Square for a day and had all of her wares stored there in preparation for the show. On the night she planned to leave, Fanny put Jane to bed and instead of leaving, stood at the door and stared at Elisa who was preparing for bed as well. Lord William had been away for two weeks.

"Is there something you wanted, Fanny?"

When she did not respond, Elisa turned to her and saw there were tears in the maid's eyes.

"You're leaving, aren't you?"

Elisa smirked. "Leaving? To where, for goodness' sake?"

"I know. Something is not right. You can't want to have a show at the square. You. ..you don't have customers who come to the square as commoners." She heaved. "And your...the art is still on display."

Elisa shrugged. "Well, let's just say I want to be sure I get more customers." She giggled. "When the rich and royals tire of me or begin to hate my style, or discover I am a slave who ran away from her farm...I will have the commoners at my side."

Fanny sighed. "I thought it was better for you to leave too." She sniffed. "I will miss Jane."

Elisa pressed her lips together. She couldn't continue the lie. Yet, she could never admit to Fanny or anyone she had decided to run away. No doubt, when Lord William returned, he would have her locked up and beheaded for posing naked for a commercial artist. She deduced as much from the little talk that went around if one was caught in such an act. Henri had been showing off her nude paintings for several weeks now, doom only lurked and if she stayed, she would regret it. Not so much for her, but for Jane. Besides, a date for the exhibition had been set and it coincided with the baron's return.

"Where do you wish to go?" Fanny asked.

Elisa shrugged. "I don't know yet. America is still at war. I just bought a cabin on a ship."

Fanny nodded. "I will miss you."

Elisa hurried to her and hugged her. "I will miss you, Fanny."

The ship sailed across the Atlantic Ocean for several months. After the first few days the captain, a middle-aged European who had been on the water more than on land all his life, noticed Elisa dressed in a superior manner, and got warm with her. He could speak six European languages and Elisa enjoyed speaking French rather than English. During one of their discussions, he suggested that Elisa do a small exhibition on the ship for travelers. It turned out the gowns were sold out and only a few undergarments remained.

"Travelers don't like to spend, Elisa," Captain O'Connor told her afterward. "For you to have such great success, I think you are on to some kind of business now."

Elisa smiled. "Thank you very much, Captain. I got orders so I might need an extra space to sew."

The captain nodded. "When we berth in the next harbor, I will ensure we reserve a much bigger cabin for you."

Hence, Elisa resumed her business on water.

She met many people, and because Captain O'Connor gave continuous news of the war in America, they cruised the ocean and never entered American territory. Her business continued to bloom on the seas and from port to port. After the first year, Captain O'Connor added her business as part of the package on his ship:

Enjoy 10% off Madame Elize Voque designer collections when you buy a luxury cabin!

In the Spring of 1866, Captain O'Connor took ill and died. Elisa was devastated. One day, the captain complained of a tight chest, the next, he was gone. A burial was organized on the ship for him, and based on his request, he was wrapped and laid to rest on the platform he'd worked for a better part of his fifty-two years, the ocean. The assistant captain, Leon, a young man who couldn't be more than a few years older than Elisa, walked up to her during the small reception in honor of O'Connor.

"Captain O'Connor wanted so badly to own this ship, but he could never make up the payments," he said. "With his death, I just want to go back home. We've worked for over six years non-stop and I'm tired."

Elisa tried to process the information. What did this mean? "Where's home?"

"England."

Elisa gasped. She didn't want to go back to England, and she feared to go to France, which could have been a great option since she could speak the language. Jane was six, and she would want her daughter to get a formal education, live a normal life again, have friends.

"I'm speaking with all those on board," Leon said. "There's a merchant here with us who has indicated interest in taking the ship. Captain O'Connor didn't entertain this, of course, because he wanted it."

Elisa drew in a deep breath. "Do I know this merchant?"

"Theodore Vernon. He's a lawyer and a banker and his family has been in the shipping industry for two hundred years." Leon shrugged. "I would not be a part of it even if he buys and he has agreed we will get to England so I could go home."

His words did not sit well with Elisa. She had never been close to him but coming off this ship would mean starting all over again for her. She had clients now. Some came on this ship just to meet her and patronize her. A new owner, a new captain or a new ship. None made her happy. She hated change, yet she couldn't but accept every major change in her life had put her on a higher level. Would this be the same?

Leon rubbed his temple. "You have up to three days to decide."

Elisa frowned. "What are my options if I choose not to continue with you to England?"

"We will dock in the next three days and we can move you to the ship going to your next destination."

"Which is?"

"I don't know, Madame Voque. You'd have to decide."

Several questions ran through her mind. Where would she go next? Not England, and definitely not Africa. The war in America had ended but she had such a thriving business on the ship, she'd decided not to return home. And what was she returning to? Though the North won, leaving the South diminished, Johnny would have died anyway, fighting for his homeland from the claims made about the casualties. She just didn't know what to think.

She drew in a ragged deep breath. "I guess I have to get on the next ship, then. And follow wherever it leads."

Once Jane was fast asleep, Elisa escaped the cabin and went to stand on the deck. The fresh breeze and sultry smells of the sea calmed her. She needed to think again for herself. Her last decision had paid off and she purred over her ability to make reasonable choices.

"It's a beautiful night, with a beautiful woman gracing it."

She turned at the voice and came face to face with... Theodore Vernon. He was still dressed as he was at dinner, in an expensive dark suit and a silk shirt opened at the throat. She placed his age at between thirty and forty. The exclusive dining Elisa used was both for its selectness, and to meet the rich, who were her primary clients. After her discussion with Leon, she had considered having a conversation with the merchant. She wanted to know his plans for the ship and if she could be included in a business arrangement just as O'Connor had done. But her request to join his table had been rudely turned down by one of his men. She suspected he knew too because of the way he glared at her across the hall through the evening. There were more than three empty seats at his table too.

"The night is lovely," she mumbled.

"I understand you wanted to sit at dinner with me, but there was an important meeting with financiers." He cocked his head. "Such a beauty would have been out of place."

Elisa despised the way his gaze roamed her body without constraint. "I would have been interested in a business meeting. Seeing I wanted to indeed talk business with you."

"I've seen some of your undergarments. Seductive!" He rested his gaze on her mouth. "What kind of business would you want to discuss over dinner?"

Elisa ignored his gesture much as it distracted her from what she had to say. "I had a deal with Captain O'Connor before he died. I make garments for men and women. I travel the world with him."

Theodore sucked in his breath and bit down on his lower lip, his gaze intent on hers. Elisa could not concentrate. He could be drunk, and the deck was deserted. She trusted no man except Johnny Holt.

"You travel the world with him?" Theodore licked his lips. "I will like that very much."

Elisa didn't breathe until she was safely behind the locked door of her cabin. What a snake of a man. She didn't care to know what he thought or did when she gathered her skirt and stomped off. He just removed himself as an option by being suggestive around her. She would never work with a man who saw her as a mere epitome of seduction or a woman for pleasure.

In the coming days, she made sure she had all her remaining meals with Jane in her cabin, and never saw Theodore Vernon again.

The nearest port was on a small island and had been built only for refueling and emergency stops. Leon made it clear his next stop after this was England and anyone who didn't want to go had to disembark. Still, they had to wait another two days before any ship arrived.

It was going to New York City.

Chapter Sixty-Two

The Asian masseur had hands so soft, Johnny for a minute thought he wore something over them today, though his hands were always so soft. For the last year he massaged Johnny once a week, his impact on his right shoulder did magic.

"Ahh, that's perfect," he moaned. "Expensive but worth it."

The masseur laughed. "I think you have said that in the past year. Every week."

Johnny groaned. "My right hand still can't hold a pen."

"But you keep coming back. Lie on your face."

Johnny obeyed. It was the worst part of the massage when he was made to move his shoulder unnaturally. He shouted and the masseur laughed again.

Johnny chuckled. "I should sue you for being insensitive to a client's pain." He sneered.

"You have made a lot of progress." He patted Johnny. "In another few years, it should be strong enough."

Johnny sat up. "Another few years of ripping me off." He winked. "Send my bill to you know where."

The Chinese man winked. "I might add a few dollars. To match up with your new promotion."

"Try that. Then I will sue you."

The masseur's laughter rang through the metal doors of the entryway and in Johnny's mind after he got back on the street. He loved to walk, and his masseur told him it was good for his weakened bones and muscles. He didn't think so, but it kept him feeling able, especially because his job required him to sit at a desk for long hours, brooding over reports.

His office, just a couple blocks down from the masseur's also housed the courthouse, which was convenient. He hated to admit the true reason to himself but being a defense attorney helped to tickle his ego. The same slave masters he fought and killed their sons in the war now sat across from him, begging him to do his best to win their cases. Quite ironic for a man who still boasted of being married to a slave woman. The south lost the war, and that was all he agreed to admit. The best he could do was join the forces to rebuild.

The young law student, David, who assisted him had a pile of reports waiting. Because of his injuries during the war, he relied heavily on others to write out his notes, and he had to read each one through before every case.

"A woman waits for you in your office." David glanced toward the adjoining door. "A colored woman."

Johnny arched an eyebrow. "Did she tell you what her business is about?"

"No. And she would not say her name. I think she's in a lot of trouble."

"You have a great thinking mind, David." Johnny walked to his door. "Fix me a cup of strong coffee, will you. Thank you."

Without waiting for the young man to respond, he opened the door. "Nan!"

"I killed him." She stood facing the door. "I killed Trevor."

Johnny glanced behind him and saw David hovering. He shut the door. "Please sit down."

She did not. "I heard you were appointed a director of a committee and I need you. You are important now. You can help me."

"First, the committee is for education, and not law or justice," Johnny sighed. "Second, I will rather you don't say those kinds of words." He tried not to sound harsh. "Third, I have never taken a defense in a murder case. You might want to consider getting a criminal lawyer." His stomach turned in hatred for this woman. "Trevor has a lot of money and you had access to it."

Nan's eyes brightened. "I didn't kill him for his money."

"I didn't think you would." Johnny bit his lower lip. "I'd advise you to get a good attorney who handles these cases all the time. I can give you recommendations for the best ones."

Nan was shaking her head so hard, Johnny stopped talking. "I know criminal attorneys, damn it! They are all Trevor's friends."

"You think they will be biased? It's a job–"

"No, please. I know they will be biased. They've asked him for years to get rid of me."

Johnny sighed. Under his breath, he muttered Trevor's friends were right after all. "Nonetheless, I don't do criminal cases, never have, and I won't start now." He was tempted to ask her what happened, but he could not do this without getting himself involved. "I'm sure Trevor does not know all criminal lawyers. Give me a day to contact some really good ones. From out of town?"

Nan was shaking her head again and Johnny thought to walk her out of his office. He owed her nothing. This brutish woman betrayed Elisa's trust and started the chain of events that led to where he was today, without his wife. She could be dead. His child could be dead too. He shrugged his right shoulder in a physical attempt to get rid of the past.

Nan shrieked. "Don't you get it? They are coming for me. Someone would have called the police now. They will be looking for me. Cole is going crazy right now, and Benjamin, he's berserk."

"Benjamin?"

"Our son. He saw everything." She hit her temple several times. "This is crazy. I'm crazy."

Johnny mentally rolled his eyes. To feel an iota of empathy was impossible. "Okay. I'll get someone to come here and we can discuss the way forward. Excuse me."

"They won't believe I'll come to you," Nan said.

Johnny entered his outer office where David sorted loose sheets of paper into leather bags. "I need you to get in touch with Bryan Butler. Go get him, to come with you."

David stood. "Okay. Is she going to be alright?"

"Get Butler, will you? Be fast."

Johnny stayed out of his office to avoid contact with Nan until David returned with Bryan Butler, a hairy attorney in his late twenties. Butler and Johnny had been in the war together, but Butler fought to the end before returning to get his law degree. He didn't have as many years of experience, but he was as passionate about defending suspected criminals as Johnny was not.

Butler clasped Johnny's right hand in a firm handshake. "You didn't kill someone, so who did? David said it was urgent."

Johnny spoke slowly. "I have a colored woman in my office. She killed her white lover of many years and there were witnesses when she did it."

"Hmm." Butler moaned. "Two things. She's black, he's white. She's alive, he's dead. The prosecution will seek the death penalty."

"I don't want to be a part of this case." Johnny sniffed. "I am, should I say, conflicted and I wish to recuse myself."

"Is she your mistress?"

Johnny sneered. "She's twice my age, not that it matters. And no, she's not my mistress, never has been and never will be."

"The case is too close to your heart. I get it." Butler clasped his hands. "Well, where is she?"

Johnny opened his office door and Nan startled. "Butler, this is Nan. She came to me for help and I thought you would be a better person for her."

Nan did not even look at Butler for a second. "Does he have a good record? I don't know him. Trevor knows the best lawyers. I don't want someone–"

"Listen to me, Nan. Butler is the best and I don't have any other recommendation for you. If you need my help, here it is." He waved at Butler. "Talk to your client, Butler. I'm going for a walk."

Butler nodded. "And congratulations on your seat at the–"

Johnny shut the door. In David's office, he told his assistant he needed to get something other than the office coffee.

"The new café down the road is where I'll be." He grabbed a pile of leather folders. "I will sit in there and review this. When they are gone, come get me."

"Yes, sir,"

The new café down the road had been open for several months, he never walked in because it was always so crowded, but not between breakfast and lunch. David had told him they had the best bread rolls and mustard sauce in all of New York. Well, the best root beer, too. And they served breakfast, lunch, and dinner.

Johnny got to it and stared at the name, which he'd never noticed before, "Taste of America."

"Indeed," he muttered.

He pushed the door open, and bells chimed the same time the smell of fresh rolls filled his nostrils. The café was not as small as he thought it was from outside. Several tables were empty, and Johnny found one at the end of the room in a corner, with a window that overlooked the busy street. The table sat two, and he placed his files on the other side. A young black girl walked to his table. He didn't know they had colored people working here, not that it made a difference. New York had always had many blacks working in shops.

"Good morning, sir. We're in the middle of breakfast and lunch, sir."

Johnny arched an eyebrow. "What does this mean?"

"We can only serve bread rolls and coffee, until lunch is served in an hour."

Johnny nodded. "I'll have bread rolls and coffee, then. Thank you."

The girl pulled a pencil from her pocket and a small hard paper. "How do you like your coffee, sir?"

The professionalism impressed Johnny. He'd seen this done in only a few select high-brow restaurants and not this small café on a long busy street in Brooklyn.

"Well, black. No sugar or milk. Thank you."

"Yes, sir. This will take five minutes."

She walked away and Johnny stared after her. He thought he would visit more often if their service was this good. He had no plans to have lunch, so hopefully, Butler would be done with Nan in less than an hour. He took the first folder and opened it. He glanced through the brief - another white farmer filing for compensation for his land that was devastated by the war. Even five years after the war ended, these claims endlessly continued, and Johnny drew great pleasure from winning huge sums of money for his clients. It was an anesthetic for him, a relief on his conscience for every stalk of cotton he marched over and every bullet he shot. Every mile he walked away from his father and continued to stay away. JJ Holt lived, but Johnny had vowed he would never go back home.

The girl returned in her speculated time, with a tray containing his order and a slice of butter to go with the bread rolls.

He mumbled his thanks without looking up. The hostess hovered.

"Johnny? Holt?"

Chapter Sixty-Three

Elisa's hands trembled as she picked the tray and asked her young waitress to keep an eye on the steak. She wanted to serve this patron. She only did so when the café was busy, which was strictly during meal times. Most people who walked in wanted food and so Elisa had maximized her hours by having the meal times clearly marked out so people would not mill in at every odd hour with an unfulfillable request. It also sent the message to her patrons that when they came in for a meal, it was freshly cooked.

She had seen Johnny walk in and at first, thought it wasn't him because of his awkward gait, but when he took his hat off, Elisa knew she had finally found her husband. His dark hair was shoulder length, but it was groomed, and his beard cultured. He looked distinguished, like the many businessmen and congressmen she attended to daily. She feared to speak to him. Ten years of no contact from her definitely would have sealed her fate with him, but she couldn't let him leave without a try. Her first instinct to take his order was destroyed by her unsuspecting waitress who walked over to him, naturally.

Johnny looked up when she called his name and the lights in his eyes went out. "Elisa."

He stood in that awkward manner she'd seen him walk in with and realized there was something wrong with his left side. It didn't seem to move at all. Her throat constricted and she clasped her hand over her mouth to keep from making noise with her sobbing.

"Elisa." He stepped out from behind his chair and stood directly in front of her. "Elisa."

Tears streamed from his eyes and disappeared into his beard. Elisa knew there were only two consequences of whatever she did now. She'd either lose Johnny Holt forever or have him forever. She fell into his arms and hugged his neck tight. Only his right hand came about her waist and even that had such a loose grip, but the rumbling of his chest and his crackling sobs made it clear he was in no way rejecting her. They allowed their tears to run their course and then Johnny leaned back and searched out her face.

"I'm sorry but I lost total use of my left arm–" he started to say, but she didn't care.

She cupped his face and cut off his apology with kisses. "Johnny. Johnny." She moaned.

He raised his right hand, but it barely moved past her upper arm. "My love."

Their lips met and he kissed her hungrily, just the way she remembered. This was more than she could bear and not in her open café. There was only one space they could have privacy, and that was where she led him. The pantry. Her two waitresses stared with wide eyes as she walked past them in the kitchen. But she had no eyes for anyone.

Inside the pantry, they kissed again, falling over each other.

When the kiss ended, Elisa cupped his face. "I thought I would never see you again. Nothing...no one had a clue where you were."

The truth was she didn't know where to search. She feared he'd died in the war or returned to the south. Either way, she asked but never got a helpful reply. It had occurred to her to go to Kentucky, but she feared what she would find about him as much as what could happen to her. There had been stories of lynching and all manner of treachery going on in pockets of the country.

"To think my office is just down the road from here, darling." *Bless Nan for killing Trevor*, he thought. "I've wanted to come here every single day for a long time."

The pantry was stuffy and tight and they both started to sweat, but Elisa didn't care and if Johnny did, he didn't act so.

"I want to touch you but my...my hands are not good."

She sniffed. "I don't care. I have you now. Oh, Lord thank you. Thank you, Good Lord." She ran her hands all over him, his face, hands, his chest. "We have a child, you know. A daughter."

Johnny chuckled but it ended in a sob. "She'll hate me."

Elisa laughed. "No! She loves you. She prays for you every day. She–" She swallowed. "She's a very spiritual child. I think she has visions. She keeps me strong. And she loves you so much. She tells me you are alive and we will be together again."

Johnny gaped. "Really? She's...ten now. I want to see her."

"I know. She's in school. I don't let her come here. She helps with babysitting our pastor's children after school."

Johnny heaved a heavy sigh and rested his forehead on Elisa's. "This is a dream. I don't want to wake up from it."

The pantry was too small to accommodate two people and they had to leave the door ajar. Someone cleared their throat and Elisa turned. One of her waitresses stood inside the kitchen area.

"A young man is here, and he says he's asking for...him. The owner of the paper on the corner table."

Johnny stepped out. "Must be David."

"Yes, sir," the girl said. "He says his name is David."

"He's my assistant." Johnny looked at Elisa. "Come with me."

Elisa hesitated. "I can't leave them alone here. I–Will–?"

"You know what, I'll ask David to leave."

"No, it may be important. Can you come back here when you're done at work?"

Elisa feared she'd never see him again, but it would soon be time for lunch and the café would be busy. She couldn't leave and she didn't want to stay. What if something horrible happened and she never saw him again? She'd never forgive herself.

"Come." Johnny took her hand and they returned to the café hall. David stood in front of the table Johnny had occupied. "David?"

"Butler wanted to see you."

"Did the woman leave?"

David nodded. Then shook his head. "Butler wants to call the police and since it was your office, thought you should be there. The woman refused to leave." He stole a glance at Elisa.

Johnny sighed. "Elisa, please come with me. It's just down the road. I'll let you come back before lunch is served."

Three people walked in and a waitress went to attend to them.

She smiled. "The crowd starts to come in, but I will follow you."

It was foolish to go with Johnny now, but she had been reckless to leave him before and it cost her ten years.

Chapter Sixty-Four

They were joined in holy matrimony by Elisa's priest on a private beach under the witnessing gaze of fifteen select people. Elisa knew many people from her church and café business and Johnny was already a popular lawyer in New York with the many cases he'd won for the Southerners ravished by war and their properties taken. But they wanted an exclusive occasion and only the closest people were invited. Jane stood both as the maid of honor and best man.

"Who gives this woman to be married to this man?"

Jane stepped forward. "I do."

The guests laughed, but tears gathered in Johnny's eyes. He had never seen anyone more beautiful. Since the day he found Elisa, or rather Elisa found him, their lives had not remained the same. Meeting Jane for the first time would forever be in his memory. She hugged him as soon as the introductions were made and started talking about everything he had missed in her life. She made loving her so easy for him, it was as though the gap never existed.

Jane smiled into Johnny's eyes and he broke down. Her beautiful eyes lit up a bright blue the way his did when he was so happy. She took her mother's hand and gave it to him. Elisa drew her in and the three hugged. Their guests clapped and cheered. It got emotional again when Jane stepped forward with the ring in one hand, while she held her mother's bouquet in the other.

Finally, the ceremony ended, and the bride and groom rode away on stallions. Jane was to stay with the pastor's family for a couple of days while her parents rode out to the country to visit old friends who could not make it to the wedding. To Johnny, these were not very important people, but he wanted to take the time to be alone with Elisa. There was so much they needed to talk about. Deep down, he still wanted to know why she denied him in Liberia. Maybe life had taught her a lesson and she had repented, which was good. He'd vowed he would forgive her and take her back if they ever found each other again. His love for her had no restrictions or boundaries. Still, he needed answers for closure.

They arrived at a cabin in the Queens area just before sunset. Johnny had chosen this because it reminded him so much of the farm in Liberia and the stream where Elisa got her first white stone, which she left with the local woman, Bomi, for him. There was no stream, but it had tall trees that shaded the cabin with beautiful spring leaves. They could go for long walks or long rides through the woods and talk all they wanted.

"It's beautiful, Johnny," Elisa exclaimed. "The old couple you spoke about lives here?"

Johnny took her hand and walked to the cabin. "No old folks live here, darling. I just wanted an excuse to be alone with you for a few days." He pressed a kiss to her forehead. "We've not had a minute together in ten years."

She giggled. "You're right. I got very jealous of you and Jane."

"Are you referring to the most adorable person on earth?"

Johnny pushed open the cabin door and Elisa exclaimed. The furnishing was modern and classy with chairs made from cane and satin covers, an oriental mat and a fireplace that looked perfect to cuddle in front of on a winter night.

She pushed herself into Johnny's arms and kissed him ravenously. The gesture got a fervent response.

After a dinner of pork and potato pie, with apple cider, which they had packed and Johnny sent with David ahead with their luggage, they lay on the mat and cuddled. Johnny searched for a way to get Elisa to talk to him, alleviate his fears and reassure him she would never leave him again. He couldn't find any, so he started with what he already knew.

"You speak so much better now, Elisa. You were educated?"

Elisa idly played with the hair on his chest. "Yes. In Liberia, after I ran from Pizzi. And later in England when I went in search of you."

"I like the way you speak." His right hand caressed her waist. "I dreamt of teaching you."

"You did. I wanted to speak like you always," Elisa sighed. "I learned French too."

"You did?" He laughed. "Now you are more educated than me."

"And Spanish too."

He raised his head. "Are you joking?"

"No. I was on this ship for two years. It was coming to New York, and their cook got sick and died. The captain pleaded with me to cook. He taught me Spanish in return. He could speak many European languages." Elisa snickered. "Those were tough years for Jane. I had to quit to allow her to live in a proper city with normal day-to-day people."

"Is that how you started selling food? Because I remember my wife was a seamstress."

"I miss it." Elisa closed her eyes. "I will do it again, someday."

"You will." Johnny stared at her. "Open your eyes." She did. "Did you become really good at it?"

She told him about her success and the Elize Voque brand. And how Henri Jean ruined it all for her.

"I knew he was no good." Johnny kissed her nose. "But everything turned out well for us."

"Yes, that's what the word of God says. It all works for our good if we love God and serve Him."

Johnny wondered how Elisa could have served God after leaving him in such a way. Could she have repented? He wanted to know. "So, you met Cynthia."

Elisa stood. "I want to show you something."

She disappeared into the single bedroom in the cabin and returned with a leather bag. Johnny watched with interest as she removed three different stacks of letters. She placed them side by side.

He leaned forward. "What are they?'

"This," she touched the one in the middle. "I wrote them from the days I had no one to give and nowhere to send. Letters to Johnny."

His head shot to her face. "You wrote me."

"Almost every week." She heaved a heavy sigh. "Every week for this, definitely."

His gaze followed her hand to the pile on the left. "And those?"

"These were given to the good Dr. Obed to help me send to you." She swallowed. "In his words, at least I didn't destroy them as Margibi did."

Johnny smirked. "Margibi betrayed us."

"He didn't." She patted the letters on the right side. "He sent them to the apartment on Oxford Street. That was the last known address Marge gave him."

Johnny gasped. "I never received a single one."

"Cynthia got all of them."

Tears sprang to Johnny's eyes, and Elisa wiped them with her kisses. "You stayed true to me. That's what matters most. Even when you didn't know what happened with Pizzi. Your heart stayed true to me, *mon cher*."

"I couldn't stop loving you, Elisa." He chuckled. "You were in my blood."

She cupped his face and played with his beard. "Pizzi scared me. Threatened to kill you if I didn't come with him. And Ms. Beth, she promised no one would harm you if I followed Pizzi." She blinked tears away. "She told me it was an insult to Africans for me to be married to you. That our relationship was a statement the whites were still our masters."

Johnny gasped. "I hope she enjoyed seeing Pizzi break her promise."

"He killed her."

"What?"

She kissed him again. "But that's not talk for today. It's our wedding night."

He moaned. "Our third wedding night. The first was in the dead house."

They both laughed.

"I have a gift for you. A wedding gift." She opened the leather bag and removed a smaller bag with white stones. "There are over a hundred, different shapes. Some are so beautiful."

Johnny sat up. "Elisa!"

She giggled. "It's crazy. I went to pick them from the stream every chance I got. It made me feel closer to you. I–"

"Elisa!" Johnny gasped. "They are diamonds! I displayed the other one you gave me in my office, and a friend saw it. We got it tested and, diamond!"

"Diamonds! Like gold? The farm stream had...oh my goodness." Her eyes widened. "Did you sell it?"

"No! I could never. They offered a lot of money, but I refused."

She laughed. "So now we have diamonds and each other."

Johnny arched an eyebrow. "And the farm is still your property. We can fight to get it back."

"No way! I'm not going back there."

He closed up on her and caught her lower lip with his mouth. "Keep that thought." He pulled at her dress with his good hand. "Right now, I need a son, and Jane needs a brother."

Chapter Sixty-Five

Johnny wanted to see samples of the Elize Voque collection, so Elisa laid the few pieces she saved, out on their Victorian bed. They were back in the city with Elisa and Jane now moved into Johnny's big house. Elisa's first thought about the three-story house was Lord William. The top floor had only one massive master bedroom she imagined could be used as a showroom.

"I couldn't sell these." She stood back and admired the layout. "I kept a piece of everything," she giggled.

For a moment, Johnny didn't say anything. He just stood on the other side of the bed and stared at the display. Elisa swallowed. She had feared he would not approve and hoped never to get to this day. But the moment they returned from their wedding getaway, he asked to see what she had left. She could have lied, because she had sold off everything on the ship except the samples when she took up cooking, but a part of her wanted him to see her work, get his opinion. She had vowed never to lie to him regardless of how painful her truths could be.

Johnny picked a piece of her chemise. He started to speak but his voice was hoarse. He cleared his throat. "This is beautiful."

Elisa exhaled. "Thank you," she whispered.

"I didn't know they were designed this way." He glanced at her. "You never wore anything like this."

She tittered. "I never knew they existed."

"You saw them in Europe?"

"No. I–I made them. Just from my imagination." *I'm depraved*, she thought.

He picked the silk drawers. It was the same one the "royal" had found *sinful*. "This–this makes me want you."

Her eyes shot to his, and she gasped. "I'm sorry you find them offensive." She started to fold them up.

"I want you to wear them for me."

Elisa gasped. "Johnny."

"Please," he whispered.

Elisa felt heat envelope her. She knew these undergarments were daring, to say the least, but she had meant for them to be. Worn by dignified women in the privacy of their chambers for their "cheating" husbands only. She remembered Fanny had warned she must not sell to an unmarried woman, and that she took seriously. The passion between her and Johnny had fired up as though the years of separation didn't exist, but she couldn't remember seeing him look so intense. Was this how men felt about such revealing underwear? She never heard back from her many patrons, but she knew she sold a lot of these undergarments.

She turned her back, suddenly ashamed. What had she hoped to achieve by making such sheer and provocative clothing? Only women of loose morals should wear them. She saw herself in the light those noble women saw her, and despite the hypocrisy of patronizing her, she must have been to them a disgusting French woman who would never be anything more than a seamstress.

"You're so beautiful, Elisa. And I want to see you in this."

Johnny's cool lips touched the base of her neck and she jolted. She hadn't heard him approach.

"I've-I never wore them before." She bit her lip. "Not sure they will fit me."

He turned her to him and kissed her deeply. "I still want you."

Cuddled in his arms later, Elisa thought of the reason she sold so many flimsy underwear, made not from the plain white cotton she knew, but of satin and lace, in daring colors. Those women must have gotten better results in their bedrooms.

"Elisa?"

"Hmm?"

Johnny ran his hand over her hip. "Would you want to sew again?"

She stiffened. "No."

"Why?"

She raised her head to get a better look at him. "I stopped. I don't do that anymore."

He leaned forward. "But you can start again. You're so good at it."

She shook her head. "The café will suffer."

He held her gaze. "I've been thinking about this for a while. The café is not your strongest forte. You sew better, you have great innovation."

She giggled, "You flatter me."

"I don't. I'd like to see you introduce the Elize Voque collection to the American society. I know many women will thank you later." He shrugged. "You have a powerful story to tell with your life, Elisa. You cook, but you sew better. You sew, but you speak best."

She laughed. "Speak? To who? About what?"

"Maybe you need to hear this small speech of mine first." He raised himself up to a sitting position. "You were taught the basics of sewing only to make soldier uniforms. But you made women's clothes for yourself, and men's clothes for me. Then you made baby clothes. That is strong talent and innovation. You are very smart, my darling."

She gave a mock bow. "Thank you, Barrister Holt."

"I'm not done." He arched his eyebrow. "Then you found yourself cooking. And you open a café and baked the best cinnamon rolls on earth, and your pies don't taste like anything anyone has ever eaten."

"I experiment, sir."

"And now you have recipes and secret ingredients and your café business is doing well."

Elisa interrupted him again. "The reason why I can't close the café."

"But listen, the best part of you has not yet been discovered. Speaking. You have a great story of hope and redemption and survival, the world needs to hear you, Miz Holt." He nodded. "And I love the way you speak. You sound so beautiful; I could lick the words off your lips." He dropped a quick kiss on them instead. "And as much as I speak only English, I can only imagine how lovely you will sound speaking French or Spanish."

"Exotic. That's how Captain O'Connor described me." Elisa threw back her head and laughed. "Oh dear, you do know how to mesmerize and confuse a woman."

"No, you think about it. Many women have not yet discovered their potential."

"Hmm, especially black women."

"Exactly. You need to speak, sweetheart. You have to." He raised his head once more. "And I never mentioned this, but I always love the design of your hair and Jane's. Who makes them for you?"

"Me." Elisa giggled. "I made hair for a living in Liberia. Taught women to do it too."

"What?" Johnny turned her face to him. "You have so much in you. You are a gift, Elisa, don't play down on your abilities. You need to teach again and speak!"

The thought formed really quickly in Elisa's mind. She had continued to write letters she termed, "letters to the future." She didn't want to forget her story, and she wanted to keep her history for Jane and any other children she had.

"You're right, Johnny, but where? How will they hear me?"

"You will speak on your platform and on others. I will get names of organizations who may be interested in your story, and we will go to them." He slapped his thigh. "You will be amazed at how much impact you will make. You will become a mentor. You may even write a book."

"Oh, my goodness. Slow down, Johnny. I can't breathe."

They both laughed.

"You are so talented, Elisa, and I am blessed to have you as my wife."

His words brought his suggestion to light. There was a huge problem, the same one she faced in Liberia and would always face.

"Acceptance. The whites will despise me, and the blacks will reject me as a betrayer," she sighed. "And what will become of my café. At least I can sew and speak, but I can't run the café with anything else."

"Your café will be fine. We will employ someone to run it."

"My recipes. Someone will steal my recipes and–"

"Then we will write a book of recipes and everyone will know they are yours originally. And you will be paid for the book, and serious café owners will only modify and not want to use them verbatim."

Elisa rolled her eyes. "You have an answer for everything when you want something."

Johnny chuckled. "I'm a lawyer, darling. My territory is advocacy."

Chapter Sixty-Six

"I was blessed to be sixteen, and never molested by a Massa." Elisa looked around the room filled with civil rights activists, most of them her color. "I watched women who were married with their husbands and their children raped and demeaned in the ugliest way. I was truly blessed."

It was her first lecture and her feet sweated in her stockings. There could be a hundred people in the room. Johnny stood at the end of the hall; his eyes keen on her. He had set all of this up and written to many organizations. His plan was to get her to go about telling her story. He believed she had something important to say to America, and the more she thought about it, the more she realized it was the truth.

"Today, I want to share that blessing. My life may have been easier than that of many of us, but see where we are today, alive, free. But are we free in our minds, and our souls and in our spirits? This is where our battle for freedom continues. To be truly free starts from within."

She spoke for almost an hour, longer than she ever imagined she could. At the end of the speech, everyone in the room rose and applauded. Tears sprang to her eyes. Johnny continued to stay at the back of the hall. He had some posters in his hand, which he shared with people as they left the hall. The poster was an invitation to another meeting the following month. Several people walked up to Elisa on the podium, some with tears in their eyes, some thanked her, some related their issues and fixed appointments with her, to discuss their issues privately.

The hall soon cleared out with only one young colored man left. His dark hair was straight, and he could pass for a white man if not for his wide nose. It was too African. He held his hat in his hand and hesitated when he got to her.

"Yes, sir?"

Elisa saw Johnny walk up from her blind side. Only three of them remained in the hall.

"My name is Benjamin Truse. I am Nan's son."

"Oh." Elisa stretched her hand to him. She saw the resemblance with Cole at once. Johnny had told her what happened with Nan.

"Thank you for coming."

Benjamin did not waste time on pleasantries. "She needs your help. Or she will be hanged."

Elisa had no idea what to say. "I'm sorry."

"Hello." Johnny stuck his right hand out before he got close enough. "I'm Johnny Holt."

Benjamin shook him. "Benjamin Truse. My mother is—"

"I know who you are. What do you want?"

"They will hang my mother and I need help." Benjamin swallowed. "Please."

Elisa sensed something was wrong. "Does she still have a lawyer?"

"She has the best lawyer and does not need us." Johnny looked at Elisa. "Let us leave, Elisa." He put his hand on her elbow and led her away.

Benjamin raised his voice. "Why would you not help me? You said in your speech you came here to help."

Johnny swung around. "Nan killed an innocent man and I have helped her to get the best lawyer possible. No other person will represent her," he snapped. "Besides Elisa is not a lawyer."

"But she's a speaker. She wants to protect black women. She wants to empower them!" Benjamin yelled. "Why won't you allow her to help us?"

"Because your mother will get what she has coming. Nan was the most despicable, disgusting and mean-spirited—"

"Johnny, dear, wait," Elisa said, softly. "Please."

The prison gate closed with a clang and Elisa jumped. This was the worst place anyone could be kept. Her heart thudded and she looked to the prison officer for direction. He only pointed down the corridor. Elisa didn't know what she would find, but she was ready to face it. Johnny had wanted to come with her, but she felt this was something she needed to face by herself, so he waited outside for her.

Nan had been found guilty already for, in the words of the prosecution, the bludgeoning death of Trevor Truse. She was described as a heartless bundle of bitterness and a danger to society. Trevor had been beaten and stabbed several times, even after he was dead. Now Nan waited to be sentenced. Butler did a great job, but Nan was just too guilty to get much help.

Elisa found a room with rows of wooden bars at the end of the corridor. A seat was placed in front of the bars so she could see everything inside. It looked a lot like Nan would be hung here if sentenced to death, because there was a hook up in the ceiling with a bit of the noose hanging down. Nan sat on a wooden bench, her eyes sunken in, her long curly hair in wild disarray. She stared blankly at Elisa.

"Hello, Miz Nan."

"I told Benjamin to leave you alone." She looked at the hook. "It's here. They keep me here to remind me how it's going to end."

"The sentencing hasn't been done." Elisa cleared her throat. "Until then."

"They will hang me. They can't wait to do it." Nan looked at her hands. "He comes every day. Asks me to join him in hell." She raised her head and Elisa saw raw fear. "They hate me. I know they will make it painful."

"I understand your fear." Elisa could feel it thudding in her chest.

"I don't want to die." Nan's eyes widened. "Benjamin, he needs me. He's a grown man, but Trevor would never let him be a man. He won't let Cole be, either."

Elisa didn't know what to say. With Johnny still angry about the way Nan treated them both, and a jury of eight white men and four white women, two eyewitnesses, Benjamin and Cole, Nan's fate was sealed. But was there a way to save her life? She could not get anything less than life in prison, but it was a second chance, a better alternative. She didn't know what to do, or what could be done. Before she came, she had spoken with Butler who was also looking for one good deed Nan had done in her life, just one person who could testify in her defense to save her life. Only her son was willing, but he had been a key prosecution witness. He would not whip up any emotion after describing in detail how his mother killed his father.

"What was your relationship with Trevor like?"

Chapter Sixty-Seven

"I met Nan for the first time when I was sixteen, a young woman who needed a mentor and a mother-figure in her life. Nan gave me that. She taught me to read and write, and she taught me to sew. From her, I learned to love sewing and creating beautiful clothes for my family." Elisa kept her eyes on the members of the jury. "You must understand that before I met Nan, I felt worthless. She gave me a sense of worthiness. There was goodness in her that drew me in. She never showed me the part of her I am about to speak of today. And I crave your indulgence to hear me out."

Johnny had told her several times she had the most beautiful voice and diction, but she didn't feel so until now, if one could judge by the way the members of jury stared at her, attentively. They seemed to soak up her words like water to a parched ground.

"Nan was born into slavery. At the age of ten, Mr. Trevor Truse started to have intimate relations with her. He insisted it was consensual, but she was ten and he was married to her half-sister at the time, and he just had a new son." She paused to let the little detail sink. "When his wife died, Truse took Nan with him and came to New York. He sold off his late wife's estate and set up a trust for their only son, Cole."

Elisa took a deep breath. "Truse never said he loved Nan. Never had a tender word for her. He never married her legally and kept her as his "slave." She never protested because she thought he would love her one day. They had a son together, Benjamin, and in her words, Nan hurt herself in such a way that she would not bring another child to this evil and unforgiving world. Not even for Trevor."

"It has been argued here that Nan was free to go and come as she pleased, but how true is this? Because freedom is only from within."

Elisa held the gazes of each member for half a second each. "Freedom is only from within," she whispered. "Nan was never loved. She was never free. Her son was the only thing she had, and her fear. Because Truse never tied her up and flogged her, but he did to Benjamin. And the last day he did this was the day he died, when Nan was pushed to the edge of insanity. She could not watch this man torture her grown son anymore. A son Trevor never allowed to be a man." She blinked. "Nan was wrong to kill anyone."

She drew in a deep breath. "Truse is not on trial today and can never be. But I appeal to you to save Nan's life, an empty life, only kept for her son's sake. It is true, Benjamin is no longer a child, but a child who was deprived a childhood will never be a free adult. Despite opportunities to study in Europe based on Nan's fight and struggle to free her son, he is not. Truse made sure by his continued abuse."

Tears sprang to Elisa's eyes. "If you have no other reason to spare Nan's life, hold on to this - she never had a life, but for her son. And without her life, he's as good as dead."

She stepped away from the stand. Everywhere was dead silent for several seconds, then the judge cleared his throat and in a gruff voice, released the jury to deliberate. Elisa rushed into Johnny's arms and heaved. Butler led them out into the hallway.

"They are not likely to return today," Butler said.

"Yes, you were wonderful, Elisa. You speak so well." Johnny nudged her with his chin. "Hmm? Are you alright?"

"No. I'm not," she heaved. She didn't think her disjointed emotional jargon had helped the case.

Johnny sighed. "They made this tougher by having the jury decide the sentence. It will be tougher to convince twelve people than one judge."

Butler waved toward the exit. "Let's get coffee. I need some."

The court clerk came out and raised his voice. "They're back."

Johnny gasped. "That's not even ten minutes."

Butler led the way back inside. The judge entered the courtroom with the jury and asked the required question. He read through the verdict quickly and asked the foreman if this represented the decision of every member of the jury. Elisa gazed at the fifty-some-thing-year-old man who stood to respond. Truse was in his age group. The judge cleared his throat, and her chest tightened. Had she said enough? The room felt empty and cold. Besides the prosecution team, Johnny and Elisa were the only other people in the room. Benjamin and Cole had chosen not to attend.

A long screech went through the room, and Nan fainted. Elisa had missed the judge's words.

She clutched Johnny's arm. "What did he say?"

"Life. She got life." Johnny exhaled. "You got them to save her life, Elisa. A woman who wanted you dead."

The judge put the court back in order and a moment before she was led away, Nan ran to Elisa and hugged her. "Thank you," she wept.

Elisa was sobbing hard herself. She hadn't thought she could convince even herself. Outside the courthouse, a reporter approached Elisa and asked for an interview. She shook her head, "No, please."

Johnny held her at the elbow and whispered in her ears. "Do it. This is a very good platform, my dear."

She sniffed. "You think so?"

"Yes, love." He caught her gaze. "And remember your line. It's become popular now."

She frowned. "What line?"

"Freedom is from within."

Chapter Sixty-Eight

Three months after their marriage, Elisa threw up on herself before she could get to a basin, minutes after she woke up. Johnny was already up and about and didn't know until they got to the breakfast table and she told him.

"You're pregnant," he laughed. "I was beginning to think something was wrong with me."

She rolled her eyes. "I have so much to do. I can't even imagine being tied down like this," she moaned. "I finally got a place I like for my sewing and I can start working with three young ladies."

"Don't sound like the women I work with." He munched on his bacon and eggs. "This is the next best day of my life."

"After what day?"

"Hmm, what day can that be?"

Elisa stared at the variety laid out on the table by her cook and house staff. Nothing appealed to her. "Do you know what I really want now?"

"What?" Johnny stuffed toast into his mouth. "I'll go across the world to get it."

"You might have to. Palm beer." She sighed, "I feel so horrible."

"Palm beer. Where on earth can I get that?"

"Liberia?" Elisa giggled. "Pizzi had his men climb the palm tree and tap it. I hated it."

Johnny snickered. "Someone is missing the *Garlic of Egypt*."

"I'm so hungry and I can't eat." She stood suddenly and rushed out of the room.

Johnny found her cuddled on the bed five minutes later, fast asleep. He shook his head, returned to finish his breakfast and left for work. He remembered Nan's admonition those many years ago.

"For the next three months, she's going to be sick until twelve noon."

He left a note by her bedside, with a promise to find palm beer or something close. The week was already a busy one, but he was willing to turn New York upside-down to please Elisa. Though she hadn't been confirmed to be pregnant, there was no other explanation for her sickness.

David had a bunch of letters for him when he walked into his office. "These two seem important, Mr. Holt."

Johnny arched an eyebrow. "What do they say?"

David fumbled with opening one. "This has a royal seal. The marriage of Viscount Gabriel of York to Lady Deborah Charring of York. An autumn wedding." David blinked. "Admits two."

"Deborah Charring whoever." Johnny groaned. "Cynthia didn't make it. And the other?"

"This is an offer for your... Your diamond? They want to pay you." David gasped. "A quarter of a million! You have diamonds worth a quarter of a million dollars?"

Johnny pursed his lips until David ended his outburst. "Do write a reply and tell them I will agree to half a million." He headed for the door.

David gushed. "Half a million!"

"I'm walking down the street. I should return in an hour or less. Any appointments should be rescheduled, David."

Johnny left the young man gaping, a smirk on his face. He did not only marry a beautiful woman, she was smart, business savvy and blessed by God. He meant it when he said he would turn the world over to please her. He couldn't think of anyone who'd sell palm beer except the Chinese, so he headed to his masseur's. He didn't have an appointment, so the young receptionist asked him to wait.

"I'm not here for a massage. I just want to know if you know about palm beer?"

The girl spoke little English. She shook her head. "Block down there. Coconut shop. Chinese shop."

"Right down the block, there's a Chinese store? Thank you."

Johnny found it easily. He had to ring a bell and a smallish man opened to him.

"I don't know if you have palm beer. It's an African drink."

The man squinted. "I have every drink. And this your hand, I can straighten it. And your other hand, I can loosen it. I see you walk all over stiff like that; I can fix you."

Johnny gasped then laughed. "Okay, I'm only here for palm beer. Can I buy some?"

"I have everything."

Johnny rolled his eyes. After another half hour, he got a small bottle of coconut water the Asian insisted was palm beer, though the milky liquid in the clear bottle had no bubbles, and he also got a "test" massage to show him the man could fix his stiffness, and a short lecture about acupuncture.

When Johnny got home, Elisa was still asleep. It wasn't yet noon so he couldn't blame her, but he wanted to be sure he got the right thing. He tapped her arm.

"Darling, I got some...some palm beer."

She roused. "Really? Thank you."

"It doesn't look a lot like beer but taste it." He helped her to sit.

She blinked. "It looks just like coconut water, mixed with something."

He chuckled. "Yes, it does. The old man who had it told me it's a special blend for breeding women."

She gasped. "You told him I'm with child? We're not sure yet."

He uncorked the bottle. "You are. Here, drink."

She took the bottle from him, drank a little and exclaimed. "Not it at all."

Johnny was about to be happy he wouldn't need to go back to the old Chinese man, but also unhappy his search had not ended when Elisa took another sip.

"But I like it. Did he tell you what he mixed? This is not quite like palm."

Johnny chuckled. "Let me have a taste." She put the bottle on his lips, and he took a small sip. "Hmm, not coconut, but not my taste either."

"Good." Elisa drank some more. "I like it and I don't have to share. Can you get some more bottles? Is it very expensive?"

"Talking about expenses, the diamond buyers got back. They want to pay a quarter; I'm asking for half."

Elisa hugged his neck. "So, get all the bottles of this drink. I'm going to be drinking it every day." She shrank back. "What's that smell on you?"

Johnny rolled his eyes. "The old man believes he can get my right side to work better and the left to come unhinged." He laughed. "He had me lie on a slab and rubbed with this stench of an ointment. Ridiculous."

Elisa looked at the drink and Johnny noticed tears sprang to her eyes.

"What's the matter, my dear? What did I say wrong?"

"You never told me what happened to you." She sniffed. "I know it's painful and it was the war, but I want to hear it."

"Remember Gilbert from back home. My friend who–"

"I remember him."

Johnny dragged in a deep breath. "Well, we met again on the battlefield. On opposite sides." He frowned. "They had lost and were on the run. One of my comrades opened fire and hit him. He fired back, but I didn't know he could. I threw myself in the line of fire. Got bullets from both sides."

Elisa put the bottle down and cupped his face. "On both sides?"

"I got a bullet for Gilbert from my side, but he turned and fired back. I got his, too."

"Oh dear."

"I lived." He sniggered. "I didn't think I would."

"And you have done well. You did not only survive, but you also succeeded." She pressed a kiss on his mouth. "And though, I hate the smell of this stuff they rubbed on you, you need to go back there and get your healing." She laughed and kissed him again.

"Oh goodness! That old man got me really tinkered, but I felt a little less numb." Johnny swallowed. "I love you so much, Elisa. You always want the best for me. And I don't know why."

"You know why, Johnny Holt. Why do you pretend?" She took a quick swig of the coconut water. "This thing helps fight nausea too, can you believe it?"

Chapter Sixty-Nine

Jacob Johnny Holt was delivered in a prestigious private clinic on a warm summer morning in 1871.

"This is exactly how Jane looked on her first day," Elisa told Johnny, when he was allowed to come in and see mother and child.

Johnny peeped into his son's tiny cot and tears filled his eyes. "He's so beautiful."

They both stared for a second and then started to talk at the same time.

Johnny smiled. "Go first, darling."

"No, you go first."

When they stopped laughing, Elisa said, "I know you will not agree under normal circumstances, but I'd like us to go to Creek View one of these days. Show the children where we are from! See your parents again."

Johnny raised his right hand and touched her nose. "Not now. Father died last week. It was in one of the telegrams I received this morning. Mother–?"

"Oh, my goodness, that is unfortunate." Elisa grunted. "Do you know what ever happened to the Spaniard, Master JJ's partner?"

"Edmond Maguerro?"

Elisa nodded. "Hmm mmm."

"Word said he died in the war." Johnny closed his eyes briefly. "Holt Land was destroyed."

Elisa moaned. "So Miz Penny can't harm you now. Seeing us may help her re–"

"I know. But the memories are hard. Maybe, someday, we will visit as a family." She opened her mouth to protest, but he sealed it with a kiss. "Now, to what I was going to say. I got the deed for your Liberia home in the mail. That's where we are visiting if anywhere."

She squealed. "You what?"

"Yes, love. Our diamond farm awaits."

The end.

Acknowledgments

I want to thank Chigozie Anuli Mbadugha, and Pastor Sunny Adediran for beta-reading this book and for their very helpful feedback.

Thanks to Stephanie Shivers for her great editing and professional feedback and Michelle Ganeles for her patience, wonderful service, and beautiful cover.

Thanks to my daughter, Oore, who heard the story the first time and thought it was worth writing.